At The Masquerade Ball

Wanda was dancing in the arms of the Czar—and she was surprised. He was young and handsome, and the eyes that looked out from behind his mask were friendly, and warm with excitement.

The masked man looked down at the frail young beauty and his heart beat faster. She was not like the sophisticated belles of Vienna, practiced in the art of pleasing men. She was sweet, innocent, enchanting . . .

The music ended and the man refused to let the girl go. After all, he reasoned, she did not know who he was—and this was his night for adventure . . .

Also in Pyramid Books

by

BARBARA CARTLAND

THE
ENCHANTED WALTZ

Barbara Cartland

 PYRAMID BOOKS • NEW YORK

THE ENCHANTED WALTZ

A PYRAMID BOOK

Copyright © 1955 by Barbara Cartland

Pyramid edition published August 1971
Seventh printing, December 1976

Printed in the United States of America

Pyramid Books are published by Pyramid Publications (Harcourt Brace Jovanovich, Inc.). Its trademarks, consisting of the word "Pyramid" and the portrayal of a pyramid, are registered in the United States Patent Office.

PYRAMID PUBLICATIONS
(Harcourt Brace Jovanovich, Inc.)
757 Third Avenue, New York, N.Y. 10017

Chapter One

"THE situation is intolerable!"

The Prince de Metternich brought his fist down on his desk with such resounding force that the gold accessories rattled from the blow.

"You expected the Czar to be difficult, dear," his wife said quietly.

"Yes, I know I did," the Prince replied, "but not as difficult as this. The man isn't normal. He is . . ." The Prince paused for a word.

"Not mad, like his father?" the Princess suggested.

"No, not as bad as that!" Prince Metternich strode across the the room, his handsome, distinguished head thrust a little forward as always when he was deep in thought. "I wish I could put into words what is wrong with the Czar. He seems at times to be two men in one body."

The Princess gave a little cry.

"It is extraordinary that you should say that, Clement! We were discussing such a possibility only yesterday and the Princess de Leichenstein said that our doctors of medicine are working on just such a theory—that a man can have a double personality and be God and Devil both at the same time."

"The Czar should be their first patient," Prince Metternich said sharply, "for at one moment he sees himself as the ruler of the world, the supreme power in Europe—at another the benign Christian benefactor doling out freedom and liberty to all men."

The Princess sighed. The exasperation in her husband's voice was very evident. She knew that he did not expect her to contribute much to the conversation. As always when he was confiding in her, he was content to talk, to clarify his own mind and his own ideas in the process.

"That is not all," the Prince continued. "Alexander is wrecking the Congress by the way in which he insists on conducting his own affairs. As you know, it was laid down very clearly that the Sovereigns should amuse themselves while their plenipotentiaries were to do the real work. The Czar breaks all the rules and insists on negotiating personally with me and Castlereagh. The wretched Count Nesselrode hardly knows what is happening from one day's end to another."

"I can see how irritating it is, my dear," the Princess said.

"Irritating?" the Prince exclaimed. "It is intolerable. It cannot continue. Something must be done—but what?"

He threw out his thin, expressive hands in a gesture of despair. Looking at him, standing with his back to the window, the pale winter sunshine illuminating him with an aura of light, Princess Metternich thought, as she had thought every day since they were married, that her husband was the most handsome man she had ever seen.

It was not that his features had a classical beauty; but they were aristocratic and there was so much character and personality in his face, such a brilliant sparkle in his eyes, such an enticing twist to his lips, that even the most libellous cartoon or drawing could not fail to make him appear distinguished. It was the face of a man no woman could fail to love, she thought suddenly, and felt her heart sink.

"What can be done? What?" the Prince asked. "If we do nothing, the Congress will fail. Already the latest *bon mot*, 'Congress dances but does not advance', is being sniggered about wherever I go. My enemies are saying this will be the greatest failure of my career and they will be right—yes, they will be right, Eleanore, unless by some miracle I can prevent the Czar from wrecking everything"

"A miracle? Isn't that asking rather a lot?" the Princess enquired with a faint smile.

"Without it we are lost," her husband replied grimly.

He walked again across the beautiful Aubusson carpet. Everything in the palace which Prince Metternich had erected for himself had been chosen by him personally. He called it 'Villa on the Rennweg', but the Emperor

Francis had already said laughingly that he would exchange it for the Hofburg.

Exquisitely designed, the Prince himself had supervised the planting of the surrounding park with its formal arrangements of rare trees and shrubs. The Villa on the Rennweg was not only the centre of the festivities but it was also the heart and soul of the diplomacy for which the Congress had been called, for the axis round which everything and everybody revolved was the Imperial Minister, Prince Metternich himself.

No-one but his wife and his secretaries knew of the great strain under which he was working; and yet there was no sign of it in his bearing, in the sparkling wit of his conversation or the ease and charm of his manner to all the thousands of distinguished guests who had converged upon Vienna.

It was in fact undeniable that Prince Metternich seemed to overshadow all the other personalities who had arrived that autumn with all the power and pomp that lay at their command. The Emperor Alexander of Russia had come with an enormous retinue, eager for the plaudits of the masses, determined that everyone should acknowledge that he and he alone had defeated Napoleon.

There was Frederick William III of Prussia, the King of Denmark, the Kings of Bavaria and Wurtemburg and the Viscount Castlereagh as personal representative of the Prince Regent of England. Gathered to meet them were all the most beautiful women in Europe and the most brilliant society of their respective countries. Emperors, Kings, Princes, statesmen, politicians, courtiers, *grandes dames*, courtesans had converged on Vienna, but the central figure was still Prince Clement de Metternich. His penetrating, clear blue eyes, broad brow, aquiline nose, pale, fair skin and gently mocking mouth seemed to remain in the onlooker's mind long after the balls, masques, parades and receptions were forgotten.

But his extraordinary political genius made him many enemies who were only too eager to proclaim that the New Year of 1815 would see him beaten and discredited.

"A miracle," he repeated now; "find me a miracle, Eleanore."

The appeal in his deep voice was something she could never resist.

"If only I could help you!" she sighed.

He walked across the room to her side and put his hand on her shoulder.

"You do help me," he said.

The simple words, spoken with a quiet affection, brought the tears springing to her eyes, but she turned her head aside so that he should not see them.

"Thank you," she whispered.

The gesture made, he turned away from her again, his brows knit, deep in the throes of his political problems, before he noticed a servant standing inside the door, waiting for permission to speak.

"Yes, what is it?"

"There is a lady here, Your Excellency. She wishes to see you privately."

"A lady? Who is she?"

"She gave no name, Excellency, but craved audience. She has come from the country."

"I cannot see people without an appointment," the Prince said testily.

"Yes, Your Excellency, that was understood; I explained, but the young lady was insistent. She was quite certain that you would wish to see her."

"Tell her she must present her credentials in the usual manner," the Prince instructed. "At the moment I am engaged."

"Yes, Your Excellency."

The servant left the room and the Prince returned to his pacing.

"I cannot allow Poland to be a sovereign state dominated by Russia," he said aloud, but ruminatively as if, in fact, he spoke to himself. "It would give the Czar domination of Europe such as Napoleon himself did not enjoy. But Alexander has set his heart on it and King Frederick William is half inclined to agree with him, if only to spite me and the English. I think that what I shall have to do is too——" He broke off suddenly for the servant re-entered the room. "What is it?"

"The lady asked me to give this to Your Excellency."

The lackey held out a gold salver on which reposed a pendant of turquoises set with diamonds. It was a pretty trifle, but not intrinsically valuable. The Prince stared at it for a long moment in silence. He remembered the moonlight on a white body, the warmth of two soft lips; her breasts had quivered beneath his hand and, as the blood drummed in his ears, he had felt the wild beating of her heart against his own.

Slowly he reached out and took the pendant from the salver.

"Show the lady in," he said.

The Princess rose from the chair in which she had been sitting.

"I will go and rest before the Ball to-night."

She was smiling as she spoke and no-one, least of all her husband, would have guessed the sudden arrow of fear which had pierced her heart. The Prince stepped forward to open the door for her and when she had left the room he walked slowly towards the fireplace, staring at the pendant that he held in his hand, the stones very blue against the hard glitter of the diamonds which encircled them.

The last time he had seen that pendant he had clasped it round a slim neck. It had cost him money he could ill afford at the time, but he had never grudged the expense. He could remember still the fragrance of the lilacs and the moonlit evenings when they had met in the little temple in the forest. He could recall the magic of those hours still, after all these years in which there had been so many other moments of magic, so many other moonlight nights. How young and rash and impetuous they had been, risking everything for those stolen kisses!

He sighed suddenly. Carlotta would be nearly forty now. It was a pity to spoil the remembrance of that youthful ecstasy by meeting again after so many years! But women were all the same, he thought, they could never be content to leave things as they were and to remain in the past.

The door was opening. Prince Metternich straightened himself and waited; and then, as someone came into the room, the faint smile on his lips faded and the expression in his eyes changed. This was not Carlotta. This was someone very different—a girl he had never seen before in his life.

She came walking towards him so lightly that she seemed almost to float across the carpet. She was wearing a travelling cloak of green velvet over a gown of white mousseline, and a tiny hat trimmed with green feathers was set on her red-gold hair. Her eyes were blue, as blue as his own, set around with dark lashes.

She reached his side and sank into a deep curtsy.

"I thank Your Excellency for seeing me."

It was an exquisite face that looked up at him—with a small tip-tilted nose, a full red mouth and those two unexpectedly blue eyes set in a tiny oval face.

"Who are you?"

"I am Wanda Schönborn. My mother said you would remember her. She has sent you a letter."

She held it out as she spoke and even after all these years he remembered the writing. He took the letter without a word, still looking at the girl who gave it to him, taking in every detail of the soft, peachlike skin, the faint colour in her cheeks, the long proud column of her neck, the way her breasts curved beneath the tight bodice of her dress.

"Yes, I remember your mother," the Prince said and wondered if it was his own voice speaking, it sounded so strange and far away.

Then he opened the letter and read:

I am very ill. The doctors say I cannot live, but when I am dead Wanda will be sent to live with my late husband's sisters in Bavaria. They are old and autocratic and do not understand young people. Let her have a little happiness before she goes, a little gaiety, a little music. Forgive me for asking this of you, but I feel when you see Wanda you will understand.

Carlotta.

Prince Metternich folded the letter between his fingers.

"Your mother is dead?" he asked.

"Yes, she died early in the summer," the girl answered; ". . . you do remember her?"

"Yes, I remember."

The sudden smile which came to her lips was like the sun breaking through an April sky.

"I am so glad. I was half-afraid, you see, that she was mistaken. When people are ill, they get fancies; and my mother was ill for a very long time."

"Yes, of course I remember her," the Prince repeated; then, looking down into the blue eyes with their dark fringed lashes, he said a little harshly, "How old are you?"

"I shall be eighteen next month."

"Next month!" the Prince repeated under his breath, "and you are christened Wanda?"

"Wanda Maria Clementina, to be exact," she smiled.

The Prince gave a little exclamation. If he wanted proof, here it was. Clementina—his own name—and the memory of those evenings in the little temple came flooding back so that for the moment it was not Wanda who stood there, but Carlotta, holding out her arms to him, her lips warm and eager for kisses, her slim body trembling, as he had trembled too with desire and happiness. But Carlotta's eyes had been grey and Wanda's were blue—as blue as his!

With an effort the Prince realized that the girl was waiting for him to speak, looking up at him with an interrogating look on her face. He remembered then why she had come and that she would be waiting to hear his verdict, to know if she might stay, if he would allow her to take part in the festivities.

"So you are to go and live in Bavaria," he said, playing for time, trying to collect his thoughts.

"So my mother told me. I try not to think of what it will mean to be without her. I have nowhere else to go, nowhere . . . but oh! how I hate the idea!"

There was a sudden note of passion in the clear, young voice.

"You dislike your relatives?"

"Not only that, they are kind enough, but because I must leave all that is familiar . . . and Austria, too, my own country."

"You love Austria?"

"Of course."

As always when an idea came to him it seemed as if a sudden flash revealed its place and position in the intricate human chessboard on which he moved the pawns. The miracle he had prayed for—it was here.

"You say you love Austria," he said quietly; "in which case, will you do something for your country?"

"But of course—anything!"

"You are sure of that?"

"How can you ask me to tell you in words? Give me something to do and, however hard, however difficult, I will do it—I promise you that."

"I think I believe you," the Prince said slowly; "and now, before I say any more, you must forgive me for forgetting my manners. You have come a long journey and must be tired and thirsty. Sit down and I will pour you some wine."

"No, no, there is no need," Wanda said with a quick

gesture of her hand. "I stopped at an inn on the outskirts of Vienna. I wanted to tidy myself before coming here."

He smiled at the slight air of coquetry about her. At the same time the shrewdness of his mind appreciated her good sense. She had wanted to make an impression. From her point of view a good deal hinged on this interview, so she did not come to him travel-stained and dusty; she had prepared herself, she had even eaten and drunk. It showed a forethought which he of all people appreciated. Her blue eyes were not the only thing she had inherited.

"At least I can offer you a seat," the Prince said with the smile which no woman had ever been able to resist or refuse.

She accepted the chair he offered her and sat upright but with an inherent grace, her body still and attentive, her eyes dancing with excitement and anticipation.

"Before you came I was praying for a miracle to help me in a dilemma," the Prince said quietly. "I believe you are the answer to my prayer."

"What can I do?"

"That is what I am going to tell you; but you will need courage and intelligence; above all, you will need your wits about you."

"I am not afraid."

"Very well, then. I will try to explain as simply as possible what I wish you to do. As I expect you already know, a Congress of the Great Powers has been called to draw up a formula of lasting peace for Europe. In my own opinion, peace can only be secured if there is a relative equality both in status and position where Russia, Prussia, Austria and France are concerned. In other words, a balance of power."

"I think I understand."

"You will appreciate that I am putting this as simply and in as few words as possible."

"Thank you."

"The Czar of Russia—the Emperor Alexander—wishes to make Poland into a sovereign state under his dominion. Austria cannot agree to this and both England and France feel the same. The Czar is being difficult; he is a strange man—at times an idealist, at others a shrewd and calculating schemer."

"He sounds frightening."

"The greatest difficulty in a position like mine is to keep a jump ahead of one's opponents and this can only be achieved when one has some idea of what they are going to say or do. Do you understand so far?"

"Yes, of course."

"One of the easiest ways of anticipating what one's opponents' attitude is going to be is to learn of their plans from those with whom they associate, and since the beginning of time women have been the confidantes of men."

"And are you asking me to help in such a way?"

Wanda's tone was quite steady and he liked the way that her eyes did not fall before the penetrating gaze of his.

"That is what I am asking of you. You are new to Vienna, you are beautiful, no one will know anything about you."

"But the Czar . . ." Wanda's hands fluttered a moment in her surprise, ". . . he may not like me. . . . I may not interest him."

"That of course remains to be seen. The Czar has a *penchant* for pretty women and yet you need not be afraid of him. You must forgive me if I speak frankly. It is best for you to know these things. He has a mistress, Madame Marie Narischkin, with whom he has lived for a great number of years; but so as not to embarrass the Empress Elizabeth, who is here with him, Madame Narischkin is stopping on the outskirts of Vienna.

"She has an extraordinary ascendancy over the Czar, for while she herself indulges in many and frequent love affairs, she expects from him complete and utter faithfulness. My informants tell me that he observes this to the letter, if not in the spirit. He likes women, he makes love to them and has an insatiable curiosity about them, but that is all—do I make myself clear?"

"Absolutely. But how shall I meet the Czar? How shall I begin?"

"Everything will be arranged," the Prince answered. "All you have to do is to seize your opportunity, when it comes and then listen, listen to everything he says. All men talk, whether they be Emperor or lackey, Prince or pauper. They talk if the women they are with are sympathetic and they receive even the slightest encouragement."

"And afterwards?"

"You tell me what has been said. We have got to be very careful about this, you and I."

"In what way?" Wanda enquired.

"Vienna at the moment is a whispering gallery; nothing goes on in one house or palace which is not known in the next—even the walls have ears. If you are to do this work for Austria, it is essential that no-one shall know or even guess what you are about."

"Of course. I understand that."

"Very well. You do not know me, you have no connexion with me, we have never met. I will make arrangements for you to stay with someone eminently respectable who will give you the entrée to all the most exclusive gatherings and the best parties. You will be introduced to Vienna as your mother's daughter. Few people knew that Carlotta and I were friends; no-one must guess that you and I are even so much as acquaintances."

"But I shall see you again?"

The impulsive question brought a smile to the Prince's lips.

"You will see me very often," he said. "In public and in private, but we must be very discreet. Can you do this for me, little Wanda? I am asking it of you only because I am desperate."

Wanda's eyes softened.

"You know that I would do anything you ask of me. My mother spoke of you often and she told me what a very wonderful person you are. I have learnt from her and from other people how much Europe owes you."

The Prince smiled at the admiration in her voice.

"You will hear very different stories if you stay long in Vienna," he said. "Lord Castlereagh, for instance, calls me 'a political Harlequin'."

"How dare he!"

"He is entitled to his own opinion just as you are entitled to yours. You must not show your partisanship too obviously. You are quite sure that you are not afraid to do this? If you would rather draw back, I shall quite understand. I will arrange for you to stay in Vienna, to attend balls and all the other gala occasions and this conversation between us can be forgotten."

Wanda stood up and with a swift movement laid her hand on the Prince's arm.

"I don't think you quite understand," she said. "When I told you that I love Austria, I meant that in all sincerity. I am ready to die for my country if it should be asked of me; and if, as you say, there is a small way in which I can be of use, then I am proud and honoured to be chosen."

The Prince put his hand over her small fingers. They

were warm and alive and he saw, too, that her cheeks were burning with the intensity of her feelings.

"I am proud of you," he said softly and saw the gladness light her whole face and make her for the moment almost breath-takingly beautiful. "But now you must go," he added. "It is not wise for your carriage to stand outside the door any longer. Make no secret of the fact that you came here and waited for an audience but that I was unable to see you. If anyone asks you why you called immediately on your arrival in Vienna, it was because you thought it polite to pay your respects on entering the capital.

"You will go from here to the house of the Baroness Waluzen. She is a distant cousin of my wife and she can be trusted. But even to her it is wise to say as little as possible. Arrangements will be made later for any communications you may have for me to be carried by safe hands. The first thing you have to do on arriving at Baroness Waluzen's is to rest so as to be ready to attend the Masked Ball to-night."

"A Masked Ball?"

"Yes, Masked Balls are one of the great highlights of the Congress. At them the guests of Austria, Sovereigns, Princes, statesmen and notabilities of other countries, mix freely with the crowd. Anyone may dance with anyone. All wear dominoes and masks, but I will see to it that before you arrive at the Ball you will know how to distinguish the Czar of Russia."

"Shall I dance with him?"

"You must make sure of it. A chance encounter is always much more exciting than a formal introduction, specially to a man who is suspicious."

"I can hardly believe it is really going to happen."

Wanda spoke the words almost beneath her breath; and then, as if the excitement of it all was too much for her, she gave a little cry that was half a sob.

"It is all so wonderful. Thank you! Thank you!"

She bent down and brushed her lips against the Prince's hand, and as she raised her face again to his, he saw that her eyes were shining like stars.

"I was so frightened when I came here, so afraid you would turn me away," she said; "and now everything is changed. I am happy, so happy that I cannot put it into words or thank you."

"There is no need for words," the Prince said. He put

his fingers under her chin and held her face for a moment so that he could look closely at it. "You are not very much like your mother."

"And not in the least like my father," Wanda added, artlessly.

"No?"

It was a question, but she did not understand it. The Prince let her go and walked to the writing desk. Sitting down, he penned a brief note and brought it to where she stood by the fireplace, watching him.

"This is for the Baroness Waluzen," he said. "You will stay with her and she has also my instructions to buy you anything you need to wear. I promise you that socially you will not find Vienna dull."

Wanda gave a laugh of sheer happiness.

"Dull!" she exclaimed. "I am not afraid of that." She took the letter from him, turned towards the door then stopped. "There is one more thing," she said. "May I have my pendant back? It was my mother's."

"Of course." The Prince drew it from his pocket and held it out to her.

She took it from him.

"My mother told me to keep it always. It was given to her by someone she loved very deeply."

"Did she tell you who it was?"

"No, but I guessed."

Blue eyes looked into blue eyes. The Prince bent his head and kissed the little fingers that held the necklace.

"I am glad your mother did not forget me," he said gently.

"As if anyone could!" she answered.

Chapter Two

PRINCESS KATHARINA raised two white arms above her head, stretched and, moving with exquisite grace, rose from the bed on which she had been lying.

Although it was still afternoon, the shutters were closed and the big, blue-panelled bedroom in the Hofburg Palace was lit by candles held in heavy gold candelabra decorated with cupids.

She stood for a moment in the centre of the room, silhouetted against the light, and the soft diaphanous folds of the garment she wore, completely transparent, showed her figure to be as perfectly proportioned as that of a Greek statue.

"A beautiful, naked angel," a deep voice said from the bed.

Katharina turned swiftly.

"Who told you I was called that?"

The man watching her laughed.

"Who? All Vienna of course. Let me think who it could have been who mentioned it last—the Emperor? the Cardinal? Or perhaps . . . could it have been . . . the inimitable Prince Metternich himself?"

She laughed a little at that, but her eyes were serious as she answered:

"No, not him. He, I think, has forgotten. It was a long time ago."

"Could anyone ever forget you?"

"Do you think that impossible?"

She moved back towards the bed to sit down at his side. He was lolling back against the pillows, the golden brown of his sunburnt skin sharply in contrast to the linen and lace. Here, obviously, was no frequenter of salons, but a

17

man who was used to the open air, to hard riding, to sport.

The Princess bent forward to lay her hand against his brown cheek, but he caught it in his and covered the palm with kisses, hungry and passionate, the impetuous kisses of youth which is never satisfied, never satiated.

"You are lovely. Metternich spoke the truth."

"Why do you keep reminding me of that time so long ago?"

"I am telling you that I see what he saw—a beautiful, naked angel."

"I remember only how young I was, how happy—as young as you are now."

"You couldn't have been as happy," he replied between his kisses.

"But I was." She threw back her head a little, her eyes half-closed as her thoughts drifted sensuously back into the past. "I shall never forget that day," she went on. "Something had gone wrong, I was angry. I rushed to the Legation in my *carrosse* and as it drew up I did not wait for the footman to get down from the box, but sprang out myself and rang the bell with my own hands.

"I remember standing there tapping my foot on the step, my cheeks hot with the fury of my feelings. A servant opened the door, but my ringing had been so imperative that the Minister had risen from his desk and entered the corridor to see what was happening.

"He told me afterwards that he expected to find one of the Imperial couriers. Instead, he saw me standing framed in the sunlight against the dark hallway . . . and I saw him! We stood looking at each other. Quite suddenly the world slipped away and I could not remember why I had come or why I was there. I only knew that the man in front of me was like Apollo descended to earth.

"Clement said my dress—the very latest directoire fashion—was completely transparent against the sunlight—'a beautiful, naked angel' he called me.

"I can only remember his eyes as he stood looking at me and the feeling in my own heart that I had been waiting all my life for that very moment."

Katharina's voice quivered and trailed away. There was an oriental mysticism about her when she spoke like that, Richard Melton thought. Then suddenly, he sat up in bed and, putting his hands on her shoulders, shook her lightly.

"Forget the past," he said; "I am here and there is to

be no other man in your life or in your memories—do you understand?"

She laughed at his jealousy, her eyelids drooping over her eyes so that for the moment she seemed shy and helpless; then she opened them again to reveal the darkness of a rising passion so that the man looking down into them felt that he was lost in some strange whirlpool.

He pulled her down on to the bed beside him, his hands running over the smooth, silky skin, his lips buried against her soft neck where a pulse throbbed wildly. He felt her teeth fasten themselves in the lobe of his ear and then their desire became a burning fire which consumed them both . . .

Later—much later—Katharina rose and crossed the room to the dressing-table.

"It is time you got dressed," she said. "We were speaking of the day I first met Clement. I remember that he was wearing an open silk shirt and a purple silk dressing-gown trimmed with sable, and he was so bemused by my appearance that he even forgot to beg permission to change into more formal clothing."

"And did he remember to ask you why you had come?" Richard enquired.

"I told you, I forgot what it was at the time and I have forgotten now."

"I dare say the Czar would remind you, or I am sure that Volkonski could find it on the files; the memory of the Imperial Secret Service is proverbial."

The note of sarcasm in the speaker's voice was very apparent. Katharina turned round to look at him, a jewelled hairbrush in her hand.

"Why do you dislike our secret service so much?" she enquired. "You never miss an opportunity to be unpleasant about it."

"I dislike the system," was the reply, "and I detest the idea of anyone spying—especially you!"

"Who told you that I did?"

"The Czar, as it happens. He spoke of you as his most beautiful and most skilled agent."

Katharina shrugged her shoulders.

"Why worry? As I have told you, those days are past now."

"Unless he has need of you again."

"Not at the moment. Metternich is his most bitter enemy, but I am no longer any use to him in that quarter."

"Women should be kept out of politics and out of diplomacy, too. It is a dirty game at the very best."

Katharina laughed, the sweet musical sound which seemed to ring round the big room.

"There speaks the Englishman. Wouldn't I know that sentence came from English lips, into whatever language it might be translated?"

The man on the bed rose and came across the room. He wore an elaborate dressing-gown of sapphire blue velvet, and watching him through the big silver-framed mirror on the dressing-table as he approached behind her, Katharina made a little *moue* of pleasure with her lips.

"You are such a boy, Richard," she said softly.

"I am twenty-five the day before Christmas, and I am *blasé*, sophisticated, and exiled from my own country. Does that sound very youthful?"

She laughed again and threw back her head to rest it against him as he stood behind her.

"You make me feel young," she murmured, "and that is enough."

He could see the rounded column of her throat and the nakedness of her beautiful body reflected in the mirror. He reached forward to cup her breasts with his hands. Katharina, however, pushed him away from her.

"No, no, you must be good now. It will soon be time for me to dress for dinner. The Czar will be expecting to see you. You know how it irritates him if he is left too long without knowing what any of us are doing."

"I'll tell him if you like."

"My dear, he will know already. One of Prince Volkonski's men will have reported that you were seen entering my room and when you leave he will hurry to his master with the information that you have left."

"Damn Volkonski and his blasted impertinence! One day I shall wring his neck."

"And then you will be exiled from Russia."

"It will still leave me half a dozen other countries in which I can find sanctuary, but I don't wish to leave you, so Volkonski's neck is safe."

"He should be grateful."

Richard bent to kiss the point of her bare shoulder.

"I have no wish to depart," he said, "but it is draughty in the passage outside and the agent of the Imperial Secret Service is doubtless feeling the cold."

He moved across the room without another word, jerked open the door and closed it noisily behind him.

Princess Katharina gave a little sigh. Richard was too English, she thought, ever to accept foreign methods of life easily or with a good grace. They had had these arguments before and often she had had to use all her tact to keep him from doing injury to some servant who had been ordered to report on their movements, or to some lackey who had been listening at the door under Volkonski's instructions.

It was part of the life that she knew. In Russia there were spies everywhere. She remembered that her husband, Prince Peter Bagration, before he was killed in battle, had also resented the spies who shadowed them wherever they went.

In Austria it was just the same. It was well known that every detail of what occurred in the Hofburg Palace and in the whole town was reported daily to the Emperor Francis by Baron Hager.

It was true that Katharina had herself been an agent for Russia. She had been sent by the Russian Government to dazzle Clement Metternich and the fact that she had fallen in love with him, desperately and overwhelmingly, had merely made her assignment easier and more pleasant. Both Katharina and Clement were enthusiastic agents of their respective governments and perhaps the fact that they were both violently partisan to their own cause helped rather than detracted from the joy and ecstasy of their love for one another.

Katharina, beneath her childlike appearance, was extremely intelligent, but what was more, she believed fervently with all the fire of her oriental ancestors in the greatness of Russia and in the part her country must play in world affairs.

Once, wearing only a filmy pink *négligé* she had been sitting on the arm of Metternich's chair. They had dined together in her boudoir and as they talked they sipped slowly the liqueurs which the servants had left beside them before discreetly withdrawing from the room. Clement sat staring into his glass and she knew by the expression on his face that for a moment he had forgotten love and was thinking of politics. But as if he felt her silence calling him, he turned his head.

She stared down at him, her arm thrown lightly about his shoulders, and then, as they looked at each other, the pupils of her eyes suddenly became larger, darkening until they covered almost the entire iris. She bent forward, trembling, to kiss his lips. He reached up his arms and drew her on to his knees, kissing her wildly, till he felt her lips open beneath his, her whole body tremble with passion. Forgotten for the moment were all intrigues, Russia, Austria, everything was laid aside except this wild desire for each other. Then with her heart against his, Katharina whispered:

"Oh, my Clement, what a terrible thing it would be if Russia and Austria should ever go to war with each other! If we were to be on opposite sides I could not bear it! It would kill me! And yet, why should I worry? It is inconceivable that any nation could go to war against the government you represent."

Metternich had laughed at that and a few minutes later, still with their arms around each other, they were talking and arguing about world affairs. Katharina, unlike any other woman he had ever met, had the ability to pass from moments of infinite tenderness and passion into intellectual discussions as astute as those a statesman or a diplomat might have with him.

How happy they had been! Katharina gave a little sigh now as she thought of those nights of love and argument, when passion and politics were indivisibly mingled and the hours had slipped away too quickly for them to keep count of them.

How could Richard Melton or any other man understand what it meant to be loved by Metternich and to love him? She supposed there would always be part of her heart which belonged to him. Yet while she was still beautiful, still desirable, there would be many other men in her life.

Richard was one. There was something about him which attracted her wildly, something that made her heart beat more quickly, when he came close to her. She must be lovely for him to-night; and even at the thought of it, she bent towards the mirror and saw the tiny, almost invisible lines at the corner of her eyes, the first warning that youth would pass and beauty would fade. For the moment they were easily disguised, but the day would come . . .

Katharina felt herself shiver; then imperiously she rang the bell for her maids. She wanted massage, a bath, and the skilful applications of lotions, perfumes, ointments and powders before she could attend the Ball to-night.

In his own room Richard Melton changed slowly into the coat and breeches fashioned by Weston of Bond Street, which made many of the noblemen at the Congress eye him enviously. He was almost too broad-shouldered for the languid elegance which was required of a Georgian dandy; but when his valet had finished arraying him, his cravat was tied to his liking, and he assumed the proper bored expression of a buck who had been everywhere and seen everything, he was not displeased with his appearance.

He had just picked up his watch to set it in the pocket of his vest, when there came a loud knocking at the door. His valet, a small, bow-legged Cockney with a scarred cheek, went to open it. An aide-de-camp in a resplendent uniform stood there.

"His Imperial Majesty, the Emperor of Russia, requests the company of Mr. Melton," he said in stilted English.

"Orl right. Say 'e'll be along in a jiffy."

Richard's Cockney valet shut the door sharply.

"The Cock o' the Roost wants yer, Guv," he announced unnecessarily. "Lor, lumme, you can't get a moment ter yourself in this place, can you?"

"True enough, Harry, but beggars can't be choosers."

"Now don't you start talking about beggars, Guv; we ain't down an' out yet by a long chalk."

"Not as long as we stay here, Harry; and while we do so, it's no use your forgetting which side our bread is buttered."

"I'm not forgetting that, Guv, but I'm not taking a lot o' foreign sauce with it, neither. These chaps give me the creeps, hanging about the place with their slit eyes. And what they put up with, too! If anyone treated me as they're treated, I'd kill 'em, that's what I'd do."

"I can quite believe it," Richard said drily; "but if we don't want to start looking for somewhere else to lodge, you had better keep such sentiments to yourself."

"Mum's the word, Guv; I can keep me chaffer close," Harry said cheerily, and added more quietly, "You 'aven't 'eard anything from England, 'ave you?"

"Only that my devoted cousin, the Marquess, is in good favour in Carlton House Terrace. He was dining with the Regent last week."

"Blast 'is eyes! I 'opes all 'e puts in 'is gizzard chokes 'im."

"A sentiment with which I fervently concur," Richard Melton said with a sigh, "but unfortunately the Bible tells us that the evil flourish like a green bay tree, and doubtless my honourable cousin passed a very enjoyable evening."

"You should 'ave seen the Prince yourself, Guv, and told 'im the truth."

"Now, Harry, we've been through all this before," Richard answered, "and you know no-one would have listened to me. I was alone when I came upon the unfortunate Mr. Danby lying in his blood and there were three of them to swear that I had done it."

"Lor', Guv, you'd no quarrel with the poor gent."

"They would have sworn I had. No, Harry, there are times in life when one has to accept the inevitable and that was one of them. At least the Marquess paid my debts and gave me five hundred pounds for my journey!"

"Fine and dandy of 'im, I'm sure," Harry said sarcastically, "the tallow-faced cull! One day 'e'll get what's coming to 'im."

Richard could only hope that Harry was being prophetic. He certainly had no love for his cousin, the Marquess of Glencarron. Richard could see his dark, spiteful face now as it had been when he stepped from the library window at Melton House into the moonlit garden. How he had cursed himself afterwards for being such a fool as to go to his cousin for help at such a late hour! But the duns had been pressing him and when he found that his cousin had already left White's, he had gone to look for him at his home.

It had only taken one glance round the small, paved garden for him to realize what had happened. Charles Danby was lying sprawled on the grass and the blood was seeping in a dark flood over his white shirt just above his heart. He had known by the attitude of the men standing beside his cousin that they were perturbed and worried by his sudden appearance; and then he remembered that the Marquess had been warned only a month earlier that the Regent would have no more of his duelling.

It was hard for a brilliant swordsman and a man with a fiery temper to control himself, but the Marquess had been duelling for too long and the mother of his latest victim had gone to Carlton House and made things very unpleasant. He had been warned that the next duel would be his last, and now he had fought it.

Then, as they all stood looking at each other in silence, the Marquess whispered to the men on either side of him, and Richard saw a crafty look come into his eyes and knew, almost before he spoke the words, what he was going to say. It was clever, Richard had to allow that, clever enough for him to see no other way out of it than to agree that his debts should be paid and that with five hundred pounds in his pocket he should accept voluntary exile from England rather than face the consequences of being tried and convicted of a duel he had not fought.

"We were lucky to have somewhere to go," he said aloud, following the train of his own thought; then, without listening to Harry's blasphemous reply, he went out of the room and down the passage.

The best rooms in the Hofburg had been divided between the five Sovereigns and their suites; but as the Czar had brought a greater entourage than any other, he had undoubtedly the lion's share of the palace. The *salon* which he had taken as his private sitting-room was a charming apartment overlooking the formal gardens and decorated with furniture and pictures of great antiquity and value. The walls with their panels picked out in gold leaf and the huge sparkling chandeliers glowing iridescent from the painted ceiling were a fitting background for the good looks of the man who occupied them.

Alexander I was thirty-seven, but he looked much younger. He had fine, regular features, a good complexion and a tall, majestic figure, and with his golden blond hair, which usually was dressed like that on the heads of cameos or ancient medallions, he seemed to have been predestined to wear a crown. As one of his critics had remarked, he played the rôle of monarch to perfection.

As Richard came through the doorway, the Czar greeted him with a smile that had a captivaing quality about it and said with a boyish impulsiveness:

"Richard, I have an idea!"

"An idea, Sire?" Richard enquired.

"Yes, for to-night. You remember it is the Masked Ball —we are all going; it is expected. Well, I want you to go as me!"

"As you, Sire? I am afraid I don't understand."

"Yes, yes, it is quite easy! We are all to be masked, we all wear dominoes; but everyone knows that I and the other Sovereigns are not so completely disguised that people cannot recognize them. At the last Masked Ball I dispensed with all decorations beneath my domino except *l'Epée de Sweden*. To-night I shall do the same, but you will be wearing my uniform and I shall go as an ordinary gentleman."

"I see the idea, Sire, but do you think we shall deceive anyone?"

"Why not? Have you forgotten that we are cousins?"

"Very distant, Sire. It is true that my great-grandmother was a Bagration, but I have always thought that I looked unexcitingly English."

The Czar linked his arm in Richard's and drawing him to the mantelpiece stood with him facing the gilt-framed mirror which surmounted it. The ornaments of Sèvres china were in the way and impatiently Alexander thrust them aside, Richard bending forward to save, by a hair's breadth, a vase from destruction as it toppled on the edge of the marble shelf.

"Now look!" the Czar commanded.

Richard did as he was bid and had to admit that there was, if one looked for it, a distinct resemblance between them. They were both fair and of the same height and almost the same build—only Richard's shoulders were broader. They had the same firm chin, well-moulded lips and finely chiselled nose. It was in their eyes and expressions that the greatest difference lay. The Czar had the look of a visionary and an autocrat, while Richard seemed to regard life with a lazy indifference.

"You see what I mean?" the Czar said. "You can arrange your hair as I do mine! I will send you Butinski, my own barber, and, wearing a mask, no-one will know that you are not me. My skin is fairer than yours, it is true, but cosmetics can remedy that, and if you enter the room with the other Sovereigns no-one will suspect for a moment that *l'Epée de Sweden* graces your coat and not mine."

"And you, Sire?" Richard asked with a smile.

"To-night I shall be at liberty to dance with whom I please, to hear the truth from lips which would otherwise school themselves to say what they think I want to hear. I want to find out, Richard, what the ordinary men and women in Vienna think of my championship of Poland, of the part I have played in saving Europe from Napoleon."

"I can see that this may lead to a lot of trouble, Sire," Richard said drily, "but, if it pleases you, I am game."

"I knew you would not fail me," the Emperor said, "and I shall look forward to to-night. I have had a difficult day.

Metternich was more obstructive than usual. It seems incredible that in the whole of this great gathering of peoples I should be the only one to interpret the ideals and principles of Christian liberalism."

He spoke with a sincerity which made it very clear to Richard that he believed what he said; and yet, knowing the autocracy and the Imperialism of the Russian Court, it was hard for anyone to credit that the Czar could really expect Congress to visualize him in such an unlikely rôle.

"Is the Empress to know of this plan?" Richard asked, determined if possible to sidetrack the Czar from expounding his ideas on the Polish question, which he had heard far too often.

The Czar frowned.

"Certainly not," he said. "No one is to know, not even Katharina."

"I doubt my ability to play the rôle of Emperor half so cleverly as you will play the part you have undertaken," Richard said, "but I will do my best."

The Czar looked him over quizzically.

"We will, of course, wear powder to-night," he said. "I know it is out of fashion in England, but here it is still 'de rigueur'. Don't forget to lighten your skin. I wonder if I should look well if I were sunburnt?"

"The ladies of Vienna assure me that Your Majesty's appearance could not be improved upon," Richard replied.

The Czar smiled.

"The ladies! Ah! but then they are always flatterers; but honestly, Richard, have you ever in your life before seen so many beautiful women gathered together in one place?"

"Never, Sire," he answered truthfully.

" 'Their stature is like to the palm trees and their breasts to clusters of grapes'," quoted the Czar.

Richard tried not to smile. He was used to the Czar sprinkling his conversation with Biblical references, but he thought this one belaboured the point.

"The Congress is unique in that, if in nothing else," Alexander went on, "and I saw someone today who surpasses all the beauties I have seen already."

"Who was that?" Richard asked.

"I call her 'La Beauté Celesté'—she is named the Comtesse Julia Zichy—I must meet her again—yes, I must be certain to meet her again. Remind me to ask Volkonski to tell me all about her—he will know—in fact, there is nothing he doesn't know."

"We will see how soon he guesses what has happened to-night," Richard said.

The Czar clapped his hands together.

"It is an idea, Richard. We will test him out. Now, what I suggest is this—when the banquet is over, I shall come upstairs. You will follow me. You will put on my coat, mask and domino, and leave my apartments as if you were me, and join the Empress who will be waiting downstairs."

"The Empress will be sure to recognize me if I speak to her," Richard said.

"There will be no need to talk to her," the Czar said. "You will merely walk at her side to the ballroom. You will be late and the others will be impatient to start, if they have not left already. Once you reach the ballroom, you mingle with the dancers as will be expected."

"I see you have every detail worked out," Richard said.

"Even the smallest engagement in war is worthy of thought and preparation," the Czar said pompously.

"War, Sire?" Richard questioned.

"And in peace, too," the Czar said quickly. "To-night I am battling against the secrecy and isolation that surrounds those who wear a crown. To-night, like the prophets of old, I go in search of the truth."

"And I, Sire, on your behalf, will go in search of adventure," Richard laughed.

Chapter Three

By the time Wanda arrived at the Baroness Waluzen's house, some of the elation and excitement which she had felt while talking with Prince Metternich had begun to ebb away.

Sunset had come and gone and dusk was hanging over Vienna as her coach drove slowly down the twisting streets crowded with carriages of all sorts and descriptions. She suddenly felt very small, very young and very unimportant.

Had she really been brave enough, she asked herself, to make this journey alone to Vienna, to come unchaperoned to the greatest social gathering in the whole world? She thought of her dresses in the leather trunks in which they had been packed by her maid—an elderly woman ailing in health who had been unable to accompany her—and she felt sure they would prove countrified and inadequate.

It had been a desperate struggle to set out for Vienna against the disapproval of her father's sisters and their continual prophecy that no good would come of it. They would have prevented her if they could, but her mother's dying wishes could not be ignored and finally they had let her go, croaking like old crows with grim foreboding of what awaited her.

Now she wondered if they had not been right in their judgment. She knew no-one except the Prince. He, it was true, had been kinder than she had dared hope. She could still feel the fire of excitement within her that he should not only welcome her, but ask her to help both himself and Austria. But, whereas everything had seemed very easy and plausible when he spoke of it, now that she was alone the chill hand of fear laid itself crushingly over her enthusiasm.

How easy for the Prince to suggest that she should get to know the Czar, dance with him, make him talk to her! How difficult, now that she was alone, to visualize such a thing happening! She did not, as yet, know in what sort of a place she was to sleep that night, what reception she would get from the Baroness Waluzen, or whether obstacles from that quarter might be laid in her path to prevent her going to the Ball.

And what was she to wear? To a woman's mind this seemed to be the greatest problem of all. In a moment of panic Wanda felt that she must tell the coachman to turn round and they would return the way they had come, to home, to security, to all the things that were familiar, easy and not in the least frightening. Then she remembered her mother's face, worn and pale from suffering and yet alight with some echo of her lost youth as she said:

"I want you to be gay, darling. I want you to have some of the things I had when I was young—dances, balls and . . . beaux."

"And where am I to find them here?" Wanda had asked laughingly.

She had loved her home, perched high as it was upon the mountainside, miles from a town. But they would often go months without seeing anyone except the peasants who worked on the estate.

"No—I suppose it is impossible," Carlotta Schonbörn replied. Her eyes had closed wearily and she lay back against her pillows as if she were too exhausted to think of anything but sleep.

A few days later, however, the spark of interest had re-ignited itself.

"Wanda, I want you," she called one morning. "Come here and close the door."

Wonderingly, Wanda had obeyed. When she drew near to the bedside, her mother stretched out and took her hand in hers.

"Listen, my darling," she said. "I have a plan. I have learned that there is to be a Congress at Vienna."

"Everyone knows about that," Wanda answered. "They are to plan a lasting peace."

"Let us hope they can achieve it," her mother said; "but do you know what that means? There will be balls, parades, masques, dancing and music. I am determined that you shall be there."

"But that is impossible. How can I?"

"It can be arranged," the Comtesse had answered. "It must be arranged!"

It became an obsession with her during those last weeks when she lay dying, forcing a reluctant permission from her sisters-in-law, telling Wanda what she should do, writing her letter to Prince Metternich with the last remaining strength of her frail body, and finally taking the turquoise pendant from a secret place and laying it in her daughter's hands.

"Give my letter to the Prince yourself," she said. "Trust it to no-one else. I know how in those vast Chancelleries the servants and secretaries lose these things or do not trouble their employers with them. If he will not see you, send him this pendant. He will recognize it."

Wanda had felt faint with terror when the moment came and the Prince had refused to see her, and in a last despairing gesture she had drawn the pendant from her neck. As she laid it on a gold salver where a supercilious lackey had looked at it suspiciously, she had known then what a gambler feels when he stakes his entire wealth on the dice or a turn of the cards.

She shut her eyes now as she remembered how her heart had leapt when the servant returned to say the Prince would see her. Once again she felt the touch of his lips on her fingers. Was she to fail him now, was she to be so faint-hearted that she would not go on when already she had achieved so much? She gripped her fingers together to stop them trembling and as she did so she realized that the carriage was turning into a narrow, semi-circular drive.

In the darkness the grey-turreted *schloss* seemed immense and grimly unwelcoming. Then the front door opened. Wanda steeled herself to descend. The obvious surprise of the servants as they viewed the travel-stained coach as she walked up the steps and into the marble hall did nothing to calm her anxiety.

"I have a letter for the Baroness Waluzen," she explained. "Kindly convey it to her."

A powdered footman took the note, another showed her into a small ante-room and hastily lit the candles. There was no fire and Wanda felt herself shiver. Suppose the Baroness would not see her, suppose she could not stay here! Must she go back to the Chancellery or should she try to find an inn where she could be accommodated for the night?

She had been told that all Vienna was full, that every hole and corner was occupied and that unexpected visitors had to sleep in their carriages or, if they were not wealthy enough to possess one, on a seat in the Prata.

Despite every resolution she began to tremble. She realized now that she was very tired, and although she had told Prince Metternich that she had eaten before visiting him, she had only been able to force herself to swallow a mere mouthful. She had been much too excited to feel either cold or hunger. But now it was different. This waiting was intolerable, she thought, and turned to see a footman in the doorway.

He led her across the hall and down a long corridor hung with portraits; then a door was opened and she found herself in a brilliantly lit *salon*.

It was the strangest room that Wanda had ever seen, for it was so crowded with furniture, china, ivories, glass and silver that it was difficult to know how one could cross it without bumping into something. For a moment she thought, in all the jumble of treasures, that the room was empty, till she saw, sitting by the fireplace, an old woman.

She had a wrinkled face and white hair piled high on her head in the fashion that had been the vogue at the end of the eighteenth century. Despite her age she carried herself as stiff and straight as a ramrod. She wore a profusion of sparkling jewels round her neck and on her wrists, and the hand that she held out towards Wanda was glittering with rings.

"So you are Carlotta Schonbörn's child!" she said in a voice deep and rasping, rather like the croak of some exotic bird.

There was something birdlike, too, in the turn of her head, in the bright, inquisitive stare of her eyes which seemed younger than the rest of her body.

"Yes, Madame," Wanda answered, as she sank in a deep curtsy.

"You're pretty, too. I remember your mother when she was first married. I never expected her to be happy—your father was far too old for her and a monstrously dull man."

Wanda did not know what to reply to this and so she

said nothing, merely standing before the Baroness, finding it hard not to keep glancing at the chains of diamonds and sapphires which encircled her neck, or the tinkling bracelets of rubies and emeralds which glittered with every movement she made.

"You are not the least like him," the Baroness said, speaking as if to herself, ". . . and blue eyes . . . I wonder! Yes, I wonder!"

"Wonder what, Madame?" Wanda enquired.

"Was I speaking aloud?" the old lady said sharply. "It is a bad habit I have acquired through living so much alone. You must help me be rid of it—for I understand you have come to stay with me."

"If you will have me, Madame!"

The Baroness laughed at that, a little cackling laugh which seemed somehow to have little humour in it.

"The Prince Metternich has decreed it!" she said. "Don't you know that anything the Prince wants he gets? We all obey him in Vienna. You will find that out before you have been here very long. And now, you had better rest, for I understand we are to go to the Masked Ball to-night."

"You are going, too, Madame?"

"Of course! Did you think to leave me behind? I may be old, but not so old as to prefer my bed when I might be watching other fools enjoying themselves. There will be plenty of time to rest when I am in the grave. Away with you, child, and sleep if you can. You haven't got much time!"

"But . . . Madame . . . what shall I wear?" Wanda asked.

In answer the Baroness picked up the Prince's letter which lay in her lap and, lifting a diamond-framed quiz-zing-glass, looked at it again.

"The Prince says you are to be suitably dressed. How like a man! Where does he expect me to conjure up a robe at this hour of the night?"

"I . . . I . . . have two ball gowns . . . Madame," Wanda faltered. "One of them is white gauze, trimmed with turquoise blue ribbons . . . it seemed very lovely when we had it made . . . but now that I have come to Vienna . . . I am not so sure."

"Your mother chose it?"

"Yes, Madame."

"Carlotta's taste was good. I think we can be sure it will

pass muster for to-night; or if not, you can always wear a domino. I will find a mask for you."

"How can I thank you?" Wanda asked. "I feel there is so much I ought to say and yet I don't know how to say it."

"There is nothing to say, child," the Baroness answered; "I obey the Prince and if I am to enjoy obeying him, then so much the better. I think it is about time I had someone young about me. When one is old, nothing is so ageing as being alone."

"Thank you, Madame—thank you!"

Some hours later, when Wanda was dressed, she realized that she need not have been afraid that her white dress with the turquoise ribbons tied beneath her small pointed breasts, would disgrace her. It was simple and unsophisticated, but it became her better than anything more elaborate could have done. She clasped her mother's turquoise pendant round her neck, carried her gloves of the same colour and went down to the *salon* to meet the critical eyes of the Baroness, holding her head high and no longer afraid.

She had slept peacefully the exhausted, relaxed sleep of a child and now her eyes were shining and her hair, brushed by the Baroness's maid, had dancing red-gold lights in it as it caught the gleam of the tapers in the crystal sconces.

If the Baroness had seemed fantastic before, her appearance was now breath-taking. She wore an elaborate gown of green satin in the very latest fashion from Paris, cut exaggeratedly low over her withered chest and revealing her thin, blue-veined arms and bony shoulders. But her neck was hidden by row upon row of fabulous diamonds, the bodice of her dress was positively armoured with them, while a tiara of great height and brilliance decorated her white hair. Wanda was so awe-struck at the Baroness' jewellery that she forgot for a moment that she was waiting for a verdict on herself.

"You look very nice, my dear," the Baroness said in a surprisingly gentle tone, then added with a cackle of laughter, "This will give them something to talk about— Spring and Winter side by side!"

"We shall be masked, won't we?" Wanda enquired.

"I doubt if a mask will prove a sufficient disguise where I am concerned," the Baroness answered drily, "but at

your age you want to hide as little of your face as possible.
You will see that it is the older women to-night who wear
the heaviest disguise, hoping to ensnare some man who
would not look at them otherwise. Fancy dress is for those
who need to be fancy. Here is your mask."

She held out as she spoke a minute little mask of
velvet. It was only a strip of ribbon with its two large
holes for the eyes and when Wanda had fixed it on her
face she realized that it gave a subtle allure to the white-
ness of her skin and brought out the fiery depths of her
hair. It was provocative, a challenge in its very brevity.

"And now let us have dinner," the Baroness said and
preceded Wanda into a huge dining-room where footmen
in red and gold uniform stood waiting to serve them.

It was a meal such as Wanda had imagined existed only
in books—chosen for its subtle flavours with sauces which
left no doubt that the chef had a genius all his own. There
was a different wine with every course.

The Baroness ate with relish and Wanda realized that
this type of elaborate dinner was prepared for her always
whether she was alone or had guests. It was almost laugh-
able to remember the simple meals which they had
enjoyed at home and which she had thought so good. There
was no comparison between them and what she was
eating now; and yet she had been trained to appreciate
good taste whether she met it in art or music or cuisine.

It was nearly nine o'clock when at length they rose
from the table, and when the carriage was announced at
the door they left at once for the Hofburg where, as the
Baroness told Wanda, the Ball was taking place.

As they joined the long rows of carriages and coaches,
all travelling in the same direction, Wanda felt an almost
breathless sense of excitement within her. It was as if the
curtain were rising on a play at the theatre, but this time
she had a leading part to play.

She had not mentioned to the Baroness that there was
any reason for her going to the Ball save to enjoy herself.
But she thought perhaps the old woman's intuition had
told her that the Prince had other reasons for wishing her
to be there. Wanda knew that the Baroness was watching
her with those shrewd, twinkling eyes which seemed to
miss nothing, and as they drew near to the Palace she
said:

"Don't be afraid, girl. People who are afraid are no use

to themselves or to anyone else. It is courage that wins battles."

"I am not afraid now," Wanda said. "There was only that one moment before I arrived at your house when I wanted to run away."

"But you didn't," the Baroness said.

"No, of course not," Wanda said.

"That is all that matters. A man or a woman who tells you they have never felt afraid is a liar."

There was no time to say more, for the footmen were letting down the steps and opening the door of the coach.

Inside the Hofburg all was light and colour and the chatter of a thousand tongues. The ancient residence of the Kings of Austria had been specially chosen for these ingenious character masques in which the incognito of the domino often lent itself to the masterpieces of intrigue with which the capital was rife.

Wanda saw a huge hall magnificently lighted, and exquisitely decorated with garlands of flowers; running round it there was a circular gallery giving access to many rooms arranged for supper. On the floor seats covered in red and gold were disposed like an amphitheatre and seated on them, watching the dancers, were crowds of guests, some of whom wore dominoes, while others were attired in elaborate and often fantastic fancy dress.

There were several orchestras playing waltzes and polonaises, and in the adjoining galleries minuets were danced. Everyone was masked and it was obvious at the first glance that pomp and ceremony had been laid aside and that there was almost an air of Bohemianism in the great ballroom. Women were laughing provocatively, defying their partners to guess whether they were of honourable birth or merely courtesans from the streets outside. Men in strangely painted masks and completely enveloping dominoes might be Emperor or prentice, courtier or knave.

The music, which was incessant, seemed to throb in everyone's veins and for the first time in her life Wanda saw people dancing with an abandonment that had something almost pagan about it.

The Baroness led the way across the ballroom. As they wound their way between the dancers, Wanda realized that the Baroness was correct in thinking that everyone would recognize her despite the mask of green satin she was wearing to match her gown. People spoke to her on all

sides, some respectfully, some with a note of jesting
familiarity in their voices as if a long acquaintance entitled them to special intimacies.

"I have just said," one man remarked with a wink at his
friends, "that Vienna presents a panorama of Europe and
no panorama of Europe would be complete, my dear
Baroness, without you."

"You were never distinguished either as a flatterer or a
wit, my dear Count," the Baroness replied crushingly and
went on again before her discomfited admirer could think
of an answer.

At last she came to rest and seated herself at the top of
the room where, Wanda guessed, other ladies as distinguished as she was herself had gathered together deliberately; and then, before Wanda could speak the question
which trembled on her lips, someone asked it for her.

"Are the Sovereigns here yet?" a woman in a yellow
domino enquired.

"I think I can see them coming now," was her companion's reply, a big man with a red beard, which must
have made it easy for his friends to identify him.

"How can you know?" the woman asked.

"They have come to mingle with the *hoi polloi*," her
companion remarked, "but they appear very conscious of
their condescension. Watch for the King of Prussia. He
has on these occasions the heavy self-consciousness of a
bull entering a field of cows."

"Hush, hush!" the lady in yellow said hastily.

Then Wanda heard a voice in her ear.

"The Czar," it whispered, "is wearing a black cloak
spangled with stars over a white uniform on which he
wears only one decoration."

The voice was so low that for a moment she could
hardly believe her own ears, and then as she glanced
swiftly round she saw the mask of a monkey slipping away
from her side into the gyrating crowd. It was a man who
had spoken, but now he was gone! The Baroness had heard
nothing.

"There is the Duchess of Oldenburg," she said, pointing
out a woman dancing past, "sister to the Czar. She thinks
she is disguised, but I would recognize those pearls anywhere. They are too fabulous to be imitated."

"Does that mean that the Czar is here?" Wanda asked.

"I expect so," the Baroness answered indifferently; and

then, as Wanda looked about her, a clown wearing a painted mask bowed low before her.

"Fair Nymph, honour me by treading this measure in my arms. Refuse me and I die!"

Without asking the Baroness' permission, Wanda accepted the invitation; she wanted to have a chance to look round; she wanted to find the Czar; yet she wondered what, when she had found him, she should do next.

She was whirled away in a jogging polonaise and just as her companion swept her round, she saw him—saw a cloak of black covered in silver stars; saw, too, that it was thrown back a little to reveal all too clearly to anyone who was looking the sparkle of diamonds against a white uniform.

With a cleverness Wanda had not believed possible of herself she managed to slip from her partner's arms, lose him on the crowded floor and make her way back again through the encircling couples to where she had seen the Czar standing alone looking at the throng.

Richard, as it happened, was feeling cross and uncomfortable. The Emperor's coat was too tight for him and, having agreed to this masquerade, he had, at the last moment, taken a dislike to it. They had dined well and he should have been ready to enjoy himself with the abandonment that comes from good food and plenty of wine.

The Emperor Francis was by every count a generous host. The Congress was costing him an incredible sum, for all the expenses of the guests at the Hofburg were paid by him. He was entertaining month after month five Sovereigns, two hundred and sixteen heads of families and a host of lesser princes, ambassadors, envoys and their hangers-on. Almost every day dinner was laid on forty tables.

On nights like this not only those who were staying in the Palace were wined and dined, but a host of other guests were invited to the banquet which preceded every ball. Richard had never cared for mass entertainment and to-night was no exception. What had put him in an ill-humour, too, was that at dinner he was not seated, as he had expected, next to Katharina, but between two ladies-in-waiting, neither of whom interested him in the slightest.

The meal, as far as he was concerned, was therefore drawn-out and dreary and things were not helped by the fact that the Empress of Russia chose, after dinner, to engage him in conversation. Richard had tried to be sorry for the Empress Elizabeth, knowing that she was neglected by the Czar, but he found himself, instead, sympathizing with her unfaithful husband.

She had not, even in her youth, been as alluring as Marie Narischkin and now she had lost even the attractions she had possessed when she first married. She had let herself grow fat and her face was covered with blotches and pimples. She was not a clever woman and she did little to uphold the dignity of her position. She might be lonely and she undoubtedly was, but she made no effort to gain popularity and generally avoided all ceremonies and public appearances, however beholden she might be to appear at them.

It was, therefore, in quite a wrong spirit that Richard, wearing the Czar's clothes and his black and silver cloak, came downstairs to the ballroom. He was amused to note, as he left the royal bedroom, that the sentries at the door presented arms without a second glance at him and that, as he moved down the corridors, those who met him bowed or curtsied and no pretence was made not to recognize him because his face was masked.

As he caught a glimpse of himself in the mirrors, he had to admit that the Czar's barber had done his work well. He undoubtedly looked extremely like the Emperor Alexander, or rather, he looked like the Emperor ineffectively disguised by a mask and patterned cloak.

"I wonder how many hours I shall have to endure this?" Richard asked himself as he walked into the ballroom. He knew that he could not go to bed before the Czar and he half hoped that the truth, when he heard it, would not be so alluring as the Emperor anticipated.

He decided not to dance but to go and get himself a drink. He turned to walk towards one of the refreshment rooms, when suddenly there was a hand on his arm and a little voice said breathlessly:

"Please, you will break my fan! Oh! you've stood on it!"

He felt something beneath his feet and looking down perceived that a stick of mother of pearl belonging to a painted fan was snapped in two. He bent to pick it up and rising, saw a little heart-shaped face with very clear blue eyes shining through the black velvet of a tiny mask. Her hair was the colour of chestnuts. He wondered if he had seen her before and decided that he had not.

"I am afraid your fan is broken."

"Alas! and I was so fond of it."

"I will have it mended for you."

"It is too much damaged for that."

"On the contrary. There is a man somewhere in the town who can mend anything—except hearts, of course."

She smiled at that and he saw there was a tiny dimple on the left-hand side of her mouth.

"Let us move out of this crowd and talk about it," he suggested, "or would you rather dance?"

"Could we . . . could we dance?"

"But, of course."

He put his arm round her. He had not imagined that anyone could be so light. The orchestra was playing a waltz and Richard remembered that he had once found waltzing quite enjoyable before he had decided that dancing with the young ladies who frequented Almack's bored him. They swept round and round. She did not talk. He liked her for that; and when at length the music stopped, they found themselves opposite an ante-room decorated with banks of flowers and great ferns, and it seemed almost as if they had moved into a fragrant garden. It was dimly lit and they found two seats set discreetly behind a floral screen.

"Let us sit down," Richard suggested.

She obeyed him and then, as he turned to look at her, her eyes fell before his and he realized that she was shy.

"Tell me about yourself," he said gently. "Who are you?"

"My name is Wanda," she answered. "I believe it is not correct to give one's whole name at a masked ball."

"No, of course not," he agreed, remembering that his name, too, must remain secret.

"Tell me instead why I have not seen you before."

"That question is easy to answer. I only arrived in Vienna this evening."

"This evening! Then this is your first sight of Congress at play?"

"My very first."

"And what do you think of it?"

"Isn't it presumptuous to think anything on so short an acquaintance?"

"It depends on whether you make up your mind about things quickly or slowly. Personally, I always find my first impressions are the correct ones."

"I only hope mine are."

"Now, you must tell me what your first impression is."

"To-night the Congress seems to me like . . . an enchanted waltz," she answered slowly.

"A very lovely description," he answered.

She was looking up at him and their eyes met. For a moment there seemed nothing more to say. Perhaps that waltz they had danced together had been enchanted.

"Wanda! I like that name," Richard said ruminatively. "I don't think I have ever known anyone called that before."

"I have always wondered what one's name means to other people," Wanda said. "To oneself it is so commonplace because one is used to it. Names to me have a very special meaning."

"I wish I could tell you mine," Richard said, "but not to-night."

"No, not to-night," she answered, and he saw her glance down at the sparkle of diamonds which showed beneath the folds of his cloak.

He remembered suddenly she had guessed him to be the Czar, and a sudden devil within him prompted him to behave as he thought all young women expected an Emperor to behave. He reached out and took her hand in his.

"You are very lovely, little Wanda. Am I the first person in Vienna to tell you that?"

He felt her fingers tremble.

"Yes," she whispered.

"Don't you think we ought to do something to celebrate this evening of your arrival?" he asked.

"What . . . what do you mean?"

How young she was, he thought. She made him think of spring, of the daffodils blooming in the park at home, of birds singing in the rhododendron bushes. He had a sudden vision of Katharina, of her face looking down at him as he lay on her bed. He had not realized until this moment how old she was.

He hesitated before he answered and then, prompted by some feeling he did not understand, he said:

"Shall we slip away from this crowd and go and have supper somewhere alone?"

He saw her hesitate and knew, by the sudden tenseness of her body and the fluttering of her fingers beneath his, that she was frightened.

"I will bring you back safely. I promise you that."

"You promise?"

It was the question of a child wishing to be reassured of its fears of the dark.

"I promise," he repeated.

Chapter Four

RICHARD hired a carriage at the door of the Palace and he and Wanda drove to one of the small restaurants off the Prater. He had been there several times before, found it quiet and attractive, and he thought now it would be the place where they would see no-one who would be particularly interested in their appearance. Not that anything one did in Vienna these days was likely to be surprising.

He was well aware, however, that there were other factors to be considered, and while Wanda was seeking her cloak he had taken the opportunity of changing the star-spangled disguise he wore for something quite different.

In one of the corridors near the entrance he saw a man asleep. He had obviously indulged too freely in the good wine and was sleeping off the effects on one of the gilt and brocade couches placed in uniform rows along the corridor beneath the Imperial portraits.

Swiftly Richard untied the dark blue cloak the reveller wore and took, too, his wide-brimmed satin hat trimmed with cock's feathers. It was but a matter of seconds to slip off the cloak given him by the Czar and place it beneath the cushion of an empty arm-chair.

The cloak he had purloined was more voluminous than his own and could be tied with ribbons down to the waist. This effectively concealed his uniform and beneath it he undid the sparkling *Epée de Sweden* and put it in his pocket. When Wanda re-appeared and he went towards her, she looked a little startled for a moment at his changed appearance. Then she smiled.

"We don't want anyone to know that we have left the ball," Richard explained in a low voice.

"No, of course not," she answered, thinking of the Baroness and wondering what she would say when she realized that her charge was nowhere to be seen.

"We won't be long, will we?" she asked a little apprehensively.

"You can trust yourself to me," he replied, and slipping his hand beneath her arm, he led her down the corridor and into the big entrance hall where guests were still arriving.

As Richard had anticipated, there were only half a dozen other people in the restaurant and they were not easy to distinguish, for the tables were arranged in small alcoves decorated with imitation vines. One could sup and drink in almost complete isolation. There was an orchestra composed of half a dozen men in national costume and there was an atmosphere of warmth and welcome which made Wanda exclaim as she sat down at the table allotted to them:

"I like this place. What is it called?"

"The Golden Vine," Richard told her; "and now I am going to order you something to eat and some of the special wine for which this place is famous."

He liked the way she accepted his decisions without argument and without comment, and when the waiter had withdrawn he said:

"Take off your mask. I want to look at you."

She raised her hands obediently to the little strip of black velvet which lay across her eyes; then, in the light of the candles which stood on the table, she turned her face towards him.

He had expected her to be pretty, but not as lovely as she was. Her eyes, seeming almost too large for her small face, were like an English sky in summer, and the unusual combination of the red-gold hair, blue eyes and dark lashes left him for the moment speechless as he sat looking at her, wondering if ever before he had seen anything quite so young, so fresh and so entrancing. Under his scrutiny she grew shy and her fingers went to her cheeks.

"Why . . . why do you look at me like that?" she faltered.

"I was thinking how different you are from anyone I have ever seen before."

"Is . . . is that a compliment?"

"Of course. Don't you want to be different?"

"I have never thought about it. I'm afraid I know very

little about the world or other people. I told you I only arrived in Vienna to-night."

"And why have you come?"

"My mother, before she died, wanted me to go to balls, masques and receptions like other girls."

"And now you have been to one, what do you think of it?"

"Could they all be as wonderful?"

He laughed at the artlessness of her question.

"I wish I could answer yes to that, but you will grow satiated with them. You will find them dull simply because to-day's rout is horribly similar to yesterday's, and to-morrow's will be no different. It is sad, but everything palls when it becomes too familiar."

"Everything?" she asked.

"Everything," he repeated firmly, "even people."

"No, no, that is not true. The people one loves grow dearer and more precious. One's appreciation of them grows. It doesn't diminish."

"You must have been fortunate in your choice of friends —or should I say . . . lovers?"

There was a sudden harshness in his voice. She laughed at that, easily and spontaneously.

"I have no lovers. You are the first man I have ever been alone with, except my father and some of his elderly Army friends who used to come and stay at the *schloss* from time to time."

"Is that really true?" Richard asked, thinking of the women he had known—the gay, fashionable young ladies of St. James's, who always seemed to have started flirtations in their cradles, to have had beaux waiting for them at the schoolroom door.

"You can believe me," Wanda assured him, "because you see, I always tell the truth."

"Always?"

"But of course. It is wrong to lie and very uncomfortable."

"Perhaps you have never had any secrets?"

She flushed a little at that and looked away from him. She had suddenly remembered that for the first time in her life she had a secret, a secret so big, so terrifying that she felt it must be written on her face in letters of fire.

But when the food and wine arrived, she forgot everything but her pleasure in being in new surroundings. She found it, too, increasingly easy to talk to the man who sat at her side. Had she ever really believed, she asked herself, that Emperors were different from ordinary human beings? There was something strong and protective about him, she felt safe and secure in his company, and in her innocence she did not ask herself what would have happened had she felt otherwise.

He had not removed his mask, and she knew that he would not wish to be recognized in such a place and therefore she made no comment on the fact. She was unimportant, a nobody, and so it did not matter what she did; but she could see his eyes watching her and for the first time in her life she was very conscious of being a woman.

The wine was delicious and though she was not hungry after her dinner, she forced herself to eat a little of the excellent dishes he had ordered.

"Tell me more about yourself."

There was a deep note in his voice and she thought suddenly that his slight accent when he spoke Austrian was one of the most attractive things she had ever heard.

"There is so little to tell," she answered. "I wish you would tell me about yourself. You asked me what I think of the Congress—what do you think about it?"

His answer to that sort of question, she thought to herself, was perhaps the sort of thing the Prince would want to hear. Her companion only laughed.

"To talk of the Congress in Vienna is as banal as talking about the weather in England," he said.

"Do people talk about it all the time?"

"All the time!" he assured her solemnly, "when they are not speculating as to who is making love to whom!"

"Is there time for love-making when everyone is so busy?"

"What are they busy at except making love?" Richard enquired. "Oh, I'm not talking about the ministers—they do a certain amount of work, it is true, although they have time for their recreations as well—but the rest of the people, the Sovereigns and their suites are here for amusement, and what could be more amusing than love?"

He spoke cynically, almost bitterly, and then looked down to see a troubled expression on the little face beside him.

"What is the matter?" he asked.

"I was trying to understand," Wanda answered; "you

see, love has never seemed to me something to play with or think about frivolously. It has always seemed . . . sort of . . . sacred."

Richard was silent. He thought of the *affaires de cœur* being carried on, schemed and indulged in by every sect and section of the social throng gathered in Vienna, secularizers and secularized, mediatizers and mediatized, poets, gamesters, bankers and delegates—they all seemed to be playing the same game with the same greed and yearning for emotional excitement.

He was no different from the rest of them. His *affaire* with Princess Katharina was a mere gratification of his senses—nothing more and nothing less. It took this simple child to show him the truth of it and for a moment he was ashamed.

Then he laughed at himself. Was he becoming maudlin that he could believe there was anything else in life but the seeking of pleasure wherever one might find it? This love Wanda spoke of existed only in the fairy-tale books. As for being sacred, he had known a great number of women in his life and there had been nothing sacred about any of them. All the same, it would be a shame to disillusion her.

"Tell me more about your kind of love," he said. "I am afraid I am as ignorant on the subject as you are about the social exercises of Vienna."

She guessed that he was mocking her and he felt as if she withdrew into some inner fastness of herself where he could not reach her.

"I must not bore you with my chatter," she said with a dignity he had not expected. "As I have already told you, I am very ignorant."

He found himself capitulating to her sweetness.

"Forgive me," he said humbly. "I am not laughing at you. It is just that I, too, am ignorant. We have lived in different worlds. Perhaps your values are truer than mine."

He felt her soften at that and remembered that she thought of him as an Emperor, divorced from the human problems and the ordinary simple things of life.

"Tell me your thoughts," he pleaded.

"It is hard to put it into words," she answered slowly, "but I have always dreamed that perhaps one day I should fall in love with a man who would love me in return and then I could dedicate my life to making him happy. Surely, if one loved someone enough, it would not be difficult to forget oneself completely and think only of him?"

"Do you think any man is worthy of such unselfishness?"

"The man I loved would have to be or I should not love him," she answered, and her smile was the loveliest thing he had ever seen.

"You are making me almost believe that dreams might come true," he said.

"It cannot be hard to believe that here," she said softly.

She raised her eyes to his and he held his breath for a moment. The music of the violins filled the room, the orchestra was playing a waltz, its haunting melody seemed to enfold them. There really was something enchanted about this moment. He had a wild desire to gather her up in his arms and take her away, away from Vienna, from the people with their chatter and gossip which besmirched everything and everybody, away to somewhere where they could be alone, entirely alone, and where the world could not encroach upon them.

Then the music stopped and he came back to earth and remembered his own position—penniless, a hanger-on at a foreign Court because he was exiled from his own country. He remembered his obligation to the Czar, the part he was supposed to be playing to-night, and knew that even by being here with this girl he had picked up in the ballroom at the Hofburg he was jeopardizing his position as a royal favourite.

"We must go back."

With an effort he forced himself to call a waiter and ask for the reckoning.

"Is it time to go?" Wanda asked.

"People may be wondering what has become of us."

"Yes, of course."

She started guiltily as if she too had been touched by a magic wand which made her forget time and responsibility. Then, as she picked up her mask to put it over her eyes, Richard laid a hand on hers.

"I shall see you again," he said.

"Do you really want to?"

The ingenuousness of her question seemed to fire him far more effectively than any coquetry would have done.

"I want it more than anything else in the world," he answered and was surprised at the sincerity in his own voice.

"I am staying with the Baroness Waluzen," Wanda answered, "and my full name is Comtesse Wanda Schonbörn."

"We shall meet again, to-morrow if it can possibly be managed."

He saw the light leap into her eyes and knew she was glad, as glad as he was himself. His hand still enclosed hers and he felt his own heart beating surprisingly quickly.

"Did you really think that all this could happen to-night and we could either of us forget about it?" he asked in a low voice.

"I shall . . . never forget."

They were both very still and then, as her eyes dropped before his, he rose to his feet. They left the restaurant and re-entered the carriage which was still waiting for them outside. As the door shut and they were together in the warm darkness, he said:

"I, too, shall never forget to-night."

He heard her draw in a deep breath and then, before he had time to think about it, before he could consider anything but the thumping of his own heart, she was in his arms.

He heard her give a litle cry of surprise before his mouth found hers. Her lips were soft and yielding. It was a kiss such as he had never known before, a kiss which had some strange spiritual quality which was quite unlike the kisses he had given and taken so passionately and so hungrily from so many women. And then, as if the coach had flown to their destination, they found themselves at the door of the Palace.

There was no time to say anything. A linkman opened the door and helped Wanda to dismount. Richard followed her, pausing to pay the coachman. Then, when he looked round again, he found that she had vanished. She had not waited for him in the brilliantly lit hall. There was no sign of her in the corridors leading back to the ballroom.

For a moment he contemplated going in search of her; then he remembered his commitments and went instead to where he had hidden the star-spangled cloak beneath the cushions of the big arm-chair. He found it crumpled but safe and, slipping it under his arm, repaired to a cloakroom, where he changed and replaced the Swedish decoration on his coat.

Slowly, with a nonchalance he was far from feeling, he sauntered back to the ballroom. He stood at the end of the room deliberately conspicuous, letting his cloak fall back a little to reveal the glittering decoration.

As he stood there, he was conscious that he was looking for Wanda, looking for her everywhere amongst the dancing laughing throng whirling around him. The merry-making and the excitement had increased during the time they had been away. The dancers were looking dishevelled and it was quite obvious that the wine had played its part in accentuating their sense of enjoyment and fun. A little Columbine, oblivious of the fact that she was half-naked, was being carried high on the shoulders of a big man dressed as a pirate. Richard recognised one of the Russian envoys and wondered if the Czar was enjoying himself as much as at least one of his subjects, and then he felt a hand clutch his arm and heard Katharina say:

"Where have you been, Richard? The Czar has been looking for you."

"Is he still here?" Richard enquired.

"He has retired and you are to go to him at once."

"To hear is to obey," Richard said mockingly. "May I escort you, Madame?"

He offered her his arm with exaggerated deference. She was looking very beautiful to-night in a dress of deep blue which clung to her figure. There was a crescent of diamonds in her hair to represent the moon. Her shoulders were very white, her heavy-lidded eyes dark and mysterious and as she moved beside him with a lightness that was characteristic of her, Richard thought, as he had thought so often before, that despite her fair skin, Katharina was completely and absolutely oriental.

"I missed you for a long time," she said when they were out of earshot of the crowds moving in and out of the ballroom.

"How did you know I was not the Czar?"

"Is a woman ever deceived by the man she loves?" Katharina enquired.

"Someone told you," Richard said. "I do not believe you guessed."

She flashed him a glance from underneath her eyelashes which told him he had hit upon the truth.

"The Czar was wrong," he said: "he imagined that

for once he would be able to escape the eternal vigilance which surrounds him."

"No one knows but me," Katharina said quickly, "and Butinski."

"Butinski?" Richard repeated, wondering who that might be.

Then he remembered—the Czar's barber! So she was keeping a check on the movements of her royal master, as he kept a check on hers.

"Are you cross with me?" Katharina's voice was soft and seductive; and now, as they climbed the wide staircase she put out her hand towards his cheek, but he turned his face away from her.

"You know how much I dislike that sort of thing," he said.

"Darling, you make a magnificent Emperor."

Richard did not answer. They had reached the Czar's apartments and he stopped just out of earshot of the sentries.

"Are you coming in with me?"

"No, I am going to my bedroom. I . . . I am not sleepy."

The invitation was very evident in her eyes and on her lips.

"The Czar may keep me," he said stiffly, and turning away from her walked towards the guarded door.

On returning to the ballroom, Wanda ran first to the place in the amphitheatre where she had left the Baroness. When she saw that she was not there, she panicked; perhaps the old lady was angry and had gone home in disgust. Then she remembered that the supper rooms were a more likely place to find someone who did not dance, and hurrying up the stairs to the circular gallery she went from one room to another until finally her search was rewarded.

At a big table occupied by many men and women as distinguished as herself, the Baroness was just finishing supper. As Wanda came to her side, she glanced up at her quizzically, but her words were commonplace.

"Are you enjoying yourself, child?"

"Yes, Madame."

"Are you ready to go home?"

"If you are, Madame."

"Very well. Give me your arm."

Wanda did as she was bid. She was well aware, as was the Baroness, that many curious glances were cast in their direction; but she was not introduced and, with the Baroness leaning on her arm, they went slowly from the supper room and down another staircase to the entrance hall of the Palace. It was only when they got into the coach and the Baroness sank back against the soft cushions as if she were tired that she said:

"I saw you dancing with the Czar. Did you find him a pleasant companion?"

"Yes, he was very kind," Wanda answered. "How . . . how did you recognise him?"

"I am not bird-witted," the Baroness retorted. "Besides, the Emperor Alexander courts recognition. Everyone in Vienna knows that."

The Baroness asked no more questions, although Wanda felt instinctively that her curiosity was aroused. When they reached the Baroness's home and were going up the stairs together side by side to their bedrooms, she heard the old lady say, almost under her breath:

"You are young . . . too young for this sort of game."

Wanda bade her hostess good-night and found the maid waiting up for her to help her undress. Only when at last she was alone in her bedroom did she put her fingers to her mouth and touch her lips wonderingly and allow the memory of what had happened to her to sweep into her consciousness, ecstatically and with a sense of wonderment.

He had kissed her! She could feel the touch of his lips on hers. Time had stood still. She had no idea how long he had held her close in his arms, her head against his shoulder. It was almost as if he had drawn her soul from her body and she had for a moment been transported by a happiness and a joy beyond anything she had ever dreamed of.

He had kissed her! For a moment she could think of nothing else. It all had happened so unexpectedly, yet it seemed to her as if the whole evening had been a prelude to that moment.

Then, slowly, as she stood there in the strange room, her elation ebbed away from her. He was an Emperor, the Czar of all the Russias, and she was allowing herself to think of him as if he was merely a man. He had a wife and a mistress. Had she gone mad to allow such liberties even in the interests of her country?

Roughly, with a sudden revulsion of feeling, Wanda rubbed her lips fiercely, as if she would rub his kiss away from them. She had been told to dance with the Czar, to get to know him. She had obeyed, but he had told her nothing that could be of the slightest interest to anyone save herself.

The Baroness was right, she was too young and too inexperienced for anything like this. She was letting her emotions become involved. She was letting her feelings superimpose themselves upon her intelligence. She knew what the Prince wanted of her. She must think only of that.

She was shivering as she blew out her candles and crept between the sheets of the big canopied bed.

In the darkness she tried to recapture her feelings when she had told Prince Metternich she would die if necessary for the country she loved. But all she could remember were two eyes looking at her through the slits in a mask and lips which seemed to ignite in her body an unquenchable flame of delight.

Chapter Five

RICHARD awoke with the feeling that he had been dreaming. Then, as gradually his eyes focussed to perceive the familiar objects in the room, he saw Wanda's fan lying on the dressing-table.

From his bed he could see the broken pieces of mother of pearl shining in the pale sunshine which was seeping through the uncurtained window. He had drawn the heavy brocade curtains and thrown back the shutters last night to stand for a long time staring out at the star-strewn sky, hearing very faintly in the distance, as though it was little more than the breath of the night itself, the strains of music.

'The enchanted waltz' Wanda had called the Congress, and he thought now that the whole evening had been enchanted. Could the girl he had met casually in the ballroom of the Hofburg have really been as attractive as he had thought at the time?

It seemed to him that all his life he had been pursuing women and when he had caught up with them they had proved sadly disappointing. If they were beautiful, their conversation was banal to the point of exasperation; if they were intelligent, there had been something about them—perhaps some quite small thing—which had repulsed him on closer acquaintance.

There had not been a jarring note the whole of the time he had spent with this unknown girl. How simple she had been in her enjoyment, how spontaneous in her laughter!

It was the fashion among the young ladies of St. James's to be *blasé* and the bucks and dandies who were his friends when he was in London had made it the fashion to yawn through every type of entertainment and to swear that even the most acclaimed beauty made them die of *ennui*. A great deal of it was pretence, of course, but one must move with the fashion and he had grown used to languid voices and bored faces.

Here in Austria things were different. Foreigners were much more volatile and certainly in most cases far more entertaining. In the weeks that he had been in Vienna he had spent the majority of his time with the emotional, capricious Katharina. He had enjoyed himself and he would have been a churl to deny it. No one could have been more generous with her favours—but it was after all just another love-affair.

What he had felt last night was something very different, so different that now in the clear light of the morning he did not believe it was true.

He rang the bell by his bedside, but a few minutes passed before Harry came hurrying into the room.

" 'Wake early, ain't you, Guv?" he asked cheerily.

"What time is it?" Richard enquired.

" 'Bout 10.30 and I'd said ter mesel', I said, 'It'll be noon before the Guv ope's 'is peepers or I'm a Dutchman.' "

Harry started to tidy up the clothes which Richard had thrown on a chair the night before.

"Must 'ave been sober as a judge, by the look of you," he added.

"That's enough, Harry," Richard said. "I don't know why I put up with your impertinence."

"I'll get your shaving water," Harry grinned. " 'Er 'Igh and Mightiness is expectin' you to breakfast, so you'd better look yer best."

He went out of the room and Richard could hear him whistling as he went down the passage. He tried to frown, but only managed to smile. It was no use being cross with Harry. He was not a conventional valet and nothing would ever make him one.

He had come to Richard originally as a groom, in a flush period when he could afford a stable full of horses and half a dozen men to look after them. Then, when things deteriorated, the servants had gone, one by one, until only Harry was left. He had not worried if his wages were paid irregularly of if his duties ranged from cook to butler.

He took everything in his stride and gave his master

an absurd, touching devotion which Richard knew could not be bought for all the gold in Europe. But he said what he thought and no one could stop his saying it. He had taken a dislike to Princess Katharina—not that that was anything unusual, because he was habitually jealous in one way or another of Richard's ladies. Perhaps he was all the more vulnerable where she was concerned because she was a Russian. He had loathed the whole Russian nation from the moment they had joined the Czar's entourage.

Richard was half-afraid that one night he would find Harry with his throat cut from ear to ear or with a knife sticking in his back. At the same time it was a relief beyond words to have him with him in his exile. Harry was a link with England, a link with the only place in the world where Richard wanted to be and which was barred to him perhaps for ever.

He wondered with a sudden sense of desperation what the future held. Was he to spend the rest of his life driven from foreign capital to foreign capital? A hanger-on of Princes, an impecunious courtier who must pay for his supper by making love to unattractive women or by picking the pocket of some unsophisticated young nobleman sowing his wild oats?

The idea was frightening, and a sudden nostalgia brought Richard from his bed to stand at the open window.

Below lay a courtyard and beyond it were the formal gardens of the Palace. There was the iridescent glitter of a dozen fountains, a magnificent array of statuary, a vista of artificial lakes, a Delphic temple set among the elegant uniformity of cypress trees. But Richard saw instead the untidy, badly clipped lawns of his home in Hertfordshire, the rough parkland sloping down to a twisting trout stream and rising again towards the thick woods which sheltered the pheasants.

What did he want with balls and masques and diplomacy? He wanted only the bitter wind blowing up the Lea Valley, the smell of the earth in his nostrils and the sound of the huntsman's horn in his ears.

His reverie was broken by the crash of the door being kicked open by Harry as he entered with a jug of hot water in one hand and a shaving-bowl in the other.

"Met one of 'er 'Igh and Mightiness's slit-eyed slaves along the passage," he said cheerily. "You're to get along there pronto. There's no rest for the wicked, as me old mother used to say."

"Hurry up and shave me," Richard said wearily, turning from the window. "And be careful your hand doesn't shake like it did yesterday morning or I'll knock your head off."

" 'Twas that filthy drink them Russian gave me," Harry replied; "vodka or some such outlandish name it's called. Looks like gin, tastes like muck, and five minutes after you've 'ad it, 'as the kick of a mule in your innards! I was so foxed I thought me 'ead would burst when I woke. I'm sticking to ale from now on, not that you can get a decent pint outa England."

"You know, Harry, you're an ungrateful cove," Richard said.

"Ungrateful, Guv? 'Ow's that?"

"Well, most people would give their soul to be in Vienna now. The whole world's here! The *haut ton* of Europe are fighting to get in, paying a fortune for the chance of a bed however uncomfortable it may be; and here you are, lounging in the Emperor of Austria's Palace, the Hofburg itself, and all I hear is grumbles."

Harry sniffed.

"Emperors, Kings, Princes and the like may be swell bleaters, Guv, but they're not much different to you and me when it comes to peck and booze. They all bleed if you prick 'em."

"I'll prick you if you make me bleed," Richard snapped. "Is that blood on my chin?"

"Not a sign nor sight of it," Harry answered cheerfully; "now keep still, Guv, she won't care for a phiz with 'airs sprouting round your jaw like the quills of an 'edgehog."

"Who won't?" asked Richard, who was only half attending to what Harry was saying.

" 'Er 'Igh and Mightiness, o' course. You're breakfasting with 'er. 'Ave you forgotten?"

"Who said I was?"

"It's a command orl rite," Harry said. "Won't stand no refusals, she won't. Don't forget, Guv, those five 'undred sparklers or what's left of 'em ain't going to last for ever."

"Damme, Harry! must you continually rub my poverty in my face?" Richard asked. "You seem to forget that this is the first time for many years I have been solvent.

My clothes are paid for, your wages are up to date. 'Pon my soul, we've never been in a better position financially."

Harry put the shaving bowl down on the table with a bang.

"That's orl rite, Guv," he said quietly, "but this time when we comes to the end o' everything we can't go 'ome."

"Blast you for reminding me!" Richard ejaculated.

There had always been home to run to when all else failed. The house was dilapidated, the chimney post falling down for want of repair, the grounds neglected, the rooms dusty, but it was still home, still a place he could call his own, and he loved it. It was one thing he could not pretend about. He loved it.

"This time we can't go home!" He repeated the words aloud; they sounded like a death sentence.

There was silence between the two men all the more poignant because it said so much in leaving so much unsaid. It was not Richard's fault that the estate was as it was. His father had gambled everything away and although his wealth, as the second son, had not been considerable, it would have been enough to keep him and his family in comfort if the craving for cards had not meant more to him than his family—more in fact than life itself. He had died a gambler's death and Richard's inheritance had been a pile of debts.

The vision of a grey stone house with the woods beyond it faded. He had got to face facts. He was in the Hofburg by the charity of the Czar of Russia.

Slowly he took a white silk shirt from Harry's hands, put on the long, tight trousers that Weston had made for him and which the Prince Regent himself had declared were the best fit he had ever seen. Then he slipped on his blue velvet dressing-gown. It took several minutes for Harry to arrange his hair in the style which had been the admiration of all the best clubs in St. James's.

When he was finished, one had to peer closely to see the resemblance to the Czar which had been so predominant the night before.

"You'd better put my riding things out," Richard said as he turned towards the door. "I shall go riding this morning before luncheon."

"That's if 'Er 'Igh and Mightiness lets you," Harry replied irrepressibly. "Here's 'opin', Guv."

Katharina's room was lit by candles. There were a

dozen placed on either side of her bed where she sat as
it were enthroned among her pillows. Her bare shoulders
were encircled with pale pink gauze, a fold of which
was draped over her fair hair.

"Richard! I thought you were never coming."

There was a lilt of gladness in her voice although her
red lips pouted a little reproachfully at him. As he entered
the room, he was conscious of the heavy fragrance of
the roses which stood on every table. Katharina's favourite flower surrounded her always, whatever the time of
year or wherever she might be.

Richard, moving to her side, repressed the thought that
what Katharina's roses cost in a year would keep him
in luxury; and then, as he bent his head over her hand,
her fingers tightened on his.

"You never came to me last night," she said softly.

"The Emperor kept me late," he lied.

"Are you sure?"

"And I thought you would be tired."

"Were you really thinking of me?"

Her tone was sweet enough, but he looked at her
sharply.

"Your breakfast is waiting," she said and indicated a
table set a little way from the bed. It was covered with
silver dishes and bottles of several sorts of wine, but
Richard looked at it distastefully. He had felt hungry
while Harry was shaving him, but now his appetite
seemed to have gone. He had half-hoped as he came
along the corridor that there would be other people at
breakfast with Katharina this morning. He felt a *tête-à-
tête* was going to be awkward, though why it should
be he was not for the moment prepared to admit even to
himself.

All over Vienna people of importance were entertaining their friends to breakfast. It was an accepted time
for hospitality on the part not only of those who, like
the Ministers of State, had something important to discuss,
but also of those who were so frightened of missing one
moment of the festivities that they must start the day
with a reception even if it involved forgoing some precious hours of sleep.

"It is hot in here," Richard said sharply, "and I hate
breakfast by candlelight."

"We will have the shutters open," Katharina said,

smiling at him fondly as if he were a petulant small boy rather than a disagreeable man.

She reached out her hand for the bell by her side.

"I will open them myself," Richard said hastily, and pulling back the pink satin curtains he unlatched the panelled shutters.

The sun came streaming in and as he turned from the window towards the breakfast table he thought how artificial and theatrical Katharina looked in her great bed with its fat, winged cherub in gold leaf and the heavy spread of white ermine.

"Darling, you are cross this morning," her voice caressed him across the distance between them. "Can the rôle of Emperor have given you a headache?"

"Perhaps," Richard answered, "and it is the last time I play a rôle of any sort in somebody else's coat."

"You didn't tell the Czar it was too tight for you, I hope?" Katharina said. "He is very vain about his figure. It would annoy him considerably for him to think that your shoulders are broader than his."

"He was not interested in my experiences last night," Richard replied, "only in his own."

"He enjoyed himself, I think," Katharina replied. "Enormously."

There was no doubt about that. Richard had found the Czar literally bubbling with excitement at the success of his incognito. Fortunately he had made the acquaintance of two quite humble ladies of the town who regarded the Emperor of Russia with awe and quite unbounded admiration.

He had listened to compliments about himself which had made his heart swell with pride and there was no doubt that for him at any rate the evening had been an unqualified success.

"No one must know that we changed places, Richard," he said earnestly when he had recounted all his adventures. "No one had even the slightest suspicion. I watched you standing at the end of the ballroom and I thought you looked exactly like me."

"I appreciate the compliment, Sire," Richard bowed.

"Only Butinski knows our secret," the Czar went on, "and he is discretion itself. He would lose his life rather than betray me."

Richard debated for a moment whether he should reveal the fact that Butinski was in Katharina's pay. Then he decided to keep silent. Let them all spy on each other. It was none of his business. If Katharina watched the Czar and the Czar watched Katharina, what the hell did it matter?

It was all too fantastic to be credited, Richard thought, just as the Czar himself was a bizarre, incredible character. He listened to the Emperor of all the Russias boasting conceitedly of his success with two cheap little prostitutes, while in the corner of the room, harshly austere among so much magnificence, stood the small bed with its hard leather mattress on which the Czar always slept and which travelled with him wherever he went. Beside the bed lay a Bible which Alexander read far into the night.

Who could understand such a man, a dual personality if ever there was one? And Katharina?

Richard raised his eyes to her face. She had a faint smile on her lips as she lay back amongst her pillows.

"Watching me eat must be very boring for you," he remarked.

"Why?" she questioned. "I am hoping it will make you more genial, more ready to be kind to me."

He thrust his plate away impatiently.

"I want to go riding this morning."

"Oh no, Richard."

"Why not come with me?"

"I hate riding. Besides, I want . . . you. You never came to me last night."

"I have told you that the Czar kept me late."

"That is not true! You left his room at ten minutes past two."

Richard rose from the breakfast table with such violence that the dishes clattered together and a glass of wine was spilled over the white cloth.

"Curse your eternal spying!" he said. "I will not be watched and pried on by you or by anyone else. I shall do what I please and go where I please. This continuous espionage is intolerable!"

He walked across to the window and stood with his back to her. He could feel his anger hot and violent within him and he was breathing quickly with the violence of his rage. Then he found her close beside him, her body pressed against his, her arms reaching up towards his neck. She was wearing only a diaphanous nightgown.

He could feel the live warmth of her nakedness against him as she looked up at his scowling face.

"Darling, I am so sorry. I didn't mean to make you angry. I want you . . . you know that . . . and I waited for you a long time last night."

"I apologize for losing my temper."

The words were clipped and cold and it was an effort for him to utter them.

"Kiss me, Richard, to show that you forgive me."

He bent his head obediently but his mouth avoided her eager lips and rested instead on the softness of her cheek. She smelt of roses, the heavy, exotic fragrance of roses in a summer sun.

"Richard! . . . Oh! Richard!"

He knew what she wanted; but somehow, as automatically his arms went round her, he could not hold her as closely and eagerly as she wanted to be held.

"Love me, Richard, please love me! See, I am pleading with you."

The words were hardly above a whisper. There was no escape from them. As he looked down at her, Richard saw the glint of passion beneath the heaviness of her lids, saw her red lips part voluptuously, and felt the excited quickness of her breath which moved her small pointed breasts.

There came a sudden knocking at the door.

"What is it?" Katharina's voice was sharp and shrill.

"A message from His Imperial Majesty, Your Highness."

Slowly Katharina disengaged herself from Richard and, moving without haste, walked back towards the bed and climbed in. When she had arranged the pillows behind her head and covered herself with the silk, lace-edged sheets, she called out:

"Come in!"

A servant entered with a note. She read it quickly.

"Tell His Imperial Majesty I will wait upon his wishes," she said.

The servant bowed low and went from the room, shutting the door behind him with an ostentatious quietness which Richard found extremely irritating.

"The Emperor wishes me to drive with him in the Prater before luncheon."

Katharina's voice was icy; they both knew this was a reprieve from the intensity of the moment.

"May I accompany you?"

"No. You wish to ride."

"I would forgo that pleasure if you have need of my presence."

"I have no need of you when I am driving with the Czar."

"Shall I leave you now so that you may dress?"

"I must ask you to do that without delay. I have not long in which to get ready."

"Very well."

She reached for the bell, rang it, then extended her hand towards him. He took it and then, as his lips brushed her skin conventionally, she drew him towards her.

"Richard, my darling, why do we quarrel?" she asked, her tone tremulous. There was an expression of pain and unhappiness on her face which Richard had never seen there before. It moved him as nothing else would have done, but, when he would have spoken, even as his arms went out towards her, the door was opened.

Katharina's maids came hurrying in and there was nothing he could do but straighten his back and walk from the room without another word.

Back in his own bed-chamber, he flung on his riding clothes with the impetuous haste of a man who feels he might be pursued. His ill-temper was upon him again and he swore at Harry when he spoke to him. He knew he was behaving like a boor both to Katharina and to his valet, and yet he was not quite certain of the reason for his churlishness.

After riding for an hour so hard and at such a pace that his horse was lathered with sweat, Richard felt his bad humour ebb away from him.

It was hard to be angry with a magnificent specimen of horseflesh between his legs, the sun on his face and the sharp, invigorating frost of a December morning, sparkling in his veins like wine.

He had ridden out from the city into the countryside and now he turned and came back along the Prater. The huge chestnut trees at least a century old were leafless now, but under them drove the carriages of the multitudinous guests in the capital, while riders of all nationalities mounted on every breed of horse joined the promenade which in itself was a social reception.

The King of Prussia was galloping along with only

a solitary aide-de-camp for company; Lord Stewart, the eccentric English Ambassador, was driving a four-in-hand which would have won the approval of the most critical *habitués* of Hyde Park. Behind him in a coupé was his reticent brother, the Viscount Castlereagh, with his gorgeous, diamond-loving wife. Following them, in an elegant chaise, Richard saw the Czar with Katharina sitting beside him.

She caught sight of him at the same moment that he saw her, and, sweeping his hat from his head, he rode up to the carriage. It had stopped beside an unpretentious phaeton in which was seated the Emperor Francis of Austria, accompanied by his third wife, Marie-Louise.

As Richard drew near, Katherina looked up at him and he knew by the expression on her face that there was no need for him to make his apologies. She understood what he wanted to say, yet at the same time his heart sank because she was so understanding. She was loving him too much for comfort, too much for it to be a light, amusing *affaire de cœur* that he had intended when he first kissed her and felt her lips respond and answer the hunger of his own.

"You have enjoyed your ride?"

"It has blown away a lot of cobwebs."

"I am glad."

She gave him her hand, but he was not smiling as he watched her drive away at the Czar's side. Instead there was a frown between his eyes and he was so intent on his own thoughts that a carriage turning out of the Prater into another avenue had almost passed before he realized who was in it.

He had only a glimpse of her, sitting there straight and alert on the extreme edge of the seat, her eyes wide with excitement, her face framed by a little green velvet bonnet trimmed with swansdown. She was as lovely as he remembered her to be.

Wanda did not see him. Her eyes were on the circus erected opposite the lawn set aside for fireworks where, to attract custom for the evening performance, elephants and horses were being paraded by their trainers to the strident music of a brass band.

"A child at a party!"

Richard found that he had said the words aloud and knew he desired more than anything else at that moment to take Wanda to the circus, to watch her face as the acrobats swung dizzily above the crowds, to hear her laughter at the antics of the clowns, to feel her tremble at the roar of lions.

'A child at a party'—and why should he not play host? He would call at the Baroness's house that very afternoon. He would not tell Wanda his secret in so many words, but she would guess that the night before he had been masquerading as the Czar and that would be that! No-one could expect him to give up a desirable acquaintance with a lovely woman because the Emperor of Russia wished to have a double who would take his place when it pleased him to play truant.

Richard felt suddenly very light-hearted. His mind was made up—he would ask Wanda to come to the circus with him to-night. He rode home, smiling and bowing affably to surprised acquaintances who had previously received very little attention from him. He spoke appreciatively to the groom who took his horse at the door of the Hofburg and went upstairs humming a tune which had lingered in the back of his mind since he had heard Harry whistling it earlier that morning.

As he changed his clothes, he talked so gaily and so happily that when he left his room for the Banqueting Hall, Harry stared after him and scratched his head.

"That's women for you, all the world over," he muttered to himself. "Cast you down an' pick you up and then it's a tanner to a monkey they'll cast you down again."

Harry was more prophetic than he knew. After luncheon, when Richard was planning to leave the Palace and visit Wanda, he received a message that the Czar wished to see him in his private sitting-room. Hurriedly, for he was impatient to be off, Richard obeyed the Imperial summons. Katharina was with the Czar; he looked at her enquiringly as he entered the room, wordlessly asking her what this was about. But Katharina's eyes would not meet his.

"Richard, I have some good news—indeed splendid news," the Czar began.

"Indeed, Sire?" Richard answered with a question in his voice.

"Katharina has brought me information of the greatest value," the Czar went on, looking at her with a fond tenderness.

Again Richard tried to catch Katharina's eye and realized with a sudden sense of discomfort that she was deliberately avoiding him.

"Had you any idea who the lady was with whom you spent the evening last night?"

The question was so unexpected that for a moment Richard could only stare at him.

"I . . . I understood her to be the Comtesse Wanda Schönborn," he said at length.

"That is right; that is who she is," the Czar agreed, "but did you guess that she is Metternich's latest spy?"

"It's a lie! It is not true!"

Richard wondered if it was his own voice that spoke the words.

"I am delighted to say it is true," the Czar contradicted. "Katharina, with brilliant intuition, was suspicious that this girl might not be all she seemed, so she asked Prince Volkonski to make enquiries. He has discovered that the girl in question is the daughter of the Comtesse Carlotta Schönborn, who was for a short time, many years ago, a close friend of Prince Metternich.

"There was no scandal, no open talk of a liaison, but the Prince stayed at her husband's *schloss* one spring and we have reason to believe that the Comtesse had a devotion for him till her death a few months ago. She sent her daughter to Vienna and the very first place at which the daughter called on arrival was at the Chancellery."

"This is pure invention, Sire," Richard said hotly. "The Comtesse Wanda has never met Prince Metternich."

"That is what she told you, I assume," the Emperor smiled, "and that is precisely what I expect she was told to tell—not you, my dear Richard—but me! You must remember it was I whom she was seeking, I whom she thought she was meeting, I to whom she was speaking."

"What other proof have you?" Richard asked curtly.

"Proof enough," the Emperor answered. "Prince Metternich sent her from the Chancellery to the Baroness Waluzen. The Baroness had never seen her before and she was not expecting a visitor, but she greeted this unknown girl as an honoured guest. Why, you may ask yourself. And the answer is not difficult to find. She had received her instructions from that king of intriguers—Prince Metternich himself. There was to be a Masked Ball at the Hofburg last night, so the Baroness escorts her *protégée*. And who is it the young lady meets? With whom does she make it her duty to become acquainted? Who but the Emperor Alexander of Russia, the man whom Metternich fears, the man of whose thoughts and actions he wishes to keep track and whom day by day he is finding it increasingly difficult to oppose!"

"I have never heard a story that is more far-fetched and less likely to be based on fact, Sire," Richard said coldly.

"I am afraid I must disagree with you, my dear Richard. I think the case is admirably proven and I can assure you that Volkonski seldom makes mistakes. The Comtesse Wanda is Metternich's latest weapon against me! But the thing which delights me is that no-one except we three here in this room knows that she did not, as she thought, meet the Czar of Russia, but Mister Richard Melton. She did not suspect you?"

"No, Sire."

"That is just what I hoped, and now for action!"

"What do you mean, Sire?"

"I mean, my dear Richard, that you must continue to play this part. Can you understand what a god-send this will be? I can defeat Metternich at his own game. I can tell him what I wish him to know through the mouth of one of his own spies."

"You wish me to do this for you, Sire?"

"Wish? I command!" the Emperor said. "No, no, Richard. I had forgotten you are not my subject. I cannot command you to do anything—you are my friend. Big things are at stake at this conference. You know how I have set my heart on obtaining sovereignty for Poland. Metternich is my enemy, and a bitter enemy to the Poles who look on me as their champion—nay more, as their salvation. For our friendship's sake I ask your help and I know that you will not fail me."

The Czar's charm was proverbial, but Richard knew with a feeling of despair that it was not charm which made it impossible for him to refuse Alexander's request. Neither was it because his own comfort and security depended on his compliance. There was something deeper than that—a feeling of being in debt to someone who had extended to him the hand of friendship, a feeling that he could not, in honour, refuse to pay that debt now that payment was asked of him. Desperately he tried to prevaricate.

"I shall play the part so badly, Sire. Would it not be wiser for you to see the Comtesse Wanda yourself?"

"No, no, Richard! That would spoil everything," the Czar replied impatiently. "Our strength lies in the fact that as far as Metternich is concerned I can be in two places at once. He will think that he has me tied down when all the time he is being hoodwinked. Besides, I enjoyed my brief freedom far more than I had even anticipated. When you take my place—I can be you."

"And does Prince Volkonski agree to this?" Richard asked.

"The Prince does not know, my dear fellow. He thinks it was I who danced with the Comtesse last night. We will continue to let him think so. Katharina has been of great service to me in suspecting that this young woman was not the innocent she appeared."

"The Princess is very astute," Richard said, his voice like ice.

He cast round despairingly for any loophole of escape, but there seemed to be none.

"Have you considered, Sire," he said at last, "that it will be impossible to keep up this pretence? Last night I wore a mask, it was easy to deceive the Comtesse for, being new to Vienna, she had never seen Your Majesty. But can you imagine her being so easily tricked in a week's time?

"Under the chaperonage of the Baroness she will go everywhere in Vienna, she will see the Czar of Russia at every important occasion, at every ball, every parade, every reception, in fact, whenever she goes out. She was, for instance, in the Prater this morning. Our resemblance is not so striking as all that. Without a mask no-one who has seen you at fairly close quarters is going to believe that I am Your Imperial Majesty."

"I have thought of that," the Czar answered triumphantly. "You will continue to wear a mask when you meet the Comtesse in secret. And you will arrange to meet her to-night at the Razumovsky Palace."

"The Russian Embassy, Sire? Is that possible?"

"It will be arranged."

"Do you think the Comtesse Wanda will come there unchaperoned?"

"I am sure of it. Her instructions from Prince Metternich will be to make contact with the Czar how and when she can. She will not refuse to meet me, however strange the circumstances." The Czar paused for a moment. "We must send her a message—that is the most difficult part. If we appear too eager, Metternich may be suspicious. Did you make any suggestion of meeting each other again?"

"No, Sire," Richard replied stiffly.

"There is a fan in your room," Katharina said, speaking for the first time. "Was it hers?"

The look Richard gave her was almost one of hatred.

"Is there anything that your spies don't ferret out?" he enquired beneath his breath.

"A fan, that is splendid. You can return it," the Czar suggested.

"It is broken, Sire."

"Then we can send her another one. What can be simpler? And with it a message without a signature to say that a carriage will call to take her to supper with him who sends the fan."

"You think of everything, Sire," Richard remarked ironically.

"I pride myself on my imagination, Richard," the Czar smiled, "but it is you who should be congratulated. You played the part allotted to you to perfection and nothing could have been more fortunate. Nothing could have pleased me better than that Prince Metternich should walk into a trap of his own setting."

"You are still quite convinced that it is a trap?" Richard asked.

Before the Czar could reply, Katharina answered his question.

"You can rest assured, Richard, that Wanda Schonbörn is Clement Metternich's latest and most cleverly chosen spy . . . and we know how fond you are of spies—wherever you may find them!"

Chapter Six

THE Prince de Metternich threw the papers he held in his hand down on the desk and turned towards his wife with the gesture of a man who rests his shoulders of a heavy burden.

"A small victory," he said. "A very small one and yet I am human enough to be elated."

"It is wonderful that something has been decided," she answered. "I began to think your meetings would end in nothing but talk."

"The Russians seem to be determined that the Congress shall go on for a thousand years," the Prince said grimly. "What we achieved to-day only concerns France, and therefore Talleyrand and I were able to reach agreement. Tomorrow we start again on the Polish question."

"Forget it for the moment," the Princess said gently. "It is time you had a little relaxation. Are you going out?"

"I have a number of calls to make," the Prince replied, "business as well as pleasure, of course, but I find these last few weeks I have been sadly neglecting my social duties."

"Everybody has been longing to see you," his wife assured him. "I have promised to call on Lady Castlereagh this evening, otherwise I would offer to accompany you."

"We shall meet at dinner," the Prince said, and raising her hand to his lips, he kissed it before, with a smile, she went from the room.

The Prince stood for a moment after she was gone, looking contemplatively at the closed door; then he walked to where a long, gilt-edged mirror stood between two windows overlooking the garden. He regarded himself for some seconds, noting his broad brow, clear blue eyes, aquiline nose and what so many people had described as his 'exceptional dignity of bearing'.

"You are forty-one," he said aloud to his own reflection; "where is your youth, your *joie de vivre?* Have the affairs of State robbed you of everything?"

He gave a little sigh and turned towards the open window. "A few hours' leisure," he murmured, "and I have no idea what to do with myself."

It was indeed an unusual state of affairs. Always before in his life the Prince had found himself embroiled in some passionate and exciting love-affair, however strenuous the calls of diplomacy.

He possessed to an extraordinary degree the ability to love one, two·or three women simultaneously, caring for each in a different way and utterly sincere in his love and affection for each particular woman.

It was also, though no-one believed it, entirely incidental that his love-affairs quite often assisted his political ambitions. Whatever information reached him through those who loved him, it came freely and without calculation on his part. And yet now, for the first time for more years than he could count, he was free of love.

He stood at the window, thinking of the woman who had meant so much in his life—Constance de la Force, who had been his first adolescent passion. She had been lovely, with her hair growing in a widow's peak on her white forehead, shell-like ears and tinkling laugh. He had adored her with a youthful whole-heartedness which he had never been able to recapture.

He would never forget the first night they had spent together at her house in Strasbourg. It was dark when their chaise had paused before a wrought-iron gate, but the lamps flickered on lilac bushes in full bloom. The door of the house had opened and he bowed, ready to depart now that he had seen her home in safety. But instead she had taken his hand and led him into the·hall and up the stairs to her boudoir.

"Wait for me," she had whispered before she vanished, leaving him to the confusion of his thoughts. When she returned, her only garment was a white batiste *négligé* edged with soft Valenciennes lace. Slowly she walked towards him and the robe fell away from her breasts, leaving them framed enticingly between billows of lace. A feeling of awe, almost of reverence, stole over him. He felt himself tremble, and a strange exultation seemed to run through his veins like quicksilver. Then, with a cry, he buried his face in her bosom and felt her hands on his hair. . . .

Constance de la Force had borne his child and for her and Carlotta Schonbörn there would always be a special place in his heart.

Katharina Bagration had been the next woman who had really mattered in his life. Their love-affair lasted for a number of years and he knew that her combination of oriental softness, Andalusian grace and Parisian elegance, together with a quick, intelligent brain, was something he might never find again all in the body of one small, exquisite woman.

After Constance and Katharina, the canvas of his life became filled with beautiful women. There was the Duchess of d'Abrantes, a tiny feminine creature whose husband had been one of Napoleon's greatest generals. Poor little Laure! He sighed regretfully as he thought of her. Even now she could tempt him with her wide-set slanting amber eyes and her tenderly curved mouth. She had high breasts, a minute waist and lovely narrow thighs, but it was the smooth contour of her throat which gave her a dramatic distinction. Long and supple, it could strike every graceful, insolent, languid and amusing attitude.

He could give her senses a fulfillment which they had never known with her greedy, conquering husband.

"Closer, hold me closer," she demanded of him once. "I am so alone . . . I want to be part of you."

Tightening his arms, he had looked down at her passionate little face. Her eyes were closed in ecstasy. Then his mouth came down on hers and her shuddering sigh mingled with the soft rustle of the silk cushions beneath them.

But the Duchesse d'Abrantes had not been the only one who had to be kept from the Congress. Caroline Murat, Queen of Naples and Napoleon's sister, tall, splendid to look at, with a keen intelligence, had written to him the most eloquent and pleading letters asking that she might be present. Prince Metternich's *affaire* with her had been full of excitements until her fiercely possessive nature and her almost insane jealousy made him wish to be free of her.

Caroline Murat had been kept from the Congress as had another beauty—the very determined, very charming Wilhelmina, Duchess of Sagan. She had filled a need at a most critical time in his career. Hers was a world of laughter, frivolity and delightful little conceits. She had been with him all through the campaign of 1814 when the allied armies marched towards France.

Each day they made a rendezvous for the next, Wilhelmina going ahead in her carriage, while he went on horseback. Wearing a grey frock coat, and a grey tall hat, he was as completely at home in the midst of the marching army as he would have been in the Prater. When the day's march was ended, he and Wilhelmina dined and spent the night together.

But while she had seemed indispensable in war, in peace the Duchess of Sagan had been told firmly but courteously that the Congress of Vienna would require the Prince's complete devotion for several months.

So many women! Yet now, at the moment, he was alone —alone and forty-one. He felt his age weigh upon him heavily. Even at an optimistic guess he had lived half his life. What lay ahead? He thought of all he had achieved in these past years when by his own personal efforts he had made himself the most talked-of, the most feared man in Europe; yet, for the moment, his life was empty of love.

Eleanore he had never loved. Theirs had been an arranged marriage and it had turned out far better than he had ever dared to hope. They lived together as intimate friends and she gave him a companionship which he knew now was more lasting and in many ways more valuable than the ephemeral loves which came and went as easily and as surely as the seasons of the year succeeded one another.

And yet he could not live without love. Women were as necessary to him as the very air he breathed. He turned to the window with a sudden feeling that something was about to happen. He had a premonition of it in his bones. What was it that made a man feel that adventure was waiting round the corner, that something exciting and wonderful lay just out of reach? The conviction was there—he would not deny it, and there was a smile on the Prince's lips as he walked down the stone steps to where his carriage was waiting.

He decided to call first on the Count Karl Zichy. The Count was one of the most distinguished and generous hosts in the whole capital. He had opened his town house to the Congress and the Prince had been told by innumerable people how charming were his receptions, how distinguished the gatherings that could be found under his

roof. It was unfortunate, the Prince thought now, that he
had been unable to make a formal call on the Count before
this, but he had so many demands on his time and he
received so many invitations that to accept even a hun-
dredth of them would have made his work at the Chancellery impossible.

However, he would make up for lost time and stay a
little longer with the Count than was necessary; and then
there were several hostesses he must honour before he
returned home to change for dinner.

It seemed to the Prince, who was deep in thought, that
it was only a few minutes before the horses drew up outside Count Karl's house. There were a number of carriages,
several just driving away from the door, others waiting
until their owners wished to leave. On the pavement was
the usual group of curious sightseers, craning their necks
to see who was arriving, striving to guess who this or that
foreigner might be.

At the sight of the Prince there was no doubt of his
identity. Whenever he appeared in public, the populace of
Vienna were delirious with joy. Whatever credit the Czar
might take to himself, to them Prince Metternich was the
conqueror of Napoleon, the deliverer of Central Europe
from the might of the French oppressor. They cheered him
now as he stepped out from his carriage, hats and handker-
chiefs waving excitedly. And as he smiled his acknowledg-
ments, the women's eyes grew tender and there was that
soft look on their lips which seemed to come to every
woman's mouth, whether she was young or old, when she
looked at his face.

The Count's house was large and magnificently furnished. The servants in yellow velvet livery trimmed with
silver lace led the Prince to the huge reception rooms
where a large gathering of people was congregated. He
moved slowly across them in search of his host. It was late
and the Count had left his position at the door where he
had earlier received the guests.

The Prince made slow progress—there were so many
people who wished to speak to him, so many women holding out their hands invitingly, so many representatives of
foreign powers hoping for a word or a glance which would
tell them that they and their masters were for the moment
basking in his diplomatic good books.

And then he saw her! She was walking away from him,
moving from one group of people to another, and she was

so devastatingly beautiful that he felt impelled to watch every movement she made with a breathlessness which was almost painful in its intensity.

She was wearing a grey gown and over it a little emerald-green velvet jacket. There were two green tassels fluttering from her hat, which appeared to cry aloud that it came from Paris and had been fashioned to call attention to her calm grey eyes and the clear perfection of her white skin. She was not very tall and her heelless Empire shoes made her appear even smaller than she was.

As if the intensity of his gaze arrested her very movement, she suddenly stopped, hesitated and looked round at him. They might have been alone at the ends of the earth. The people chattering and moving around them ceased to exist; they looked at each other and it seemed to the Prince that her eyes widened ever so slightly before, with a faint smile at the corner of her lips, she turned and moved away.

For a moment he thought he had lost her. Impulsively he stepped forward as if to go after her.

He felt as if he must forget everything—conventions, diplomatic upbringing, even his pose of distraction which was so characteristic of him. He had a wild desire to call out to her, to tell her that she must not leave him, that he must speak to her now at this very moment or go crazy at the delay.

Then he saw that she had gone in search of Count Karl Zichy. She was pointing out to him who had arrived and the Count's rather heavy face lit up with pleasure as he came hurrying across the room towards the Prince.

"Your Excellency, this is a great honour. You are indeed welcome to my house."

"I have neglected your kind invitations for too long, Count," the Prince replied. "I must make my excuses for not having come before and also tell you how delighted I am to be here."

"May I present my daughter-in-law, Julia?"

She was standing there at her father-in-law's side, and now at last the Prince could take her little hand in his and raise it to his lips. He felt his heart turn over at the touch of her and he knew then that he was in love—overwhelmingly, wildly in love with a woman who attracted him at this very first sight more than any woman had ever done before.

"I want to talk to you alone."

She looked slightly surprised at the urgency of his tone, but without argument and without question she led the way through the crowded *salon* to a small anteroom opening out of it.

Like the rest of the house it was decorated in exquisite taste and its soft maroon hangings and quaint old carved mirrors seemed to make a perfect background for her beauty.

"Who are you? Why have I never seen you before?" the Prince questioned.

"My father-in-law has told you who I am," she replied. "My husband and I have come to Vienna to help him entertain because, as doubtless you know, he is a widower."

Her voice delighted him. It was low and soft and very sweet. Voices had always had a particular effect upon him, and now, when she spoke, he felt as if she calmed and soothed him so that even the violence of his excitement died away into something quieter and deeper.

"Tell me what you think about Vienna."

He asked the first thing that came into his head because he wanted to watch that lovely serene face with its steady grey eyes.

She told him then how much she was enjoying herself, how she found the capital gayer than anything she had ever known before. How it had been amusing to take part in the *tableaux vivants* in which she had appeared in a picture representing Louis XIV kneeling at Mme de la Vallière's feet, and how she had been entranced by a performance of Beethoven's 'Fidelio', when, in spite of being stone deaf, he had conducted a new composition himself. She was looking forward, she continued, to taking part in the Imperial Carousel, where knights-at-arms were to fight for the favours of twenty-four ladies who had been given the title of 'belles d'amour'.

She talked on, describing this function and that, and it seemed to the Prince, listening to her, that never before in the whole of his life had he been so at peace with the world. This was happiness as he had never before known it, to feel charmed and invigorated without recourse to passion, without even a word of tenderness passing between himself and a woman.

After perhaps twenty minutes the Comtesse rose to her feet.

"Your Excellency will, I know, excuse me," she said, "but I must attend to my other guests."

For a moment the Prince stared at her, then he turned and walked from the house as if he were a man in a dream.

He went to no other reception that evening, but drove home, and Eleanore found him sitting alone before the fire in his study when she returned an hour later.

"Back already!" she exclaimed as she came into the room, and a sudden fear went through her that he might be ill. But as he turned to look at her she saw his face and knew that what she had been dreading these past weeks had happened.

Her husband was in love again! No one should ever guess, she had vowed to herself once, least of all Clement, what agony his *affaires* brought to her, how each one was like a knife wound in her heart. She had married him knowing that he did not love her, knowing their marriage had been arranged by his family because she was one of the richest heiresses in Europe.

The fortunes of the Metternich family had never been at a lower ebb than at the moment when Eleanore Kaunitz had consented to marry young Clement Metternich. The victorious French Army had overrun the Austrian Netherlands, occupying the left bank of the Rhine where all the Metternich family properties were located. The lands were confiscated in the name of the grande nation, leaving Clement's father, Count Georg, in the most desperate circumstances, his diplomatic posts swept away and his ancestral properties lost.

Clement and his parents arrived in Vienna stripped of property and wealth, but their relations began to be busy on their behalf. It was a cousin acting as hostess in the Kaunitz household who introduced Eleanore to Clement. The Comtesse Eleanore was engaged to a County Balffy, but as soon as she saw the young Metternich she was only too eager to break her engagement and agree to any plans that his relations might make for marriage.

She knew why he was marrying her, knew that her social position and her money mattered far more than anything she might be herself; but she did not care. She fell in love with him as so many other women in the past had done and so many more were to do in the future.

She loved him wildly, passionately, crazily; and yet, because she was intelligent, she knew that she was not beautiful enough to hold him by her physical charms. She schooled herself fiercely, with an iron discipline which had something heroic in it, to give him all that he asked of her, but to demand nothing.

Gradually, with a cleverness that he never recognized, she began to make herself indispensable to him. He grew to rely on her, to be grateful that she was always there, to confide in her, not only about his diplomatic difficulties, but about his personal ones.

Eleanore thought sometimes that she must cry out in sheer agony to hear him speak of his love and desire for other women, yet he never knew that she was anything more than interested in a friendly manner.

"It is so wonderful to be able to tell you these things," he would say, and she would smile understandingly at him and try to help him to untangle the intricacies, the plots, schemings and infatuations which at times made his life utterly chaotic.

Sometimes she could do more for him than just listen. There had been that terrible time in Paris when he had been making love to two women at the same time, two who were widely different both in looks and in character. One was Caroline Murat, Queen of Naples, strikingly beautiful and as passionately strong-willed as her brother, the Emperor. The other was Laure, Duchesse d'Abrantes, who offered him a tender, selfless love and a devotion which was to endure throughout her life.

Caroline's nature was one of fire, turbulent and possessive. She had originally claimed the greater share of Clement's affection until gradually Laure d'Abrantes occupied his time and his heart. He went more frequently to her apartments, he appeared with her at public gatherings until the headstrong Queen of Naples vowed publicly that she would recapture her distinguished lover at any cost.

Caroline had in her service a handsome footman named Prosper who was a great rake amongst the maids of the household, and she decided that he should try his charms with the Duchesse d'Abrantes' maid, Babette. Her butler arranged for a meeting between the two servants, and Prosper, well supplied with money by his mistress, in a short time produced tangible results from his courting. He brought to the Queen of Naples a little bundle of letters which he had bribed Babette to steal from her mistress's writing-desk. They were tied together with ribbon and Caroline could hardly wait to be alone before she tore them open to find, as she had expected, that they were the love letters of Clement Metternich.

After reading the letters Caroline knew that she had in her hands a weapon of the most deadly sort. A weapon, moreover which, if skilfully used, would vanquish completely her rival for Prince Metternich's affection.

Sending for her carriage, she set out for the Palace of the Duchesse d'Abrantes. Sweeping in with Imperial haste, which made up in theatrical impetuosity what it lacked in dignity, she told Laure of her discovery and to prove to her that she was in possession of the letters she quoted extracts from them aloud.

"I am going to give these letters to the Press," she finished. "The publication will bring disgrace not only on you and the Austrian Minister, but also upon your husband."

Laure sprang to her feet.

"Do you really mean," she asked, "that you would cause a scandal at this moment, when you know as well as I do that Clement is conducting the most delicate negotiations with the Emperor? He would be completely ruined!"

"I do mean it," Caroline replied fiercely.

"Then you don't love him," Laure cried. "You could not love a man and even consider such a vile action. You wish to destroy him out of sheer jealousy. I will give him up."

"It is too late," Caroline answered. "I had thought of that originally; but now that I have seen these letters, I want only to make him suffer and you as well."

Her dark eyes were flashing with fury as she stood there, towering over the tiny Duchesse like some avenging goddess; but Laure was unafraid.

"You do not understand the meaning of the word love," she said quietly. "You are a wicked woman, Caroline Murat. I love Clement with all my heart, but rather than he should be harmed, I will go out of his life and never see him again. I will promise you that on my oath in return for those letters."

But Caroline's jealousy had made her impervious to pleading or to any sort of bargain.

"I shall publish them," she retorted, hating the frail little Duchesse because she knew Laure could give Clement Metternich something that it was not within her power to give to any man. She departed in a fury; and because the Duchesse d'Abrantes really loved the Austrian Minister she went in despair to call on his wife.

Eleanore listened sympathetically with a calmness which

helped the tearful Duchesse over the most difficult parts of her story.

"Thank you for telling me, Madame," she said when the tale was finished. "You are not to worry. I promise you everything will be all right."

As soon as the Duchesse had left, Eleanore went to visit the Queen of Naples. She saw that Caroline was surprised to see her and she wasted no time in coming to the point.

"You have in your possession certain documents which my husband intended only for the eyes of the Duchesse d'Abrantes," she said calmly.

Caroline's lips tightened ominously, but the expression in her eyes was one of astonishment.

"I know all about you both," Eleanore explained; "there have never been any secrets between my husband and myself. We have a perfect understanding on such matters."

"You must be a very exceptional person," Caroline retorted acidly.

"My husband is an exceptional man," Eleanore replied, "and I cannot allow you to hurt or disturb him, which I understand is what you intend."

"Who told you this?" Caroline asked.

"That is immaterial," Eleanore replied; "but I understand, on good authority, that you intend to make public the letters which he has written to Laure d'Abrantes. I cannot conceive any valid reason which could cause you to take such a decision."

"I have a reason," Caroline cried, "and it is a good one."

"I doubt that," Eleanore contradicted. "I am Clement's wife and if I do not take offence at his actions, it is not for anyone else to do so. I am quite undisturbed by the revelations which have come into your hands relating to the affection between my husband and the Duchesse d'Abrantes."

Even while she argued Eleanore realized that after the first shock of her visit, Caroline's resolution to make trouble had not been altered. She was hating Clement at that moment, hating him all the more because she loved him so desperately.

Eleanore knew that nothing she might say would help matters, so she decided upon a desperate course. She drove to Fontainbleu and asked for an audience with Napoleon. She was shown immediately into the Emperor's study. He was writing at his massive desk which was covered with reports, diagrams, military documents and a well-marked map of Russia. He was wearing the dark green uniform of the Old Foot Guards with its white revers. He rose and greeted Eleanore courteously:

"You have asked to see me, Madame Metternich. What can I do for you?"

Without the slightest hesitation or embarrassment Eleanore told him of the delicate situation which had arisen between the Duchesse d'Abrantes and his sister Caroline Murat.

"Unless something is done to prevent the Queen from carrying out her threats, Your Majesty, there will be a great scandal. It will be a scandal which, as I need not point out to you, Sire, will embarrass your own Imperial House just as it will embarrass the best interests of the Austrian Minister.

"My husband's position in Vienna is serious enough as matters are at the moment. There are many there who blame him for representing too eagerly the interests of France. A scandal involving him now with the Queen of Naples would not only seriously interfere with the work he is doing on behalf of his own government, but might well react unfavourably to Your Majesty."

Napoleon listened attentively. He was shrewd enough to realize that Eleanore was being very clever in the way she was putting the situation to him, but he was obliged to admit there was a great deal of truth in what she said.

He thanked her for being brave enough to come to him.

"You can rely on me, Madam. I will bring this to a finish and at once."

Eleanore thanked him profusely and made ready to leave. At the door, however, the Emperor detained her for a moment.

"*C'est un diable* that husband of yours," he exclaimed with a twinkle in his eyes. "It seems that all the ladies at my Court have lost their heads over him."

Eleanore gave a little sigh and then she smiled.

"Can you blame them, Sire?" she asked softly. "I cannot see how any woman can resist him."

It was not the women who could not resist the fascinating Prince de Metternich, whom she minded, it was the fact that he himself found them irresistible. She had been happy at Vienna since the Congress started. There had been no one in his life. In his conferences with her when the day's work was done or when they breakfasted together, they talked of his troubles with the Czar, his points of difference with the other plenipotentiaries.

Yet now the blow had struck. She had not been expecting it and therefore it hurt all the more. He was in love. She knew it by that strange, exalted expression on his face, the faint smile at his lips, the look of rapture in his eyes. He was like a man who had had a sudden vision of the Holy Grail and who could not focus his gaze again quickly upon mundane matters.

The discipline Eleanore had imposed upon herself for so many years made her speak naturally and quietly as if she had noticed nothing. Moving to the Prince's side, she held out her hands towards the fire, the long thin fingers heavily weighted with rings. Her hands were Eleanore's most beautiful feature and she had often wished that Providence had been as kind when it came to her face.

"I went to Lady Castlereagh's," she said. "She was covered in diamonds as usual and there seemed to be even more dogs about than there were the last time I visited her. Then I went on to a reception given by Princess Paul Esterhazy. The Baroness Waluzen was there and she had brought with her a young girl. She has only just arrived in Vienna and is entranced with everything and everybody, a charming child! I took a great fancy to her. Funnily enough she reminded me of someone I know, but I can't think who it may be."

With an effort the Prince forced himself to listen. What was his wife saying?

"You say . . . this girl is enjoying herself?" he asked.

"Tremendously, from all accounts. She seemed to find everything, even the most commonplace things, exciting and different from anything she had ever known before. She is so pretty, Clement. I would like you to see her. Her name is Wanda Schonbörn."

"I have seen her," the Prince replied.

"Then you will agree that she is very pretty," his wife said.

"Yes, very pretty."

"I think it must be those brilliant blue eyes with that red hair which is so striking," the Princess went on. "They are almost as blue as yours."

She waited for her husband to say something, but there was no answer. The Prince was staring into the flames again. For a moment Eleanore contemplated asking him of whom he was thinking, and then she repressed her curiosity. He would tell her all in his own good time, she knew that. She shut her eyes for a moment. She felt as if the room spun round her . . . another woman to hear about, to dream about and to envy. Oh, how she envied them, these women her husband loved!

Would this one be tall or small, dark or fair, clever or stupid? It was impossible to guess where his affections might lead him. He had no type which attracted him particularly, but whoever he loved would have something unique about her, something a little different from other women, something, Eleanore thought despairingly, that she herself had never possessed.

She would hear all about her—of her virtues, her attractions, her enticements! But for the moment he wanted to be alone, he wanted to think of this new star which had flashed upon his horizon. He wanted to reach out his arms towards the unknown in secret and in silence.

Gathering up her furs which she had put on the chair, Eleanore went softly across the room until she reached the door and then she looked back. Her husband had not even realized that she was leaving.

"Don't be late coming up to change for dinner," she said, and knew despairingly even as she spoke that he had not heard her.

Chapter Seven

THERE was no light by the private door through which Richard left the Hofburg at ten o'clock that night. Everything had been arranged for his departure by the Czar himself. He came out of the Imperial apartments wearing a wide-brimmed hat pulled low over his forehead and carrying a mask on a stick which he kept raised to his eyes.

He wore a black evening cloak over the civilian clothes which the Czar himself used when he wished to be incognito.

As Richard stepped through the doorway, the sentries presented arms. He hurried past them down a narrow staircase which led to a private door opening on to a deserted courtyard. A carriage was waiting there; but otherwise, as far as Richard could see, there was no one in sight. Yet he was certain that Baron Hager would report this very movement to the Emperor Francis next morning.

As the carriage started off, he threw himself back against the cushions with an ill-humour that he thought sourly could only bode ill for the assignation which lay ahead.

He could no longer deny what a shock it had been to learn of Wanda's perfidy. He had been thinking of her all day, even as he had dreamed of her last night; but now the thought of her youth and freshness was an insult all the more vehement because he had been deceived by it.

He was not foolish enough to believe that the intricacies of European diplomacy could be carried on without secret police or the employment of agents, but he had always considered that such work should be executed by those who needed money or those who had a natural aptitude for hypocrisy.

He had not believed it was a task with which a gentleman should soil his hands, and least of all a lady. He detested the thought that Katharina should have been employed by the Russian Government and then by the Czar himself as a skilled and extremely successful agent. She made no secret of her prowess, recounting her successes as eagerly and as enthusiastically as any general might speak of his manœuvres on the field of battle.

But Katharina was a Russian, an oriental, and the Russian blood in his own veins made him understand that their minds worked differently from Europeans' and more especially from those of the British.

Wanda had seemed so different, untouched by intrigue and subterfuge. It was hard to explain even to himself why a girl he had met for such a short time should make such an impression on him. He was used to beautiful women, he was used to their artifices of enticement, to the practised sweetness which fell from their too eager lips.

But Wanda had seemed original, she had not been like the others. Yet now he knew it was all an act, a rôle played so skilfully that he had been utterly and completely deceived by it.

Richard's lips were set in a grim line as he thought how easily he had been duped. He would have taken his oath that Wanda was as pure and unsophisticated as she appeared. What idiots men were where a pretty face was concerned and how cunning were women when it came to the art of deception!

He was honest enough to admit to himself that shyness and a certain timidity had always appealed to him in a woman. He supposed it made a man feel strong and masculine to be confronted with the frailty of femininity. Katharina had excited him for that very reason the first time he saw her. It was only later that he was to learn that when she veiled her eyes with her long lashes it was not modesty, but to hide her too easily awakened desire.

Katharina was at least frank. If she wanted a man, she wooed him with her lips and her naked body. She was a spy; but when a man took her in his arms knowing her for what she was he found himself wildly intoxicated by a number of things he had not suspected.

Wanda was a cheat, a deceiver and a liar. Richard found himself longing to confront her with her lie, to tell her that he knew her for what she was, to denounce her, to watch her eyes drop before his and the blush of shame creep up her cheeks.

Then he remembered his instructions. Well, if it came to a duel of wits, he supposed, inexperienced as he was, he could play a part as well as anyone else. He would give Metternich a run for his money. It would be a new thrill, he decided, to out-manœuvre one of the astutest diplomats in Europe, to play him at his own game and leave him discomfited.

The carriage drew up at the Razumovsky Palace. Richard had been there before and knew it as one of the sights of Vienna. It had taken twenty years to build. Count Razumovsky had embellished the place with all the treasures that wealth and influence could buy.

The reception rooms in their decoration surpassed any others in the whole of the country. There were galleries containing world-renowned pictures and statuary, there was a library in which the rarest manuscripts and books had been collected from all over the world. Count Razumovsky had spent so much money on the Palace that it was even rumoured his fortune had been impaired by it. But this was unlikely for his wealth, inherited from his father who had been a famous Field Marshal in the Russian Army, was enormous.

Several times since the opening of the Congress, the Czar had borrowed the Palace from his Ambassador. There he had given some of the fêtes which had equalled, if not exceeded in pomp and splendour those given by the Austrian Court.

But to-night Richard was not driven into the huge courtyard with its gilded gates and great marble pillars. Instead, as the Czar had told him had been arranged, he was set down at the side door leading on to a small dark passage, then up a twisting iron stairway which led through a secret panel into a small *salon*.

The room was empty and the trusted servant who had shown him the way up the stairs closed the panelling behind him as he stepped into the room. Richard noticed at once that the room was furnished with the same sumptuous magnificence that was prevalent all over the Palace. But there was a certain motif in its decoration which did not escape his attention.

The Dresden china candelabra, for instance, which held the flickering tapers, were ornamented with cupids and

love birds, the pictures on the walls and the painted ceiling
showed Venus in various exchanges with those who wooed
her and the designs on the coral silk hangings were of
hearts pierced with arrows.

There was a huge couch in the room covered with
cushions and there were flowers whose exotic fragrance
seemed to have an almost aphrodisiacal effect upon the
senses. From somewhere far enough away not to intrude
but near enough to be heard came the strains of music.

Richard's lips twisted in a wry smile. The Czar certainly
knew how to set the scene for a love-affair, he thought,
and decided that this was another side to the Imperial
character, as incompatible with his earnest reading of the
Bible as the fact that he kept, in a secret drawer of his
desk, a portrait of Madame Narischkin exhibiting her
charms as Aphrodite rising from the waves.

With an effort Richard remembered the part he had to
play. He pulled his hat from his head and took off his
cloak; then, throwing down the mask which he held in his
hands, he drew a small black velvet one from his pocket
and fixed it over his eyes. It was the same mask he had
worn last night at the Ball, and as soon as he had it on
he could see by his reflection in the mirror that he bore an
unmistakable resemblance to the Czar.

Butinski, the barber, had arranged his hair in the same
fashion as before, but to be on the safe side, Richard blew
out a dozen or two of the candles which lit the room so
brilliantly. Now the shadows were deeper and there was
an air of mystery about the place.

On a table in the corner Richard noted there was a
collation of appetizing dishes and several of the choicest
and most rare wines in a gold ice bucket. Picking up the
first bottle which came to his hand, he poured himself out
a glass of wine. It was cool and of a delicious bouquet, and
having gulped down the first half of his glass he drank the
rest slowly and with respect. This must have been Count
Razumovsky's choice he thought and acknowledged that
the Ambassador's taste was flawless in every detail.

As he set the glass down on the table, he heard the
sound of footsteps outside and then the door was opened.
The servants did not announce her. She merely came in
and the door was shut behind her.

She stood there looking frightened and very small. He
had, in fact, forgotten how tiny she was. She wore a dress
of some soft green material which was laced over her

shoulders and beneath her tiny breasts with silver ribbons. She might have been a nymph who had strayed from the Vienna Woods, and that quality of Youth and Spring was there just as he had remembered it from the night before.

How clever it was that she could look like that and still be Metternich's spy!

"So you came. I was half afraid you would disappoint me!"

He heard himself say the words smoothly as he walked across the intervening space between them and took her hand to raise it to his lips. Her fingers seemed to tremble in his.

"I was so frightened," she said softly, "when I saw where the carriage had brought me. I hoped we were going to that little restaurant where we supped last night."

"There was a Masked Ball last night," Richard answered. "Everyone in Vienna was disguised. To-night it would be different. You will understand that I dare not be seen."

"Then you really are . . ." As he did not speak, she continued, ". . . who I think you are. I wondered if I might have been mistaken."

"Why?"

This monosyllable came from his lips unexpectedly and sounded sharp even to himself.

"You were so different from what I imagined an . . . an Emperor . . . would be like."

"What did you expect?"

"Someone who was not quite human . . . someone I could not talk to as I talked to you. Oh, it is difficult to put into words. I . . . I kept forgetting who you were."

He found himself listening intently to her words. Then he remembered that this was all part of the act to deceive him.

"And now you are disappointed!"

The statement was a sneer.

"No, no, of course not! It is only that it is all so strange. You see, I have never met anyone like . . . like you before."

"Shall we forget who I am and talk as if we were just two ordinary people who like each other and who want to be together?" Richard enquired.

"Isn't that just what we are doing?" she replied. "What we did last night?"

"I suppose so."

"But first of all I must thank you for my present—it is

a lovely fan, far lovelier than the one I broke, which was my mother's."

"Yours shall be mended for you."

"Thank you. It is greedy, but I would like to have both. The one you have given me is magnificent and I shall treasure it, but the other has sentimental associations for me and I would hate to lose it."

"It shall be mended by the man I told you about and returned to you as soon as it is done."

"Oh, thank you! How kind you are!"

"I wonder if you will always think so?" Richard asked enigmatically. "Will you have a glass of wine?"

"A very little, please."

She watched him cross the room to the side table, then looked around her with wide eyes.

"What a wonderful room! I have never seen anything so magnificent as the entrance to this Palace—and the stairs and the corridor along which I came. To whom does it belong?"

"Count Razumovsky, the Russian Ambassador," he replied and his eyes narrowed. She must have known, for Metternich would have told her.

"I must try to remember his name," Wanda said. "It is all very bewildering, the crowds one sees and meets. All day long I have been presented to distinguished people and now I am afraid I have their names all jumbled up in my mind and I have no idea who is whom."

"You must tell me what you have been doing," Richard said. "Shall we sit down?"

He indicated the cushion-covered couch and noted that Wanda eyed it a little apprehensively and sat on the very edge of its cushioned softness at some distance from himself.

"Are you afraid of me?" he asked with a smile.

"No, of course not."

The words came too quickly and her tone was nervous.

"Then why sit so far away?"

A sudden flush came to her cheeks. She was cleverer than he imagined possible, he thought. This was undoubtedly the brilliant acting of a very experienced woman or else there had been some incredible, unforgivable mistake. And then, even as the doubt came to his mind, he knew there had been no mistake. Would any innocent girl have come here alone, unchaperoned, obeying without question a brief request in an unsigned note? No, Wanda Schonbörn had her reasons for coming and doubtless her instructions.

"Last night you did not seem afraid of me," Richard continued.

"Last night it was different," she answered. "I suppose it is being here alone in this very grand room that makes me feel uncomfortable. Perhaps really I ought not to have come."

"And yet you did."

His voice was hard.

"I . . . I wanted to see you again."

"Is that the only reason?"

He saw the blood rise in her cheeks again and now her eyes fell before his. A streak of cruelty he had never known before in his character made him long to torture her. He bent forward and took her hand.

"Can I really credit," he said softly, "that it is as a man, an ordinary commonplace man that you like me? If I could be sure of that!"

She did not answer, and looking at her downcast eyes he added:

"Can you let me hope that that is true?"

"It is true."

She looked up suddenly, her eyes vividly blue.

"As a man, not an Emperor?" Richard insisted. "That has made me very happy. Now, tell me about yourself. Where have you been to-day, what have you seen?"

"There is so much to tell that I might bore you."

"Everything interests me except lies."

He saw her swallow a little convulsively.

"The Baroness and I drove in the Prater this morning," she said hastily. "It was full of people and I thought . . . I thought . . . I saw you in the distance."

"I wish I had seen you," Richard answered. "Yes, I was driving in the Prater with the Princess Katharina Bagration."

"I saw her, too. She is beautiful, more beautiful than anyone I have ever seen in my life before," Wanda said.

"A great many people have called her beautiful," Richard agreed. "As I expect you know, Prince Metternich loved her for many years and she him."

"Prince Metternich!" Wanda's voice seemed to falter on the words.

"Yes, he is a great success with the ladies, as you will have already heard."

"I . . . had not heard . . . that."

"Indeed? But why should you? For you told me last night that you had not met the Prince—or was I mistaken?"

"No, no, I have not met him, of course. Last night I had only just arrived in Vienna. I had met no one except the Baroness."

"Yes, I remember now. Well, it augurs well for your visit that your first admirer should be an Emperor."

"Don't say it like that." The words came out spontaneously. Then she stopped. "I am sorry, Sire—that is what I should call you, isn't it? I had forgotten."

"There is no reason for any formality between us," Richard answered. "When we meet, I am incognito. And haven't you just said that you like me because I am an ordinary man?"

He would have taken her hand in his again, but Wanda sprang to her feet.

"I ought to be . . . going," she faltered.

"But why?" Richard asked cruelly. "You have only just come and we have much to talk about. We have not discussed any of the things yet that will really interest you— the question of Poland for instance. I feel sure that you would like to have my opinion on that."

"Yes, of course, if you would like to tell me about it," Wanda answered.

"What exactly do you want to know?" Richard enquired.

"I . . . I don't really know," Wanda replied. "I am sorry to appear so stupid, but when I hear people talking about the Poland question I am not certain what it all means."

Richard's lips tightened. She was being cleverer than he thought possible. A half-knowledge might have put the man to whom she was speaking on his guard. To pretend utter ignorance was to invite an explanation from him which would undoubtedly be of tremendous interest to Metternich and his Ministers.

"It is the most important problem, the essential crisis of the Congress, and anyone less politically abstruse than Prince Metternich would realize it immediately."

"The Prince has to look at everything from the Austrian point of view," Wanda said in a small voice.

"And I think of it from Poland's," Richard answered. "That perhaps is the difference between the Prince and myself. He thinks only of his own country, its needs, its aspirations, its ambitions, while I am entirely selfless, thinking not of Russia, but of Poland."

He smiled to himself as he spoke. That sort of sentence was indeed worthy of Alexander. Metternich, when it was repeated to him, would undoubtedly recognize the familiar touch.

"I wish I was clever about these things," Wanda sighed. "My father hated politics and would never have them discussed at home. But my mother always said that Metternich was the most brilliant diplomat that Europe had ever known. I would like to believe that she was right, for my country's sake."

"And if I told you she was wrong?"

Wanda hesitated for a moment.

"I should think that perhaps you were mistaken," she said quietly.

Unexpectedly Richard laughed. At least the girl had courage. As he well knew, it took courage to say that sort of thing to the Czar.

"Metternich is making a terrible mistake," he insisted. "What is more, he will find it out in a very short while."

Let the Prince make what he could of that, Richard thought. Then, bored with the whole conversation, he said:

"Now let us talk of something else. You, for instance. Where else did you go to-day?"

There was a note of relief in Wanda's voice as she began to talk of the visits she and the Baroness had made that afternoon. Richard let her chatter away for some time and then he said:

"Didn't the Baroness think it a little strange that you should come here to-night alone—unchaperoned?"

The embarrassment in Wanda's little face was so intense that for a moment he almost hated himself for wiping away her expression of happiness and making her lips tremble as she answered:

"The Baroness . . . did not . . . know."

It was a lie, and a very badly told lie at that.

"But it must have been difficult to slip out without an explanation, without leaving a message," he insisted. "Won't the servants tell her that you have gone?"

"I . . . don't think . . . so."

"I shouldn't be too sure of that. Servants in Vienna have an uncomfortable way of recounting everything they hear and everything they learn either to those who employ them or to those who pay them better."

"You mean . . . they spy?"

"But of course. Everyone spies on everyone else, and

perhaps the most efficient of the lot is Baron Hager—
haven't you heard of him yet? He is the head of the Secret
Police in Vienna—the emperor Francis' right-hand man,
an indispensable figure at the Congress."

"But what could servants learn of any import?" Wanda
asked.

"I do not think you can be quite as innocent as that,"
Richard answered coldly. "Think for instance what trouble
a spy in Baron Hager's pay could make if he was allowed
to move about in my apartments at the Hofburg and over-
hear the things I say to my Ministers and to my friends in
private. Things which should never be repeated, things
which would hurt my country as well as myself if they
came to the ears of my enemies."

He noticed as he spoke that Wanda was twisting her
fingers together, her face turned away from him.

"But don't worry," he said with false cheerfulness. "I
take every precaution that is possible against Baron Hager.
I can trust those who are around me; I am assured of their
loyalty, and I count myself singularly fortunate where my
friends are concerned."

Wanda made a little strangled sound. Then she turned
towards him impulsively. But as her blue eyes looked up
at his masked face it seemed as if she remembered something and she turned her face away again.

"What were you going to say?" Richard enquired.

"Nothing . . . nothing."

"But are you sure? I had the feeling that you were going
to confide in me."

"No, no, you were mistaken."

"How stupid of me. I am not usually so abstruse.
Another glass of wine?"

"No, thank you; I really ought to go now."

Her face was very pale, it seemed drained of all colour.

"I have a feeling you have not enjoyed yourself to-
night," Richard said in a low voice.

"It has been nice to see you again."

"I thought we should be happy here. Can't you hear the
music? It seems to me that they are playing another enchanted waltz."

"No. It is not the same."

Her voice was very positive.

"The tune or the enchantment?"

"I don't know. I only know that I must go now. Thank

you for my fan and thank you for asking me here. But I would like your permission to leave."

"Supposing I refuse it?"

She turned quickly at that, her eyes widening a little. Much as he desired to hurt her, his better instincts would not permit him to play the brute.

"I only mean that we have had no chance to talk comfortably as we talked last night."

"That is because everything is different," she murmured.

"Are we different?" he asked.

"I don't know," she answered miserably. "Perhaps it is this room, or perhaps it is . . . us."

He had a sudden feeling that she must not leave him on such a note. He told himself that he was thinking of the Czar and his instructions, but he knew in his heart that he could not bear to hear the unhappiness in her voice or see the bewilderment in her eyes. If she was acting now, she was brilliant beyond belief and would have made a fortune at any playhouse.

"Wait five minutes more," he begged. "Just to please me; and besides, your carriage will not be ready."

He thought she wished to believe this, although anyone more experienced would have known it was a palpable untruth. She sat down again and now he bent towards her and in a quite different tone said:

"I have been worried and disturbed today. I learnt something that upset me. Someone I trusted has failed me. You must forgive me if I have made you suffer for that."

"I am sorry you are unhappy," she said gently. "Being disillusioned by someone we care for hurts more than anything else in the world."

"How do you know?" Richard asked.

"It happened to me once," she answered, "and I have never forgotten it."

"You are right," he said, "disillusionment can hurt; but don't let's talk about it for the moment."

"What shall we talk about?" Wanda enquired.

"Why not you?"

"But we are always talking about me," Wanda answered. "It is a very dull subject and if it comes to that, a limited one. Tell me about Russia."

"What do you want to know? Russia's intentions with regard to Poland?"

His ill-temper was obvious and gave an unmistakable sharpness to his tongue.

Wanda gave a little sigh.

"Oh dear, we don't seem to be getting very much further, do we? Do you think my carriage will be there? Shall we ring and ask?"

"In a moment," Richard said. "When shall I see you again?"

"Will you want to see me again after to-night?"

"What is wrong with to-night?"

"I don't know exactly; it is just that everything has gone awry. Can't you feel it? We are on edge with each other. Last night was different. I . . . I thought you were my friend. I suppose that is presumptuous of me, knowing who . . . you are."

"You were my friend last night," Richard agreed.

"And to-night?"

"And to-night, too," he answered, hastily but without conviction.

She made a little helpless gesture with her hands which was somehow infinitely pathetic.

"You are upset about something," she said. "But because I do not know what it is I cannot do anything to help. Perhaps next time we meet things will be different."

"When will that be?" Richard enquired.

"I will come and see you when . . . you want me."

"Because you yourself want to—or because you think it is the right thing to do?"

He could not forbear to ask the question.

"Because I want to," she answered, quickly and directly. The blue eyes raised to his were shining with sincerity. "Please believe that; you must believe it."

For a moment they were close again, as they had been the night before.

"Are you quite sure you would want to see me," he asked, "if I was not the person you think I am?"

"More so." He hardly heard the words. Then impulsively she bent towards him. "I felt last night that it was of tremendous importance that we had met; then I remembered who you were and I wished that I might learn that you were a nobody like myself, just a man to whom I could talk, with whom I could be friends."

"If I were, perhaps you would never have noticed me," Richard sneered.

"Somehow I think these things are meant," Wanda answered. "We were fated to meet each other. Don't you feel that, too?"

"I wish I could be sure," Richard answered. "Last night I was very grateful to a broken fan. To-day I wasn't so sure."

She flushed and turned her eyes away from him.

"There is only one thing of which you can be quite sure," she said, "that is that I should want to talk with you and be with you if you were indeed nobody."

Richard had a wild desire to tell her the truth, to pull the mask from his face. Then he laughed at himself for being duped once again as he had been duped before.

"I am indeed honoured," he said stiffly.

She rose to her feet.

"Good-night," she said, and he knew, as she stood there, that she was thinking how they had said good-night last night. He wanted to kiss her again, but some fastidiousness within himself stopped him. Last night their kiss had been perfect, a spontaneous expression of happiness between two people united by a joy which could not be withstood. To-night both joy and happiness were missing.

He took both her hands in his and kissed first one and then the other.

"Good-night, Wanda," he said. "Forgive me."

"For what?"

"For spoiling our time together. It was my fault. I know that, but I could not help myself."

"Please, don't be sorry. I am trying to understand. There is really nothing one can say on these occasions, is there?"

"Nothing," he agreed a little sadly.

"Good-night then."

She turned away from him and walked towards the door. Then, as she reached it, as her hand went out towards it, he cried her name:

"Wanda!"

She turned as he bridged the space between them, reaching out towards her, forgetting caution, pride, suspicion. There was no need for words, no need for explanations. She was in his arms, his lips were on hers and he was kissing her wildly, impetuously, with the desperation of a man who has so nearly lost what he wanted most.

"Wanda! Wanda!"

He heard himself whispering her name against her lips, and then with an unmistakable sob she had broken free of him and gone before he could stop her. He heard her footsteps running down the corridor and dared not follow her.

Instead, he could only stand for a long time in the empty room, looking at the place where she had sat on the sofa, feeling the softness and fragrance and youthfulness of her still in his arms, until his elation ebbed away from him.

He laughed cynically at the reflection of his masked face in the mirror, and picking up his cape and hat went towards the panel in the wall which led to the secret staircase.

Chapter Eight

BARON HAGER drummed his spy glass in the palm of his hand, an irritating habit he had when annoyed.

"I regret that there is not more to report, Your Excellency," he said with an air of sullenness.

Prince Metternich threw the closely written sheets of paper down on his desk.

"More!" he exclaimed. "There is nothing here, nothing of the slightest import. I cannot believe that the Emperor is satisfied with such rubbish."

"His Majesty has not expressed his dissatisfaction," the Baron retorted.

His tired, deep-set eyes met those of the Prince and they were both thinking the same thing. The Emperor Francis possessed an infantile and therefore prying mind and would read with delight the secret reports supplied to him by the Baron's agents, however trivial, however inconsequential they might be.

After a moment Prince Metternich picked up the papers again.

"Do we really pay for this twaddle?" he asked, and read aloud: " 'The King of Prussia this morning visited the Archduke Charles. In the evening he went out in civilian clothes with a large hat pulled over his eyes. He had not returned at 10 p.m.' That of course is most enlightening! What chambermaid or city scavenger supplied you with that nonsense, or did you find it in the wastepaper baskets which are sorted through so assiduously every morning?"

His sarcasm had no apparent effect on the Baron who merely shrugged his shoulders.

"It must be a tragedy for you, my dear Baron," the Prince continued, his voice sharp as a razor, "to learn that Lord Castlereagh has commanded that the contents of all the waste-paper baskets at the British Embassy shall be burnt."

"I believe that order has been given," the Baron agreed. "The British Mission has also engaged two housemaids of its own. Yet one of them is already in our pay."

"Splendid," the Prince replied with mock heartiness, "and we shall, therefore, receive more of these enlightening reports on the movements of our guests."

He turned over two or three sheets distastefully before he once again read aloud:

" 'The Emperor of Russia went out at 7 p.m. with one of his aides-de-camp. It is believed he went to visit the Princess Thurm and Taxis. Every morning a large block of ice is brought to the Emperor with which he washes his face and hands. At ten o'clock he left the Hofburg by a side door and drove alone to the Razumovsky Palace, which he entered by the secret stairway.' "

Prince Metternich looked up at the Baron.

"Why did he go there?" he enquired.

"I have no idea," the Baron replied. "There is nothing unusual about his visiting his Ambassador."

"Alone? Leaving the Hofburg by a side door?" Prince Metternich queried.

"I will make enquiries," the Baron said.

He was still sullen and resentful of the contempt which Prince Metternich had shown for his reports; then suddenly there came a gleam into his eye.

"Someone else went to the Razumovsky Palace last night . . . let me think who it was . . . the Comtesse Wanda Schonbörn—a newcomer to Vienna. I do not think I have spoken to you of her before. She danced with the Czar at the Masked Ball; in fact it is reported that he paid her marked attention."

"So!"

A faint smile played round Prince Metternich's lips.

"I have somewhere," the Baron continued, rustling through his papers, "a report on her. She is staying with the Baroness Waluzen. No one was told of her arrival before she came, but the Baroness escorts her everywhere and speaks of her as the daughter of one of her oldest friends."

The Baron drew a piece of paper from the bottom of the file and put it on the Prince's desk.

"Here it is," he said. " 'The Comtesse Wanda Schonbörn

visited the Razumovsky Palace last night at approximately
10 p.m. She left three-quarters of an hour later and was
driven back to the Baroness Waluzen's house.' "

He glanced up quickly.

"The times coincide."

"So they do, my dear Baron," the Prince said, as if in
surprise.

"You are not interested?"

"Not particularly."

The Baron sighed.

"I shall bring you the reports to-morrow"

"Do, if there is anything I should know. But don't waste
my time with rubbish. I am, I may remind you, a very
busy man."

The Baron bowed, collected his reports together and,
bowing again, left the room. The Prince walked to the
window and opened it. There was something deliberate in
his attitude, as if he wanted the fresh air to cleanse the
room of the Baron's presence.

He made no secret of the fact that he disliked the
man. The Baron might have his uses and the Prince
would be the last person to dispute that, but his poking
and prying into the secrets of other people seemed to
have affected his personality so that even on sight one
distrusted him.

The Prince was still standing at the window when, a
few minutes later, he heard a movement behind him. He
turned to see a servant with a note lying on a gold salver.
There were only five words written on the white paper
when he opened it.

Please, I must see you!

The Prince sent for one of his confidential secretaries.
He gave him certain instructions and then, walking to
the fireplace, threw the note into the flames. He watched it
burn, making quite certain that not even a small particle
of the paper fell through the grate.

He was taking no chances. He imagined that he was
safe enough from Hager in his own house, but could be
sure of nothing. For all he knew, the Emperor might
have given instructions that he was to be watched and
reported on; but whether he gave the order or not, Hager
would no doubt welcome any opportunity of gaining special
information about him.

The Prince was well aware that one of the things the Baron disliked most was that he was not made conversant with all that went on at the most secret meetings of the Congress.

When nothing remained of the note but a few black ashes, the Prince rang the bell for a footman and ordered his horse to be brought to the door. It was a fine, sunny afternoon and although the wind was cold, the air had a sparkling astringent quality about it which brought a bloom to the cheeks of the women thronging the main streets of the capital.

Accompanied only by his personal groom, a man who had served him all his life and whom, the Prince believed, he could trust as he could trust himself, he set off. The horses trotted swiftly until they were clear of the carriages and sightseers, and were alone on desolate pathways in the woods outside the city.

The fallen leaves made a carpet for the horses' hoofs, the bare branches of the trees rustled against the grey of the winter sky. It was in these woods that the youth of Vienna played and made love in the summer-time. Then there would be lovers entwined under the shade of every tree and there would be the sound of singing and laughter echoing through the glades. And at night there would come the soft sighs of satisfied desire, and sometimes the sound of a young voice yodelling from sheer unbridled happiness.

To-day there was no one to be seen, until at length Prince Metternich came to a small, half-hidden temple in the very depth of the forest; and there he saw a groom waiting, holding the bridle of a riderless horse.

The man saluted smartly at the sight of the Prince, who nodded in acknowledgment.

"Are you well, Josef?" he enquired.

"In good health, I thank Your Highness."

"You've joined the Baroness' household as instructed?"

"Yes, Your Highness. I am employed as groom and my brother has taken the position of footman."

"Good! Your services will not go unrewarded."

The Prince dismounted from his own horse, his groom took the bridle and he walked along the leaf-covered path which led to the temple. As he anticipated, Wanda was waiting for him there. She was wearing a riding-habit of green velvet and as she ran towards him he thought appreciatively how lovely she was, how vivid the blue of her eyes in the sweet oval of her little face.

"It is good of you to come, Your Excellency," she said as she curtsied. "I did not mean to trouble you, but I felt that I had to see you, to talk with you."

"You have something to report, perhaps?" the Prince questioned. "Shall we sit down?"

There were wooden seats arranged round the temple. It was in the summer a favourite meeting place for lovers, of which the walls bore witness, for they were scrawled and carved with names, most of which were encircled with a roughly drawn heart.

Wanda settled herself on a bench, spreading out her skirt, before she turned to the Prince with an eagerness which told of her impatience.

"I wanted to see you because I have met the Czar," she began.

"Yes, I know," he replied. "You danced with him at the Masked Ball and you visited him last night at the Razumovsky Palace."

"You know that?" she cried.

"Yes, I know," he answered. "What transpired?"

"That is what I wanted to see you about," she said, but now she looked away from him, a little frown between her eyes.

"The Czar told you something of import, perhaps," the Prince prompted.

"I . . . I don't think so," Wanda stammered, "but that is not what I wanted to tell you. You see, I think he trusts me and if he did confide in me, it would be because . . . he looks on me as . . . his friend."

"Well?"

The Prince's reply was a question.

"I see that I am not making you understand," Wanda said. "Can you not understand the position in which I find myself?"

"A position which you have achieved with much cleverness," the Prince smiled. "I have not yet had time to congratulate you."

"Please do not do that," Wanda replied. "I am not proud of what I have done. I contrived to dance with the Czar at the Masked Ball as you wished me to do. He . . . he was very charming."

"Yes? Then what happened?"

Wanda hesitated for a moment.

"We talked for a long time. He promised to have my fan mended—that was how I got to know him, because he trod on my fan and broke it."

"A clever idea," the Prince approved. "I see you have brains, my dear."

"No, don't praise me."

"Then go on."

"Last night another fan arrived as a present, and with it a note, unsigned, telling me that a carriage would call for me just before ten. It came and I was taken, as apparently you know, to the Razumovsky Palace. The Czar was there."

"Where did you meet?"

"In a small *salon* on the first floor. I cannot describe to you which it was, the Palace was so vast that I found myself utterly bewildered."

"Yes, yes, continue!"

"He was different somehow. He spoke of how there was no one he could trust. I had a feeling that he was suspicious of me."

"Nonsense!" the Prince said sharply. "There is no reason for him to suspect you."

"I kept telling myself that. And I suppose it was my guilty conscience; but I felt unhappy. I did not want to deceive him."

"Let us be frank," the Prince said. "The Czar is the enemy of Austria. If he succeeds in his ambitions, he will have greater power in Europe than ever Napoleon enjoyed."

"I . . . I quite understand that is someting which must be prevented by you and all the other nations at this Congress," Wanda said; "but where I am concerned, it is different. The Czar seems to me a lonely person. . . . It is so difficult to put into words, but I didn't realize before that an Emperor can be just a man!"

"The man who also has the power, authority and autocracy of an Emperor," the Prince answered. "What else did he say to you? Did he speak of Poland or of me?"

"He does not seem to be very fond of you," Wanda prevaricated.

"He hates me, I know that. What I would prefer is that he should be afraid of me," Metternich replied. "Anything more?"

"Nothing really, I think," Wanda answered. "But suppose there was something? If there should be other occasions on which I should meet him and he should tell me something privately because he wants to talk with someone whom he believes has nothing to do with politics and has no interest in the Congress save as a place of entertainment is it right that I should repeat it to you?"

The Prince looked at her in genuine astonishment.

"Right?" he said. "What are you trying to tell me, child?"

"Only that my conscience is troubled."

"Austria is the thing that matters. Our country is more important than personalities, more important, if it comes to that, than our petty little consciences. In affairs of State we have to rise above trivialities. We have to look to the main issue, to the main objective. We can only, all of us, each in his own way, strive to serve our country. We cannot give more than we are capable of giving, but we can give that. And it is only by complete elimination of self that we can offer to Austria, whom we all love, a little of our gratitude for being a part of this very great and very glorious country."

As he spoke, warming to the theme, the Prince held Wanda's eyes with his. It was as if he hypnotized her so that her troubles and worries seemed to recede into the background and she felt again the warm rush of patriotism that she had felt that first night when she came to Vienna.

"I do want to help—I do," she said. "And when you are here, it seems so easy, so simple."

"Nothing is simple and nothing is easy when it comes to dealing with other people and especially those of other nationalities," the Prince said. "The Czar is an extraordinary man—no need for me to tell you that. My wife tells me that our doctors are researching on the problem of a man being two personalities in one body—that is the Czar! Remember, if he shows you one side of his character, there is another side which he keeps hidden and secret."

Wanda gave a little sigh.

"I wish you could see him as I do."

"I am afraid I should not be so sympathetic," the Prince smiled. He hesitated for a moment and then added: "Let me tell you something. We have reached a deadlock. The Congress has been in existence now for some months, but we are exactly where we were when we started in September. I am at my wits' end as to what the next move shall be. I am speaking frankly, Wanda, because I need your help. I must know what the Czar intends. I must know whether he is putting over a gigantic bluff or whether he has the power and strength to remain adamant where Poland is concerned. Won't you help me?"

No woman, however experienced, would have been able to resist the appeal in the Prince's voice. It shattered Wanda's resistance and swept away her hesitation and doubts.

"Oh, I will!" she said impulsively. "I promise you I will."

The Prince smiled at her.

"Then continue your friendship with the Czar," he said. "Find out all you can, encourage him to talk. He is, I believe, a great talker on subjects that interest him."

"I will try to do as you tell me," Wanda answered.

The Prince rose to his feet.

"You have been far more successful already than I had imagined possible. I hope, too, that you are enjoying yourself in Vienna. From all reports you are being very much admired." He turned to look at her as she stood there, vivid against the grey walls of the temple. "It is not surprising," he added. "You are very lovely, as a great many men must have told you already."

"I have no time to listen to them," Wanda replied.

"I cannot believe that," the Prince replied. "All women like to be told they are lovely, and all women like to talk of love; but let me warn you—be careful to whom you give your heart."

He was not prepared for the sudden flood of colour which came into Wanda's face. He raised his eyebrows.

"So there is someone?" he queried.

"No, no, there is no one," Wanda protested, "no one who could possibly matter to me."

"I am glad of that," he answered seriously, "for at the moment you are too important for me to want to lose you."

"I shall not fall in love with anyone," Wanda said, and he thought it sounded as if she made a promise, not to him but to herself.

"Love, when it comes, is something we cannot deny," he remarked contemplatively, and he was not thinking of Wanda.

"But suppose . . . one falls in love with . . . someone completely unsuitable . . . completely impossible?"

"It would still be love," the Prince answered. Then he returned from dreams to hard reality. "But I am sure you will do nothing so stupid. When you fall in love, it must be with someone eminently suitable, someone you can marry, someone of whom I can approve wholeheartedly."

"I shall hope that will happen," Wanda said in a low voice.

"It will, my dear, I am quite sure of it, but for the moment your task lies with the Czar. It is fortunate that there is no likelihood of your falling in love with him. They tell me that ten years ago he was attractive to women; but now that he is older and more vainglorious than ever, he is even losing his proverbial charm. Perhaps it is as well, or I might be anxious about you."

As Prince Metternich spoke Wanda knew that never in his wildest imaginings did he think she might fall in love with the Czar. He was striving to be humorous, and obediently she forced a smile to her lips. There was no need for her to say anything for already the Prince was ready to leave. As far as he was concerned, the interview was ended. There was nothing more to be discussed and he was impatient to be away.

"Good-bye, my dear."

He raised her fingers to his lips and then as she rose from her curtsy he repeated the words he had used the last time they met.

"I am proud of you," he said and went from her then without a backward glance, swinging himself so swiftly into the saddle that almost before she had reached the door of the temple he was cantering away through the woods, his groom following behind.

Only when he was out of sight did she realize that she had gained nothing from this interview, nothing save the fact that the burden he had set upon her weighed even heavier than it had done before.

But Prince Metternich, as he rode towards the city, was well satisfied. The child was intelligent. It was not surprising he thought, considering who her father was. And she was pretty enough to attract any man, whether he were Emperor or commoner. She had, too, an innate purity which should, he calculated, appeal to the Czar. He was never quite certain how far Alexander's religious instincts affected his intercourse with women; but he was an idealist in many ways, and Wanda's innocence and air of untouched freshness should appeal to him where a more sophisticated woman might leave him cold.

He was taking a long chance, of course, but no-one knew better than the Prince how important a part a clever woman could play in diplomacy. And where the Czar was concerned, it was not safe to leave any stone unturned however small, however insignificant.

Prince Metternich was so intent on his own thoughts that he had practically passed another rider moving ahead of him before he saw who it was. Then a face was turned towards him and he heard his own voice as breathless as that of a boy breathe her name.

"Comtesse Julia!"

"Good afternoon, Your Excellency. I thought I was the only person in the woods this afternoon."

"And I have been thinking the same thing," he said, his eyes taking in every detail of her appearance, the soft silky grey of her habit which seemed to echo the serene depths of her eyes, the way her hair curled from under her hat from which fell a long feather the rich, vivid blue of a peacock's tail.

She was sitting on a big black mare, a magnificent animal with a strain of Arab in her, and her groom in her father-in-law's yellow and silver livery rode almost as fine a piece of horseflesh.

"I want to talk to you," Prince Metternich said.

"Why not?" she smiled.

"Alone," he insisted, feeling as he spoke that even the grooms were an intolerable intrusion on their privacy.

She hesitated and he added:

"There is a walk to the left of us which leads down to a small lake which in the summer is covered with water lilies. Shall we go there together? It will not take long."

She smiled at the pleading in his tone.

"Why not?" she enquired gaily. "If you can forget your engagements for a few minutes, then I can forget mine."

They left their horses in charge of the grooms and walked side by side down the path which led to the lake. The wind, which had been so boisterous early in the afternoon, seemed to have died away and there was a sudden breathlessness about the atmosphere—or was it just his own feeling because they were together?

They walked until they reached the lake. It was like molten silver reflecting the clouds above it; and then, as he turned to look at her, he forgot everything save his overwhelming need for her calm serenity.

They talked, moving round the lake, hardly conscious of where they went. He watched her face. The sweet seriousness of it showed no coquettishness when she spoke to him; there was nothing flirtatious in the way her eyes were raised to his. It seemed to him that her beauty was intensified as he grew to know the curves of her face, the movement of her lips, the way she would smile suddenly and slowly, so that her whole face seemed illuminated.

He had no idea how long they talked, till suddenly he felt a splash on his face and realized that it had started to rain. Then he saw they were far away from their horses.

"We will shelter under the trees," he said, and put his hand under her arm.

The trees were so thick on the far side of the lake that although they were leafless, their branches, locked and inter-locked, provided shelter if they kept close to the trunks.

For a moment they stood there side by side and then the Prince put his arms round Julia. As if she were waiting for this moment, she made no resistance, but turned confidingly towards him and hid her face in his shoulder.

For a long time he held her close, kissing her hair just above her ear and murmuring, in a voice he hardly recognized as his own, that he loved her.

"I love you. Oh my precious lady, I loved you from that first moment when I saw you in your father-in-law's house. I knew then you were the woman I had been waiting for all my life. I can't tell you how I know that this is different from anything I have ever felt before, but it is different."

"How?"

"Look at me!"

She threw back her head and then his lips found her half-open mouth. He thought, as he kissed her, that this was the first time he had ever realized what a kiss could mean. Never before had any woman evoked such emotion within him. He felt himself tremble as he held her. He was for a moment almost faint with the violence of his desire.

"I love you." And because there seemed no other words that could be said at that moment, he repeated: "I love you . . . I love you . . . I love you!"

Then, as gently as she had yielded to him, Julia drew away.

"I love you, too," she said in her soft, sweet, serious voice. "Love came to me as it came to you, that moment when we met at the reception."

"Say it again," his voice was hoarse, "say it again so that I can really believe it is true. Oh, Julia, say that you love me."

"I love you."

He thought all the beauty of the whole world lay in her face and in her voice as she spoke; but when he would have taken her in his arms again, she said:

"No, don't touch me yet. There is something I have to say to you."

"What is it, my darling? God, how wonderful you are!"

She leaned back against the trunk of the tree. Her lips, warm from his kisses, were a bright splash of colour in the pale loveliness of her face; her grey eyes were shining. The rain was like a silver curtain shutting them out from the world so that they were alone in a secret place of their own.

"Let me kiss you again," Prince Metternich begged.

"No, wait till I have said what I have to say," she answered.

"Yes, what is it?"

It was hard to listen when his whole body ached for the touch of hers.

"I love you," she said slowly, "and I believe that you love me; but love to me is a very different thing from what is generally accepted as love by our friends."

"How can you compare what I feel for you with anything anyone else has ever felt before?" Prince Metternich enquired.

"You have loved many women before, if all reports are true."

"I have never loved anyone until this moment. I have told you my love for you is different, and I will swear on the Bible that is true. I have never said to another woman before that she was different from all other women, but I say it to you and I mean it."

"I think I believe you, darling," she said, "and if you love me as you say you do, then you will not find what I am going to ask you to do too difficult to perform."

"What is it?" the Prince enquired. "There is nothing that you could ask of me that I would not do, nothing I would not give you. My darling, must we talk when I might be touching you? I want to possess you, I want to make you mine. I want to be sure of you as I have never wanted to be sure of any other woman."

"And I want that, too," she answered softly; "I want to be yours."

"Oh, my God!"

The idea of the surrender of herself was too much for him. He took her in his arms and covered her face with kisses. He rained them on her eyes, her lips, her cheeks. He kissed her throat where a small pulse was beating wildly; then again he crushed her mouth beneath his until it was almost impossible for either of them to breathe.

When finally she disengaged herself from his arms, her breath was coming brokenly. There was colour in her cheeks and her breasts were moving tumultuously beneath the tight-fitting coat of her habit.

"You love me!"

He repeated the words as if he spoke of a miracle.

"Yes, I love you; but please, Clement, you must listen to me now. You are not to kiss me again until you have heard what I have to say."

"You tempt me beyond all endurance."

"Then I must be swift in what I have to say," she answered with a faint smile.

"Hurry then," he commanded, his eyes on her mouth.

"It is this," she said. "Love to me is too great and wonderful to be trifled with; it is, in fact, not only my body that I shall give you, but my thoughts, my feelings, my heart, my soul. I could not give that lightly to anyone who would accept it lightly. We both of us have our commitments where marriage is concerned—that is a thing apart and cannot be altered or changed; but our love is free to give or withhold. I can give you mine on one condition and one condition only."

"What is that, my darling?" he asked fondly.

"That you give me in return," Julia answered, "absolute fidelity, that you pledge me your heart and soul as I pledge you mine, forsaking all other women and being completely and indivisibly mine as . . . I shall be yours."

Chapter Nine

WANDA looked round her in astonishment. She had already grown used to seeing magnificent pomp and splendour wherever she went in Vienna; but to-night, at a fête given by the Czar in honour of his sister, everything that had happened before seemed to pale into insignificance.

The party was being held in Count Razumovsky's Palace. The vast riding school had been converted into a ballroom and the *corps de ballet* had been brought from the Imperial Theatre in Moscow. Everyone who had been invited, including Wanda, had expected to see something unusual, but even they were awe-struck at the magnificence with which everything was presented that evening.

It was difficult for anyone to surpass the fêtes already given. The Metternich Ball, where the guests sat down to supper in a grove of orange trees; Baron Arnstein's, where flowers covered the walls and staircases; and Lord Castlereagh's great Gala Ball, where his Lordship danced a Scottish reel and her Ladyship wore her husband's Order of the Garter in her hair, had already created a precedent which it was hard to rival.

But Count Razumovsky, on behalf of the Czar, was determined that the Russian Ball should be the talk of Vienna, at least until another and richer host provided an even more fantastic entertainment.

The guests had of course heard whispers of what was to be provided for their delectation. The Baroness had been told on good authority that everyone at supper was to receive a plateful of cherries which had come from the Imperial gardens at St. Petersburg at the cost of a gold piece for each and every cherry. Strawberries had been brought from the Royal gardens of England, grapes from

Burgundy, truffles from Péregord, oysters from Ostend and oranges from Palermo.

People had chattered so much about what they were to receive that it might have been expected that most of them would be disappointed. On the contrary, *blasé* though they might be from so much entertainment, the nobility of Europe were amazed and delighted at what they found in the Razumovsky Palace.

Wanda had felt almost unbearably excited ever since the invitation had come for the Baroness and herself.

"I was afraid I might be forgotten," she said as the Baroness held out the huge invitation card.

"I should think there was no fear of that," the old lady replied drily.

"I could not be sure," Wanda answered, trying to speak calmly while her heart hammered in her breast that he had not forgotten.

She had not heard from the Czar for the past week and it seemed to her as if the days had never gone so slowly or seemed so long. She would feel again those fierce demanding kisses on her mouth that he had given her before she had wrenched herself from his arms and run sobbing down the corridors of the Palace.

Why, she asked herself not once but a thousand times, had they quarrelled and been so ill at ease with each other during those precious moments together?

Had it been her fault? She could not answer that question because she could not really understand what had happened. Why had he been incensed with her, why had there been that sharp edge to his voice which had not been there that first night?

Young though she was in years, she was woman enough to know that she attracted him as he attracted her. She could feel it in the magnetism which seemed to join them together so strongly, so unmistakably that there was no need to express it in words.

She had only to stand near him to realize that her heart was beating in unison with his. Why, then, had he been so strange? What had she done to upset him? Why had she seemed at times to detect something akin to disgust in his tone?

Then his silence! That had been harder to bear than anything else. She had lain awake night after night, longing and yearning for some explanation, some word that would tell her that he had not forgotten or dismissed her for ever from his life.

She had not believed until now that anyone could suffer so much or that suffering could be so painful. It was hard to disguise her feelings and her anguish from the Baroness and she thought at times that the old lady guessed her secret.

"No, you have not been forgotten, child," the Baroness remarked drily. "But don't count on keeping the favour of Princes. They breathe a more rarefied air than we ordinary mortals, and when it suits them they use their omnipotence as an excuse for breaking every rule of normal civilized behaviour."

"Some are not like that, I am sure," Wanda answered.

"How are we to know?" the Baroness asked with a shrug of her shoulders. "And what can it matter to us who must not be deeply concerned with their lives?"

The Baroness was trying to warn her; but Wanda was determined not to listen, not to acknowledge what her heart told her was the truth.

"There are several eligible young men who are interested in you at the moment," the Baroness went on. "The Comte de la Garde-Chambonas paid you many charming compliments when he was talking to me last night, and the Comte de Rochchouart has asked if you will ride with him tomorrow morning. He is a nephew of the Duc de Richlieu and a most excellent *parti* as you must undoubtedly realize."

"He is conceited and a bore," Wanda said in a small voice.

The Baroness shook her head.

"All men are that when one knows them well," she answered, "but the comforts of a good marriage are not to be ignored for that reason or for any other."

Wanda gave a little laugh.

"I do not believe you are half as cynical as you pretend," she said.

The Baroness' face softened. Wanda was very lovely with the afternoon sun bringing out the fiery lights in her hair, with her blue eyes dancing and her red lips parted over her white teeth.

"You will follow your heart, child, I can see that. Be careful where it takes you."

"You understand really, I know you understand."

Wanda was even more sure of that on the evening of

the Ball, when the Baroness was at particular pains to see that she looked more beautiful than she had ever done before.

She wore a puff-sleeved, low-cut white tulle gown over a sheath of white satin. The Baroness let her choose leaf-green gloves embroidered in silver, and shoes to match, while for her hair, worn without powder, there was a garland of water-lily buds arranged with leaves the same shade as her gloves. She carried in her hand the beauti-fully-painted fan which had been sent to replace the one which Richard had broken.

"You'll be the belle of the ball," the Baroness told her, but Wanda had shaken her head.

"Not while Princess Katharina Bagration is there," she said and knew, as she spoke, the first pangs of jealousy.

She had seen Katharina in attendance on the Czar at every party. Two nights ago she had watched them together at the Opera, and the beauty of the older woman, with her fair hair and heavy-lidded oriental eyes, had swept away Wanda's newly found conceit about herself as if it were the burnt ashes of a very small fire.

Never, she thought, could she emulate the grace and elegance of Princess Katharina, apart from the fact that her beauty was in itself unique and quite unchallengeable. She had not been able to see very clearly into the Czar's box, but she thought that he had seemed amused and delighted with Katharina, talking with her in an animated manner, and there was, Wanda thought miserably, some-thing almost possessive in his attitude.

She had wept that night bitter tears into her pillow, trying to pretend to herself that she was lonely and home-sick, but knowing the truth even while she would not admit it in so many words. The next day there had been a military parade. She had stood on the outskirts of the great crowd while the soldiery formed a huge double square and the Sovereigns came riding on to the ground on horseback. The Czar, in his green uniform covered with decorations, had drawn great cheers from the tightly packed onlookers.

Wanda had felt her own eyes prick with tears. He was so fine, so noble that she felt he was indeed, as the Baron-ess had said, a being from another world.

She could hardly bear to leave the house in case a mes-sage arrived while she was out. But the days went by and there was nothing, just the aching fear in her heart that she might never hear from him again. Now, at the Ball to-night she would be near him.

She had no eyes for the Russian dancers who opened the Ball. She was not even interested in the lottery which in the latest fashion provided rich and beautiful prizes for those among the guests who were lucky enough to draw a winning number.

She was looking all the time at only one person, hoping among the thousands of people assembled in the vast ballroom that he, too, was looking at her. His great height and his white uniform covered with decorations made him outstandingly conspicuous. She could see him moving among his guests; but try as she might, there seemed to be no way in which she could draw near to him.

She longed to appeal to the Baroness, but the old lady had found some cronies of her own and was seated comfortably by the ballroom floor, watching the dancers and criticizing them with a caustic tongue.

By now Wanda knew many people in Vienna and she found no lack of partners. Her beauty, her lack of sophistication and her quite undisguised enthusiasm made her an instantaneous success wherever the Baroness had taken her. The Comte de Rochchouart, who was spoken of as a spoiled social lion, was very assiduous in his attentions, but Wanda hardly heard what he said, and when she danced with him she was trying all the time to watch the Czar at the other end of the room.

It seemed to her that the hours passed slowly. The *corps de ballet* made their appearance dressed as gipsies and performed exotic, sensuous dances which were greeted with great enthusiasm. Wanda could see the Czar applauding them, while Katharina stood beside him, entrancingly lovely with a tiara of roses in her hair instead of one of jewels as was worn by all the other women.

She felt in that moment that she could not bear to watch him any more. He was not looking for her, not interested in the despair which made her turn away from the voluptuous excitement of a group of Russian dancers portraying an impassioned courtship. She walked towards the end of the room where off the brilliantly lighted arena there were little alcoves, curtained and decorated with exotic flowers where two people, if they wished, could sit in almost complete seclusion.

She must find somewhere where she could be alone, Wanda thought, conscious that her head as well as her heart was aching, while she felt as if she was empty of everything save her own misery.

No one seemed to notice that she had left the throng of onlookers. Everyone's eyes were on the whirling, gyrating bodies of the dancers. She stood for a moment with her hand on the curtain of one of the alcoves and looked back. The Czar must have moved, she thought, for she could not see him. Then she felt a hand grasp her wrist and she uttered a little cry of fear as she was pulled sharply backwards. The curtain fell behind her over the entrance to the alcove and she found herself in darkness.

There was the acrid smell of candles which had just been snuffed and then, as strong fingers tightened on her waist, she was no longer afraid. She knew who was there, who had pulled her from the ballroom into the darkness and she gave a little cry of sheer joy.

"Hush!" his voice said sternly. "We do not want anyone to come to the rescue."

"You did see me then!"

Her voice was breathless.

"I have been watching you all the evening," he answered.

"That is not true," she replied; "but how glad I am that you have not forgotten me!"

"Did you really think I could forget?"

"I was hoping and praying that I might hear from you. Oh dear! I suppose I ought not to say that to you, but I am no good at pretending."

"I'm not good at it either," he answered. "We were very stupid the other night."

"Don't let us think about that," Wanda begged.

He was very near to her, but he had not touched her save for that first moment when he had pulled her by the wrist into the alcove. Now that her eyes were accustomed to the dimness she could just see the vague outline of him, his broad shoulders, the proud carriage of his head. She looked up at him, conscious that both their voices had died away and there seemed to be nothing else to say, but she could hear his breathing and knew her own breath was coming quickly through her parted lips.

"You are looking very lovely," he said hoarsely.

"I wanted to look lovely."

"For me?"

"You know that was the reason."

It seemed to her that he made a sound like a groan.

"My dear, you haunt me. Do you know that everywhere

I go I find myself looking for you? Looking for your little face with those blue eyes that make me think of an English sky, for your red lips—have you forgotten the last time I kissed you? Why did you run away?"

Wanda gripped her fingers tightly together.

"Everything had gone wrong. You were angry with me, incensed or irritated, I do not know what it was. I could hear it in your voice. I did not understand the way you spoke to me."

"Yes, yes I know," he said. "I tried to hate you, but I failed."

"To hate me?" she faltered. "But . . . why?"

"I cannot explain now—I must go, we cannot stay here."

"You must go back to your guests . . . I understand."

"Do you? Wanda, Wanda! there is so much I should like to tell you and so much that I dare not."

She heard the desperation in his voice and did not understand it. Then she felt his arms go round her. He held her very close and for a moment he did not kiss her. Instead he laid his cheek against hers and even while her whole body melted with a joy beyond words because she was in his arms again, she knew that he was suffering.

"What is wrong? Please tell me!" she asked

"I can't," he answered. "Don't talk; if you only knew what it was like to hold you like this. I have thought about it so much. I do not understand what has happened to me. I only know that I cannot get you out of my mind. Wanda! Wanda! my little love!"

He held her tighter still and now at last his mouth was seeking hers, blindly and with a kind of misery behind his kisses, which made them all the more poignant. For the first time she kissed him back and knew as she did so the rapture of giving rather than receiving. At the same moment she felt the first rising of desire within herself like a small flame flickering within her body.

His arms tightened around her and now his kisses grew more passionate, more possessive.

"Wanda, Wanda!" he was saying her name wildly, their passion igniting both of them as if with fire.

And then they heard voices outside, the sound of feet and the music changed to that of a mazurka.

"I must go," Richard said.

He knew that the entertainment was over. It was madness for him to stay here any longer. He kissed Wanda again, quickly and passionately on the mouth.

"Go back to the ballroom," he commanded. "I will leave the way I came in."

"And I shall see you . . . again?"

"Soon," he answered, "very soon, I promise you."

She clung to him for a moment and then obediently she raised the curtain and stepped out into the brilliantly lighted ballroom. Richard stood for a moment in the darkness. Then, as he turned towards the back of the alcove, a voice said:

"Very touching. Let us hope the Czar is not in the ballroom when she returns or he will be suspicious."

"Katharina!" Richard ejaculated.

"Yes, Katharina," she mocked him.

"How long have you been here?"

"Quite a long time, *mon cher*. I saw you hurry away when the Czar went to supper and so I followed you."

"I hope you were duly edified."

"I was entranced. You always told me that you disliked intrigue."

"So I do, especially when it is forced upon me."

"Well, at least we know that your masquerade is not entirely a disinterested one!"

"That, if you will permit me to say so, is entirely my business."

"Indeed?" He knew she was smiling even though he could not see her face. "I thought it was my business, too."

"Listen to me, Katharina," Richard said impatiently; "this is all very unfortunate and I am sure unpleasant; but at the same time it is not my fault that the Czar wanted to make a fool of himself and asked me to help him."

"She is very pretty, this new spy of Metternich's," Katharina said, "but is it you she loves or the Czar from whom she is trying to extract information?"

"We will not discuss her, please."

"*La!* how formal we are!"

Katharina had come nearer to him as she spoke and now he knew that she was only a few feet away from him. He could smell the fragrance of the perfume she always used, the scent of roses which was so essentially a part of her.

"Richard, are you still angry with me?" she asked softly. "It is not my fault that she is Metternich's spy. It is true I discovered it, but would you really prefer to remain in ignorance? Besides, why should you be angry with me when all I have done is to love you?"

She made the very word vibrate and now she was closer still and he could feel her body close against his.

"I am sorry, Katharina," he said quickly, "but you know what I feel about the intrigue that goes on at the Court. It infuriates me. I wish to have nothing to do with it."

"And yet you don't seem very angry with her, with the woman who is prepared to kiss you because she believes you to be the Czar. Why not kiss someone who loves you because you are you?"

Her arms went round his neck as she spoke. They were soft and warm and yet he felt as if they were bands of steel imprisoning him.

"Katharina, we must go in to supper," he said quickly. "The Czar will miss us."

"Does it matter?"

He felt her lips seeking his and then as he turned his head he felt her bite the lobe of his ear, an action that was peculiarly a part of her passion and her desire.

"My Richard!" she whispered. "Have you forgotten what we mean to each other?"

Her body seemed to entwine itself about his and he waited for the surging wave of desire that she had never failed to arouse in him. Then, almost to his own astonishment, he found himself cool and detached and quite unmoved by the quivering passion which vibrated from her. He knew then that he was free, free of Katharina and the power she wielded by the exotic beauty of her face and body.

"I want you, Richard."

It might have been the voice of a complete stranger calling to him. Very gently he unclasped her arms from round his neck.

"We must go, Katharina," he said. "You know as well as I do that there will be trouble if we do not have supper with the Czar."

For a moment he thought she would defy him. He heard her draw in her breath quickly and knew, though he could not see her, that her eyes would be dark with passion.

Without a word she turned and walked away from the alcove. He saw the curtain swing back and heard her footsteps going away down the passage. He felt a momentary relief, but knew that this was not the end of what had been a curiously unpleasant incident. Katharina would never forgive him, he could be sure of that.

As it happened, the Czar had not noticed the absence

of either Katharina or Richard from the big supper table set for the Royal party in the Banqueting Hall. He was concerned at that moment only with himself and his partner, for against all precedent and setting aside the arrangements that had been made early in the evening the Czar had taken the Comtesse Julia Zichy down to supper.

She was looking exquisite to-night in a dress of pale mauve gauze ornamented with velvet ribbons. There was a tiara of diamonds in her hair and a wide necklace of the same stones round her neck.

"You look like a Queen," the Czar told her, "and indeed you are the Queen of my Ball and of my heart."

She smiled at the fulsome flattery.

"I have christened you '*La Beauté Céleste*'," the Czar continued. "Did you know that?"

"What you say one day, Sire, is repeated all over Vienna the next," Julia answered.

"Then I shall publicly proclaim you the Queen of my Ball to-night and to-morrow all Vienna will know the reason," the Czar answered.

He bent his handsome head towards hers, but she turned her eyes away.

"I would not like you to embarrass me, Sire," she said quietly.

"Does it embarrass you to know that I admire you more than any woman I have ever seen?"

"It is very kind of Your Majesty to say so," Julia answered, "but I would rather that no one else should hear you for fear they suspect favouritism."

"What does that matter when you are in fact someone I should like to favour, someone of whom I would ask a favour?"

Julia looked at him quickly and looked away again.

It seemed to her that there could be no mistaking what he was trying to convey, and yet she thought she must be imagining it.

"These are delicious, Sire," she said, referring to the dish of Sterlets in front of her. "I hear they came from the Volga."

"All the treasures of Russia shall be yours if you will only be kind to me," the Czar answered.

"Kind?" Julia questioned, raising her eyebrows above the cool, grey eyes.

"Must I put it more plainly?" the Czar asked. "I fell in love with you the first moment I saw you; I have thought of you ever since as *'La Beauté Céleste'*—the words are already written on my heart."

Julia smiled and shook her head.

"No, no, Sire. You are mistaken," she said. "Many other names may be written there, but not mine. Besides, I will tell you a secret—I am in love with someone else."

She felt him stiffen beside her. She was speaking deliberately, making sure that this interest of the Czar should go no further. She was well aware of how embarrassing the attentions from one of the potentates could be, and she was determined that the whole thing must be crushed at its very inception.

"In love with someone else?"

The Czar repeated the words in a stunned manner, as if he could hardly believe they had been said, let alone credit them to be the truth.

"Yes, in love," Julia repeated; and now her face was suddenly radiant with a light which seemed to come from within. "Love to me, Sire, is a very serious, very wonderful emotion. It is indeed my whole life."

"And who is this lucky person?" the Czar asked.

"That I cannot tell Your Majesty for reasons you will appreciate."

"I cannot believe it." Now there was a note of exasperation in the Czar's voice.

"But it is true," Julia answered, "and I know that with Your Majesty's proverbial generosity you would not wish me anything but happiness."

She saw by the exasperation on his face that she had gone as far as she dared. She had not yet finished supper, but she rose from her chair.

"Will Your Majesty excuse me? I have promised the next waltz to the King of Prussia."

She swept down to the floor in a deep curtsy and then hurried away as the Czar sat drumming with his finger-tips on the supper table. The Empress of Austria, who was sitting on his right, turned to speak to him, but without any apology he rose abruptly and strode away.

As he went from the room, he beckoned to Prince Volkonski and strode ahead of him. He found a small ante-room that was not occupied. As the door closed behind him the Czar turned to the Prince. His face was contorted with anger, his ears reddened as he shouted:

"Who is she in love with? Why wasn't I told? What the devil do I pay you for, I'd like to know, except to learn what is happening, what is going on? Are you so blind, so deaf or incompetent that you cannot keep me informed even about the people who most concern me?"

"You are speaking of the Comtesse Julia Zichy, I assume Sire?" the Prince enquired.

"You fool, you nit-wit, who else do you imagine it could be?" the Czar fumed.

He was in one of his hysterical rages which Prince Volkonski knew too well and which, unlike most people at court, left him unperturbed.

"I am sorry, Sire, but you had not confided to me that you were interested in this particular lady. Had you done so, any information you require would be at your disposal."

"Tell me, then, with whom does she imagine she is in love? Who has succeeded in her affections where I have failed? Tell me, tell me at once, if you can do so."

"I assure Your Majesty that question is quite easy to answer," Prince Volkonski replied. "Although the Comtesse's affection is a quite recently developed emotion for the gentleman in question, it is undoubtedly, from all reports, a *grand passion* and not to be compared with any of the frivolous *affaires de cœur* which are taking place in Vienna at the moment."

"Stop your cackling and tell me whom she loves."

The Prince hesitated only for a moment. He knew he was dealing the Czar a body blow, but there was nothing he could do about it.

"The Comtesse is in love with Prince Metternich," he said quietly.

The Czar's whole countenance was now suffused with crimson.

"You lie, you dog!"

"It is the truth, Sire."

"Metternich! Always Metternich. He thwarts me at every turn and none of you does anything about it. Do you hear me? None of you does anything about it."

"I am afraid there is nothing we can do, Sire."

"Metternich! In love with Metternich!"

The Czar picked up an exquisite piece of Sèvres china and threw it violently into the fireplace where it smashed into a thousand pieces.

"God damn his soul!" he said. "He takes everything from me—even the woman I wanted for myself!"

Chapter Ten

KATHARINA entered the Czar's bedroom and stood for a moment by the door. He was well aware that she was there, but he ignored her presence, continuing to read his Bible as if every word needed his closest concentration.

Katharina let a small smile curve the corner of her lips as she watched him. She was wearing a flowing *négligé* of shell-pink taffeta trimmed with lace which rustled as she moved slowly across the room. The candlelight shone on her fair hair and gave her heavy-lidded eyes a mysterious beauty which would have attracted the attention of the Czar at any time other than now.

He was in one of his most difficult and obstinate moods. Prince Volkonski had reported his condition to Katharina and suggested that she should try to inveigle him into a better frame of mind.

"The Czar is already losing some of his popularity," he told her. "When he came to Vienna, everyone was ready to acclaim him for his stand against Napoleon and because they genuinely believed in his goodness of heart and his desire for peace. But he has antagonized too many people lately by his unpredictable behaviour."

"Yes, he can be difficult," Katharina sighed.

"Difficult?" the Prince said. "I am closer to him than anyone else; he trusts me, he knows I serve him to the best of my ability. . . ."

"You are of course indispensable," Katharina interposed flatteringly.

"Is anyone that?" the Prince asked. "It is, however, true that the Czar would not know where to obtain truthful information if I were not here. But there are times when even I feel I cannot stand any more."

"And yet he can be so charming," Katharina said.

"And so devilish," the Prince added.

Katharina laughed at the vehemence of his tone.

"I will do what I can," she promised.

The tense lines round the Prince's mouth seemed to relax a little.

"He is fond of you," he said, "genuinely fond."

Katharina shrugged her shoulders.

"For the moment! To-morrow I may be sent to Siberia. *Eh bien!* I will do what I can. Is it Metternich again?"

"Yes, Metternich again—not only because of Poland, but also because of the Comtesse Julia Zichy."

"I suspected that," Katharina remarked, "when I saw her leave the supper table last night."

"And as if that was not enough," the Prince went on, "the Czar learned this morning that Marie Narischkin is infatuated with a young Cavalry officer."

"Who told him that?" Katharina asked sharply.

"Not me," the Prince answered. "I take good care to tell him only the things I want him to know, but he has other sources of information, as you and I are well aware."

"Marie Narischkin is always the same," Katharina exclaimed. "Promiscuous and without shame! A new lover is no surprise. Yet at this moment such upsets can be catastrophic. He loves her."

"I doubt it—he has grown used to her, as a child grows used to an old and battered doll," the Prince contradicted.

"Can love become only a dreary habit?" Katharina enquired.

"In the dark all lovers are grey," he replied.

Katharina laughed, throwing back her head.

"Are you really as cynical as that?" she asked.

"Not where you are concerned," he answered, and bent to kiss her hand.

It was evening before Katharina found there was a chance of seeing the Czar alone. His day had been spent in hysterical denouncements of his Ministers, recriminations and dismissals and sullen silences, which were more frightening to his entourage than when he berated them.

It was usual for those who were to spend a part of the night in seeking enjoyment to rest before dinner. It was a time for many in the Palace not only for rest but for love; and Katharina, as she rustled down the corridors, wondered how many closed doors hid secret lovers seizing a few minutes from their arduous duties and public appearances for the carefree happiness of love.

But such secrets would not be hidden for long, she thought. Prince Volkonski would know about them before evening from the chambermaids, valets, waiters and sentries, who were all in his pay. Everything, whether it concerned the Czar, the Empress or the most unimportant little secretary, was reported to him.

As she crossed the Imperial bedroom, she knew that the time she entered the room would have been noted and that the Prince would already have been informed that she was there. She must not fail him, she thought. It was important for her to remain in his good graces.

The Czar was lying on his hard, narrow bed, which was, however, covered with a spread of gold lamé lined with sable. He wore a dressing-gown of green brocade and a diamond ring on his finger glittered as he turned the pages of his worn Bible.

Katharina swept forward and with a lovely gesture knelt beside him.

"I want to talk to you, Sire," she said in a soft voice.

"What about?"

The question was sharp and disagreeable.

"About yourself. We are all worried about Your Imperial Majesty—worried and distressed."

The Czar turned over another page and read aloud:

" *When the ungodly are green as the grass and when all the workers of wickedness do flourish, then shall they be destroyed for ever!* "

"All your enemies shall be destroyed," Katharina said consolingly, "but you must not destroy your friends as well."

"What friends have I?" the Czar asked. "I can trust no-one."

"Perhaps you set too high a standard for those you love," Katharina said softly. "You must remember that few people are as strong either in mind or body as you, Sire."

"That is true," the Czar agreed.

"Women especially, like myself, are weak and very foolish," Katharina said. "You must not judge us too harshly."

"It is impossible to tolerate some things," the Czar replied.

He was thinking of Marie Narischkin, Katharina

thought, and deliberately she turned away from that subject.

"Julia Zichy is not worthy of your interest in her."

"She is beautiful," the Czar retorted. "She is in love with Metternich! What power has he got that all women capitulate to him? Even you have worshipped at that shrine!"

Katharina shrugged her shoulders.

"He has a certain glamour about him—for a time."

"She is in love with him," the Czar repeated; "she told me so with her own lips."

"She is not the only woman in Vienna."

"And who am I to take only those in whom the Prince Metternich is not interested?" He flung the Bible down on to the bed and swung his legs on to the floor. "The man haunts me. I cannot rid myself of his presence whatever I do, wherever I go. He is like some demon that must fasten its hand into my very soul. I wanted Julia Zichy, I wanted her for myself, and why not? I am a free man, free of the vows that I have made to Marie Narischkin. She cannot expect fidelity when she herself takes lover after lover and each time expects me to forgive her. It has gone on long enough, too long. I won't do it, I tell you, I won't do it."

The Czar's voice rose to a high, hysterical note. He rose to his feet and walked backwards and forwards across the room.

"Listen to me, Sire," Katharina said, "and I will tell you a way which you can take your revenge both on Clement Metternich and on Marie Narischkin."

"Revenge?" the Czar questioned, arrested in his pacing. Katharina nodded.

"Tell me, then, tell me!" he commanded her impatiently. Katharina looked around her.

"Not so loud," she whispered. "Who knows who might be listening?" She rose to her feet and moved towards the fireplace, where a big log fire was burning. "Come and sit down, Sire," she suggested. "What I have to say is for your ear alone."

The Czar obeyed her, seating himself in an armchair on one side of the fireplace while Katharina once again sank down on her knees beside him.

"There is someone in Vienna who is far more beautiful than the Comtesse Julia," she murmured in a low voice.

"I doubt it," the Czar contradicted her. "I myself christened her *'La Beauté Céleste'* and I consider that she is without doubt the most beautiful woman attending the Congress. But what is the use of my even thinking of her —Metternich has got there first—Metternich!"

"Yes, yes, I know," Katharina said soothingly, "but Metternich is also interested in Wanda Schonbörn!"

"The girl whom Richard has been meeting? What about her?" the Czar enquired.

"Then you have not seen her?" Katharina asked. "She is very lovely and I have my suspicions that she is closer to Metternich than Julia Zichy or any other woman can be."

"I am not interested in Metternich's women," the Czar said pettishly.

"And yet supposing through one of them you could strike at him in a way that would hurt him desperately?" Katharina asked.

"How? What do you mean?" the Czar enquired.

"Wanda Schonbörn is Metternich's daughter," Katharina whispered.

"Are you sure of this?" the Czar enquired.

"As sure as one can be of anything," Katharina answered. "Prince Volkonski has made enquiries about her. The agent came back yesterday from her home in the mountains. Metternich stayed there nearly nineteen years ago when he was on holiday from Paris. When you look into Wanda Schonbörn's eyes, you find yourself looking into Metternich's."

"Can this be true?" the Czar enquired.

"The facts are indisputable," Katharina replied. "When the Comtesse Carlotta Schonbörn was dying, she schemed to send her daughter to Vienna. She talked to those around her of her devotion to Prince Metternich, and although she had not seen him for nearly nineteen years, she was certain he would help her child. Wanda Schonbörn came to Vienna and the Prince accepted her at once. She has been everywhere and met everyone. Is that an act of friendship or of something closer?"

"Does the girl know?"

"I have no idea, Sire," Katharina answered, "but it doesn't matter one way or the other. What does signify is that she is in love with Your Majesty."

"With me?" the Czar enquired. "But I have never seen her."

"You forget, Sire, that Richard has been playing the rôle of Emperor."

"So she has fallen in love with him?"

"Only because she has been swept off her feet at the idea of meeting the Czar of All The Russias, the man whom all Vienna acclaims as a hero, the greatest warrior since Alexander the Great, and a man whom women find irresistible."

"And she is pretty?"

"Lovely," Katharina enthused, "and she is young, untouched—a virgin."

"What exactly are you suggesting?" the Czar enquired.

He was sitting alert and interested in his chair, the look of rage and sullen depression had lifted from his face.

"I am suggesting," Katharina answered softly, "that she takes the place of the Comtesse Julia Zichy. Leave her to Metternich—but make Metternich's daughter yours."

"You think it would annoy him?"

"I think," Katharina answered, choosing her words with care, "that Metternich believes in your fidelity to Marie Narischkin. It is well known to everyone in Vienna that you adhere most strictly to the vow she has extracted from you."

"Why should Metternich know of such intimate matters?" the Czar asked angrily.

Katharina smiled.

"Marie Narischkin boasts of it quite openly. It is an impertinence on her part—she does not realize the great value of a love such as yours."

The Czar's eyes flashed.

"She certainly does not appreciate me," he said. "This Captain of the Cavalry—have you heard of him?"

"I am afraid, Sire, I don't associate with such people."

"It is intolerable that someone of no importance should take my place," the Czar fumed.

"Marie Narischkin will not expect you to make a fuss," Katharina goaded him. "You have always been so long-suffering, so complacent."

The Czar jumped to his feet.

"Too complacent!" he shouted. "I'll show her I'm not a lackey to be kicked around."

"And you can show Metternich, too, Sire."

"And Metternich, too," the Czar repeated. "How can it be arranged?"

"I have thought of that," Katharina said. "To-night we are supposed to be dining here. Instead you must send a message to Count Razumovsky to say that Your Majesty

will honour him by dining at the Palace. Make quite clear
that we are all to go there, including Richard."

"Yes, yes, go on."

"At the last moment, Sire, you must make an excuse to
stay here and we will go without you. You will refuse to
let us change our plans. After you have dined alone Your
Majesty will feel better and you will proceed to the Palace.
But you will enter by the side door and go up the secret
staircase to the *salon* on the first floor which has been used
before. A note will have been sent earlier in the evening
to Wanda Schonbörn to meet you there."

"What point is there in everyone being at the Palace,
too?" the Czar enquired.

"Can't you see that we do not want anyone to be suspicious of your movements?" Katharina said. "Baron Hager's
spies are everywhere. He will know where you are dining.
It is always conceivable that Wanda Schonbörn might be
warned not to go to the Palace at the last moment; but if
the Empress is there—who could object or forbid?"

It was a lame excuse, but the Czar did not realize it.
Katharina's real motive was to make certain that Richard's
evening was fully occupied. She sensed intuitively that he
would want to see Wanda that evening. If they dined in
the Hofburg and he asked to be excused from the Royal
party it would be hard to keep tracks on him. As a guest
of Count Razumovsky he would be caught, at any rate
until the Czar had finished what he intended to do.

"Yes, yes, I am sure you are right," the Czar said
decidedly.

"No one must know of your intentions, no one. You will
not speak of it to Richard, Sire?"

"No, of course not. You are certain that the girl is in
love with me?"

"Quite, quite certain. She has been swept off her feet
with the wonder of meeting the Emperor Alexander of
Russia. You must remember that she sees you every day,
watching from the crowds as you attend the military
parade or drive in the Prater. She is young, inexperienced
and unsophisticated. Can you imagine what it means to
someone like that to receive the attentions of the most
handsome, most brilliant man in the whole civilized
world?"

The Czar bent down to pinch Katharina's cheek.

"You flatter me, Katharina," he said; "but how well we
understand each other, you and I!"

"How kind you are to me, Sire," Katharina answered. "You know there is nothing I would not do for you."

"I believe that is true," the Czar said, "and Metternich will be angry about this, you think?"

"Both Metternich and Marie Narischkin will be furious beyond words."

"It delights me to think of their rage," the Czar replied. "The girl will come when I send for her?"

"Can you doubt it, Sire, when she knows she is to see you?" Katharina answered.

The Czar smiled at that. His ill-humour had completely vanished by now. He glanced at himself in a mirror over the mantelpiece.

"I will wear my white uniform," he said. "I find women always admire a uniform."

"It depends who is inside it, Sire," Katharina flattered. "You won't forget to arrange about dinner at the Razumovsky Palace?"

"I will send a note to the Count immediately," the Czar replied, "but I must dine here?"

"Yes, here, Sire—a headache at the very last moment."

"I won't forget," the Czar replied.

Katharina pressed her lips against his hand as she sank in a deep curtsy.

"She is a very fortunate young woman, Sire," she murmured, and left him preening himself in the mirror with a smile on his lips.

The Czar was still smiling three hours later when he stepped through the secret panel into the *salon* at the Razumovsky Palace. Everything had gone according to plan. The Imperial party had left for the Palace, upset and disconcerted by the news at the very last moment that His Imperial Majesty would not be accompanying them.

The Czar had dined in his own apartment and, throwing a dark cloak over his uniform, had hurried down the side staircase to where a carriage was waiting for him.

He glanced round the *salon* appreciatively. The great bowls of flowers scented the air, it was warm and a fire was burning brightly in the hearth. The lighting was discreet and his eyes did not miss the wine and cold collation of dishes in the further corner of the room.

There was a mirror set in one of the panels of the wall. He could see himself reflected in it. Butinski had dressed his hair in a new way this evening. It was very becoming, he thought, and hid the slight tendency, which was beginning to perturb him a little, to thinness above his forehead.

He wondered how far Richard had advanced in his association with this young woman. Katharina had said that she was in love with him. Katharina would know. He had no intention of admitting that he had not been present at their previous meetings—Metternich must never know that he had been clever enough to find an impersonator. There would be many other occasions when Richard could be useful to him.

He was a good boy, Richard. He would take him back to Russia after the Congress was over.

The Czar straightened a curl at the side of his forehead. As he did so, he heard the secret panel in the wall open slowly. He had a quick impression of hair such as the Venetians liked to paint, a little oval face and smiling lips, of eyes so blue that they seemed almost too large and vivid, surrounded as they were with dark lashes; and then she had run towards him.

"Oh! but you are not masked to-night," she exclaimed. "How wonderful, how . . ." she stopped.

He had put out his hands instinctively towards her and quite naturally and spontaneously she had laid her fingers in his. But at his touch her voice suddenly died away and he saw a strange expression wipe away the happiness on her face.

"What is it?" he asked.

"You . . . and . . . your voice."

The words came stammering from between her lips.

"What is worrying you?" he enquired. "Aren't you pleased to see me?"

"But of course I am," she answered. "I have been wondering all day if I would hear from you; and when your note came . . . but it is so strange! You are different. Could a mask really alter anyone so much?"

"Am I altered? What did you expect?"

"I expected to see you," Wanda answered, putting up her hand to her eyes, "and yet . . . I can't explain exactly. It doesn't feel the same."

"Is this what is wrong?" the Czar enquired, and put his arm round her.

She made no effort to resist him, but she stared at him, her blue eyes troubled.

"You are very lovely," he said appreciatively, looking down at her face.

He drew her closer as he spoke and then he bent his

head and his lips found hers. For a moment she seemed to respond; then, unexpectedly, she twisted herself free.

"Tell me what you have been doing all day," she said. "I expected to see you in the Prater or at the Concert this afternoon."

She was talking quickly in a kind of flurry, as if her words were but a screen to smother emotion.

"Don't go away from me," the Czar said. "Your lips are soft and warm, like the feathers of a dove."

She glanced at him quickly and looked away again.

"And your hair is the colour of the leaves in the autumn before the wind blows them away."

He went nearer to her as he spoke.

"'Thy breasts are like two young roses that are twins'," he quoted softly, "'which feed among the lilies.'"

He put his arms round her and drew her close. But suddenly Wanda pushed him away from her.

"No! No!" she cried.

"Are you afraid of me?" the Czar asked.

"No . . . yes . . . I don't know what to think. It is not the same—somehow it is not the same."

"Look at me," the Czar commanded, and as she did so he encircled her even closer in his arms. "You have seen me before, as I have seen you. To-night we are alone together, just you and I. And I have taken off my mask. Is it because you see me as an Emperor that you are afraid?"

"It isn't that!" Wanda answered.

"Then don't be afraid any more," the Czar said, "for I am also a man."

He picked her up suddenly in his arms and carried her to the couch covered in cushions. He set her down amongst them; then, as she tried to struggle, he bent forward to fasten his lips on hers. She tried to cry out, to free herself, but his great strength was too much for her. His lips were hard and almost suffocating and she felt his hands on the nakedness of her shoulders and at the softness of her throat.

He raised his head from hers for a moment and, gasping for breath, she cried out at him:

"Let me go . . . please let me go!"

"But why? I love you and you love me."

"It isn't right . . . it is wrong," Wanda answered, "please let me get up."

"But I don't want you to."

He looked down at her, his hands holding her prisoner, and she thought with a kind of sick horror that he was amused at her helplessness. It was like a nightmare from which she could not wake, a nightmare with the shadow of terror standing behind it.

"Please let me get up!"

She was ready to plead with him now, but there was no change in his expression. His eyes seemed to be watching her with a detachment that was more frightening than if he had been ablaze with passion. There was something sensuous and at the same time cruel about the smile of his lips.

"Let me go. . . . I insist."

"And how will you do that?" he asked. "My beloved is mine!"

He bent forward again to bury his lips in the softness of her neck. His lips were hard and possessive and she felt as if every nerve in her body was repulsed by them. She could not understand herself and yet she knew that she hated him. She was repulsed by the touch of his hands that had thrilled her before. She felt herself quiver and shrink from any contact with this man whom she had thought she loved.

"Let me go! Let me go!"

She struggled wildly within his hold and knew it was as ineffective as if she were a bird in the hand of the trappers.

"I will scream," she cried, striving wildly to keep her head. "People will come. They will find you here."

"And how will you scream if I stop your mouth with kisses?" the Czar asked.

She strove to evade him, but he was too strong for her. His mouth was on hers and his hands held her down. She could not breathe, she could not move. She felt as if she were being drowned in deep waters, as if she were lost, defeated, overwhelmed, and there was nothing she could do about it.

She strove to free herself from his mouth. She could feel his hands wandering over her body and with every last remaining ounce of her strength she strove to push him from her. She heard her dress tear, but she was utterly and completely helpless beneath him. And then, as her whole being cried for help soundlessly, yet with the desperation of despair, she heard voices.

There were cries, followed by screams shrill and insistent. The Czar heard them too and lifted his head.

"There is somebody coming!" Wanda gasped.

He raised himself from the couch.

"Fire! Fire!" she could hear the words distinctly.

The noise and tumult was coming nearer.

"Fire!"

Dizzily she tried to sit up, and as she did so, she heard the secret panel in the wall close. She put her hand to her mouth and found her lips were bleeding. She smoothed down her dishevelled dress and with a supreme effort managed to rouse herself from the couch, only to sink down again and drop her head between her hands.

The room was swimming around her; she felt faint and sick from the horror of what she had encountered and the desperate ineffective striving of her imprisoned body.

The Czar was gone—that was all she could remember at the moment; but she knew that the terror and misery in her heart had not gone with him.

Then, as if the full horror of what she had been through, of what she had feared, swept over her so that she could not face it, could not bear to acknowledge the truth of it, she felt herself falling. She made no effort to save herself, dropping forward . . . down . . . down . . . into the darkness.

Chapter Eleven

RICHARD had been restless all day. It was not Katharina's anger and jealousy that was perturbing him, it was his own feelings. He could not determine to himself exactly what he felt about Wanda.

In what seemed an incredibly short time she had encroached upon his life so that he found himself thinking of her continuously, in fact it seemed to him to be every minute of every hour. Her little face haunted him, her steadfast blue eyes stood between him and his relationship to everything and everybody.

He found himself searching for her wherever he went, watching the crowds to see if she was amongst them. Amid the dancers in a ballroom, the women riding to a hunt, people wandering down the Prater, there was always someone who reminded him of her. A glimpse of a red-gold curl, a movement of a sweetly curved cheek, a gesture of a little hand would recall her so vividly that he felt at times that she had become an indivisible part of himself.

And yet, though his lips were prepared to say, 'I love you', some cool, critical logic within his mind questioned what his heart asserted so forcibly. He had been infatuated with a pretty face before; he had known so many women and found them attractive only to be disillusioned and very quickly bored. Could it be possible that here was a woman who was entirely different from those who had passed through his life and so easily become forgotten?

Wanda was young, she was unsophisticated, she was immature. He knew all the arguments against this being a love different from all others, and yet even while he repeated them to himself his whole being vibrated with the conviction that it was different.

135

He was unable to sleep the night after the Ball and after lying wakeful for some hours he rose, dressed and went out into the gardens of the Hofburg. It had been snowing since dark, the world was white beneath a rising moon and the gardens had an unreal and ethereal beauty which made him think instantly of Wanda.

Perhaps, he told himself, it was because she had never been enough with other ordinary people to be like them. He could visualize her living a detached, almost spiritual life in the fastness of her mountain home. She had at times an ethereal unsubstantialness, and yet her lips beneath his had been mortal lips, her body trembling in his arms had been warm and pulsating.

Was Wanda different in any way from the other women he had kissed? He remembered how infatuated he had been with Lady Isobel Manvers when he first went to London. She was the toast of St. James's, 'The Incomparable' the bucks of the town called her, and yet she had let him kiss her one night in the gardens of Devonshire House. He could still remember his elation when her lips clung to his. The fragrance of her hair, the quick rise and fall of her breasts beneath her gown of silver gauze had changed him from a callow, untried youth into a man.

"I'm crazed with your beauty." He heard his voice deep and husky with reverence as if it were the voice of a stranger.

"To-morrow I drive to Guildford to stay with my Lord Sutton," she whispered. "Come with me!"

He had gone, humble with gratitude because she had invited him, and only when he reached the huge ancestral mansion of the Earls of Sutton did he understand all that the invitation implied. The wild, raffish house party of old roués and young rakes, with a number of what his father would have called 'Fast-stepping ladybirds', would not have shocked him if Isobel had not been completely at home among them.

The fact that he was accepted as Isobel's partner did not have any particular significance until he found that his bedroom communicated with hers and that she was waiting for him in her nightgown with outstretched arms.

He had enjoyed that visit, but a young dream died, and an ideal of womanhood toppled from its pedestal into the mud. Were all women like Isobel if they were given the opportunity? He began to believe they were, as they melted into his arms too easily and he discovered that his infatuation of the moment was deceiving him with his best friend.

"Kiss 'em and leave 'em," his grandfather had advised; and the old reprobate lived up to his advice until he had a stroke at the age of eighty from chasing a pretty little Opera dancer up the stairs after a heavy dinner.

Yet Wanda's purity seemed to radiate from her, as if the lamp of truth shone within the transparency of her body. He would have staked his life that he was the first man who had touched her lips. There was a lovely, unawakened immaturity about her, as fragile and elusive as the dew-drop trembling on the first flower of spring, but unmistakable, irrefutable.

Richard walked through the snow until dawn broke, and then at last he went back to his bedroom and slept dreamlessly until it was nearly noon. It was because he was late in waking that he lost the opportunity of seeing Wanda in the morning. He had meant to call on her before luncheon and tell her the truth about himself. The time had come, he decided, when he could no longer play the Czar's game of pretence.

He was not, and never could be, cut out to be a spy or intriguer. It was utterly and completely foreign to his nature and to his English upbringing. When in his youth he had stayed at various times with his grandmother's Russian relatives, he had not realized how over-ridden they were by informers and espionage.

He had suspected from time to time that things that were said were repeated, that movements were noted and catalogued, that men and women were often afraid to speak what they believed to be the truth; but not until he came to Vienna with the Czar's entourage did he realize to what terrible proportions this habit of check and counter-check had grown.

He knew now that he should never have let himself be inveigled into playing a part in the Czar's intrigues against Metternich and he knew that, at whatever cost to himself and his popularity with his Royal host, the time had come to call a halt. He would tell the Czar what he had decided, he thought, but Wanda should know first. She had been the one deceived and he owed her that, if nothing else.

By the time he was dressed and ready to go out, he was informed that the Czar was waiting for him and he was forced to accompany the Emperor Alexander on his morning round of calls made by Sovereign to Sovereign when the happenings and gossip of the previous day were exchanged and commented upon.

There was a sleighing party that afternoon at which he had also to be present. The early snow of the night before had been followed by a sharp frost and an immense crowd had gathered in the Hosefplatz where the sleighs were to meet. Those intended for the Emperors and Sovereigns were decorated in the brightest colours picked out with gold. They had cushions of emerald-coloured velvet and the silver harness of the horses decorated with the escutcheons of the Imperial House of Austria were hung with tinkling silver bells.

As soon as the sleighs were occupied, a blast on the trumpets was blown and the procession began its march. There was a detachment of Cavalry to lead the way and a huge sleigh drawn by six horses contained an orchestra of kettledrums and trumpets. After the procession had moved slowly down the principal streets of Vienna amid cheering crowds, the horses started off at a gallop on the road to the Schönbrunn Palace.

The first sleigh contained the Emperor Francis of Austria with the Empress of Russia who wore an aigrette of diamonds in her toque and was wrapped in a coat of green velvet lined with ermine. All the ladies wore velvet coats or cloaks of the most glorious colours trimmed with rare furs.

Richard had half-expected to find himself in the same sleigh as Katharina, but instead he found his companion was the Comtesse Sophie Zichy, who, the gossips had already reported, was making a dead set at the Czar. The latter had, however, been so busy pursuing her sister-in-law that he had hardly noticed Sophie, apart from christening her 'La Beauté Triviale', which was hardly a compliment after the celestial title he had given to Julia. She had, however, been included in the Imperial party, and as she chattered away vivaciously and with a charm that was undeniable, Richard found himself thinking that the Czar would be foolish to waste his time running after Julia, whose affections were already engaged, when the pretty Sophie was here for the taking.

He found, however, that his attention was wandering when the sleighs, on arrival at the Schönbrunn, formed a circle round the frozen lake which was covered by skaters wearing national costumes of the countries of Northern Europe.

As always he found himself unconsciously looking for Wanda, and he was angry that it should become such an obsession with him.

Servants in livery brought round hot drinks to those in the sleighs who did not join the skaters on the lake. The Comtesse Sophie took a glass in her hand.

"Shall we drink to your thoughts?" she asked softly.

Richard started and realized that he was being rude.

"You must forgive me," he said. "I am preoccupied with my own troubles instead of trying to entertain you."

"You must be in love," she replied. "I know the signs only too well."

"Strangely enough, that is the question I am asking myself. Am I in love? How can I be certain?"

"Only your own heart can tell you that," she replied.

"I'm afraid I don't trust my heart," Richard said.

"Then trust me," she smiled. "My intuition tells me that you are in love—perhaps for the first time in your life."

"Why should you think that?" he enquired.

"Perhaps at times I am a little clairvoyant," she answered, "and there is, too, an expression on your face and an aura about you that tells me you are on the threshold of something so wonderful that you feel it cannot be anything but a figment of your imagination."

Richard raised his glass to her.

"I drink to your charming eyes," he said. "At the same time I am wondering if you are making things better for me or worse."

Light though her words were, they had an effect upon him and by the time the sleighing fête was over and a blast of trumpets gave the signal for the return to Vienna, he was longing, as he had never longed for anything in his life before, to see Wanda.

He was sure now what he had to say to her—almost sure; and yet that cool, calculating mind at the back of his brain still questioned the fire that seemed to be rising within him.

'I want her—I can't live without her!' His body seemed to burn at the thought and yet his mind continued to laugh at it.

It was difficult to remain cool and detached about anything when as dusk fell the horses galloped back towards the city, their bells ringing across the white, snow-covered fields, the cold air seeming to have something

heady and intoxicating about it as it whipped the cheeks
of the fur-covered occupants of the sleighs.

"I, too, am in love," the Comtesse Sophie confided in
the darkness as she and Richard travelled homewards.

"Be careful," he warned her, "love can be a dangerous
emotion when it is given unwisely."

She laughed at that.

"One cannot choose whom to love," she said. "It
just happens. Haven't you learned that?"

He nodded his head, remembering that first enchanted
waltz, and that moment when Wanda had taken off her
mask and he had seen her face for the first time. Yes,
love happened, the Comtesse Sophie was right, and when
it came there was no denying it.

It was too late when they got back to the Hofburg for
Richard to visit Wanda before dinner and while he was
changing his clothes and planning to see her late in the
evening, the message came that the Czar and his personal
suite would dine at the Razumovsky Palace.

"Keep you busy, don't they, Guv?" Harry remarked.
"You'd think some of the nobs'd want to put their feet
up and 'ave a quiet evening at 'ome once in a while."

"It would certainly be a change," Richard agreed.

"If you ask me, all this 'ere dressing up and kissin'
of 'ands ain't good for yer, Guv," Harry continued.
"You're looking tired, and your visage is tallow. What
you want is a day out after the pheasants or a rattlin'
run after a fox that ain't afraid to stretch 'is legs."

"Be quiet, damn you!"

It wasn't often that Richard swore at Harry, but the
words came out vehemently now. The valet's words had
conjured up a nostalgia that was almost unbearable. He
had a sudden yearning for the empty, shuttered house that
he called home. Pheasants would be roosting now in the
woods, there would be a hunter in the stable which
would be wondering why he didn't come, stirring rest-
lessly in his box when the morning came and there was
the baying of the hounds across the fields and the sound
of the huntsman's horn.

Was his whole life going to be spent worrying about
women, drugging himself into a complacency with other
people's champagne and other people's hospitality? Richard felt that he wanted to groan at the hopelessness of
the position, instead of which he finished dressing in
silence, scowled at his reflection in the glass, and went

slowly down the corridors to the *salon* where they were to assemble before proceeding to the Razumovsky Palace.

That the Czar did not accompany them at the last moment was to Richard's mind somewhat of a relief. Although when Alexander was in a good mood his charm could make people believe they were enjoying themselves however much they might have anticipated the contrary, his presence always imposed a certain stiffness and formality on the gathering. The Empress was also at her very worst in his presence, while without him she was inclined to expand and even at times to make an effort to be amusing.

Dinner, therefore, with the Count Razumovsky playing host, was a comparatively informal meal and the excellent food and wine managed to make Richard feel in better spirits than he had been all day. After dinner they sat round talking; and though once or twice Richard looked at the clock, hoping there would be a chance of seeing Wanda, he knew as the hours ticked by that such hopes were fruitless. He was in process of stifling a yawn when at length the Empress rose to her feet.

"We must thank you again for a very pleasant evening," she said graciously to the Ambassador.

Count Razumovsky bent over her hand. At that moment there was a sudden shout outside the door. There was another cry and everyone stiffened as the door of the *salon* was thrown open.

"Fire! Fire! The Palace is on fire!"

A servant stood there, his gold-laced uniform disarranged, one side of his face blackened and dirty.

"We must get the ladies outside," Richard said quickly.

He offered the Empress his arm as he spoke, forgetting all precedence, taking command naturally without for a moment thinking that as a quite unimportant guest at the Palace it was presumption on his part.

As he hurried down the marble stairs with the Empress at his side, he realized from the clouds of smoke belching into the hall and the crackle of flames in the distance that the fire had already got a firm hold on the ground floor. Having got the Empress and the ladies who accompanied her out into the garden, Richard ran back into the Palace to see who else was to be rescued.

The Secretaries, servants and guests were already pouring out of the building from a dozen different doors and the Count was giving instructions to his staff to try to save some of the art treasures and the furniture before the flames reached them.

At the moment Richard was more concerned with animate than inanimate objects, however valuable. He found three small dogs cowering in the corner of one closed room and carried them to safety despite their struggles when they smelt the fire and felt the smoke in their eyes. As he laid them down, he felt a hand on his arm. He turned to see Katharina staring at him with a distraught expression on her lovely face.

"Richard, help me. I have just remembered something," she cried.

"What is it?" he enquired.

"The Czar!" she answered. "He is there!"

She pointed in horror towards the burning building. Amid the snow-covered roofs there rose dense clouds of smoke and one wing was already ablaze, its windows glowing with the brilliance of the flames leaping against the darkness of the sky. Even as Katharina spoke there was an explosion and part of a wall collapsed, disclosing a room crammed with treasures and masterpieces of art.

"The Czar?" Richard repeated. "But he didn't come to-night. He is at the Holburg."

"No, no!" Katharina said. "He was coming here after we had left. It was arranged that he was to go up the secret staircase to the same *salon* where you went."

As she spoke a sudden fear seemed to stab Richard.

"What do you mean?" he asked harshly. "Who was he meeting there?"

Katharina's face was very clear to him in the light of the flames and he knew the answer to his question long before she could force the words to her lips. Without a word he turned and ran towards the Palace.

"Richard! Richard, be careful!"

He heard Katharina's despairing cry, but it did not check the speed with which he was running.

He sprang into the smoke and flames which made the main entrance already a small inferno. Blinded and choked, for the moment, he thought they would overpower him and then he saw his way through them. The marble stairway was as yet untouched. He sprang up it, running with all his speed down the long corridors which instinct rather than knowledge told him led to the part of the building where the Czar would be.

He had only once been in that room which Count

Razumovsky kept as a convenient meeting place for those who wished to be secret or incognito, but fortunately his bump of locality was good, and with only a few moments' hesitation he found himself in the quieter, less ornate part of the Palace, which the flames had not yet reached.

He burst open the doors as he went—a bedroom, a small sitting-room containing a delightful collection of Fragonard's pictures, a gallery decorated with statues, several more bedrooms and at last, when he had almost begun to despair, a room which he recognized as soon as he opened the door.

For a moment he thought it was empty till, with a feeling of terror such as he had never experienced before in his whole life, he saw Wanda lying on the floor. He thought she must be dead; then, as he knelt down beside her, he knew she had only fainted. Her face was very white, but her body was warm and her heart was beating.

He bent to pick her up in his arms and as he did so she opened her eyes. For a moment she stared at him, then she gave a little convulsive cry.

"You've come! You've come! I felt sure . . . you would."

She turned as she spoke and hid her face against his shoulder. She was trembling all over with a violence that was almost frightening.

"It's all right, darling," he said to her. "I am here, and I will take you to safety."

"Don't let him . . . touch me! Don't let him . . . touch me!"

For a moment he did not understand. Then he noticed her torn dress and raising his eyes saw the cushions on the sofa dented with the imprint of a body. His lips tightened for a moment. There was an expression of murder on his face and he drew her even closer to him.

"No one shall touch you," he said. "I promise you that."

"I am frightened . . . save me!"

It was the cry of a child, the cry, too, of a woman who had been frightened beyond endurance. Very tenderly Richard rose to his feet, lifting her in his arms.

"We've got to escape from here, my darling," he said quietly. "The Palace is on fire."

"So that is what they were crying out," Wanda whispered. "Thank God you came before . . . before . . ."

Her voice broke on the word and suddenly her whole being was racked with tears. They were the tears of relief, tears, too, which could wash away, at least for the moment, the sharpness of her terror.

For a moment she sobbed convulsively and then, as Richard started towards the door, she gave a little cry.

"Put me down, please put me down."

He did as she asked of him.

"We must hurry," he said, still keeping his arms about her.

She looked up at him. Her eyes, glistening with tears, were very large in the white oval of her face.

"I do not . . . understand," she said. "I thought it was you . . . at first. It wasn't; and yet I had seen you so often and believed . . ."

"Never mind about that now. I will explain everything later. The Palace is on fire and I have got to get you out of it."

He would have picked her up again, but she stepped away from him.

"I will walk," she said. "It will be easier. Explanations don't matter now you are here, and it was not . . . you who was . . . with me . . . just now."

Her lips trembled for a moment and he knew what she was remembering; then, taking her by the hand, he pulled her along.

"Come quickly," he commanded.

They ran along the corridor, but as they reached the top of the main staircase the billowing clouds of smoke coming towards them told them it was already impassable.

"We can't get down that way," Richard exclaimed.

"Why not the staircase through the panel?" Wanda panted, but he shook his head.

"Unless the servant is on duty at the foot of the stairs, which is unlikely now, there is no way of opening the door except by the key which he and he alone holds."

"There must be another way!"

They ran back down the passage, looking for a side staircase; but when they found it, they saw the flames already licking their way up the wooden banisters.

"We've got to risk the main entrance," Richard decided. "Do you trust me?"

She smiled at that and for a moment they stood looking

at each other as if there was no need for haste, no need for anxiety.

"You know I do," she answered.

"And I love you." He knew it now. "I love you with all my heart and with all my soul. I have never loved anyone until this moment."

"I love you, too," her lips were raised to his and then as he kissed her he gave a sudden triumphant laugh.

"We are not going to die yet. Come, I know what to do."

He ran into the nearest bedroom, seized a blanket off the bed and soused it with an ewer of water from the washbasin. Heavy and sodden he draped it over his own head and then over Wanda's as he lifted her in his arms.

"Hold tightly to me, keep your face hidden, and pray, darling, as you've never prayed before," he told her.

He felt her arms go round his neck and her lips touched his cheek. Then she buried her face in his shoulder and the blanket enveloped them both. The smoke, dense at the top of the stairs, cleared a little as he went lower. Wanda weighed very little, but he could not go quickly for fear of stumbling and hurling them both into the flames which leapt crackling towards them as they consumed the beautiful inlaid furniture and brocade-covered chairs.

It was hard to see and yet he knew from the way the flames were blowing that the front door was open. It was only a question of passing through the river of fire, vivid, glowing, which lay between them and safety.

Slowly Richard descended the stairs. It was now or never, he knew that. They must be the last people left in the Palace and there was no chance of help. They must save themselves or perish. He took a deep breath and, as if she knew what was happening, he felt Wanda's arms tighten round his neck.

"God help us!" he muttered, and it was perhaps the most sincere prayer that he had ever offered in his life. And then he was dashing into the fire. He could feel the great heat of it scorch his face. He felt an agonizing pain in his legs and heard the hiss and siss of the flames against the wetness of the blanket.

The smoke blinded his eyes and filled his nostrils. He could not breathe, he could not see; then suddenly, as he fought against suffocation, he knew that they were through. He could feel the coolness of the air and felt his feet stumble on the gravel.

Then there were hands to support him, to prevent him from falling, and the chatter of a dozen voices. Someone took the heaviness of the blanket from off his shoulders. And they would have lifted Wanda from his arms, but he shook himself free of them.

"We are all right," he muttered. "I can manage."

He carried her away from the heat of the house and on to the shadows of the formal garden. He could see the little crowd of dinner guests standing where he had left them, watching the burning Palace, every detail of their white, strained faces clear in the firelight. Beyond them, kept back by sentries and servants, a huge crowd of spectators was assembling.

They were coming in great hordes from the town, the brightness of the flames against the sky a beacon to guide them to this new excitement. But where he and Wanda came to rest beside a little pointed cypress tree, they might have been in a deserted garden, for no one noticed them. They might have been alone, too, as far as they themselves were concerned.

Tenderly he set her down, and with a tenderness somehow new to his nature, noted her dishevelled hair, the way her hands went quickly to the crumpled bodice of her dress.

"We've done it!"

The words came triumphantly from his lips.

"Who are you?"

Her eyes were on his face, looking at him with an almost pathetic bewilderment in their expression.

"I am Richard Melton, an Englishman."

"You pretended to be the Czar?"

"Yes, I pretended to be the Czar."

"But why?"

"Because you were working for Metternich."

He saw the colour flush her cheeks before she raised both hands as if to hide it.

"Do you know? Does it matter?" she whispered. "I am so stupid, I might have known you would guess."

"My darling, I didn't guess, and don't let that worry you. There are so many other things to talk about."

She raised her eyes to his and her lips were parted.

"I am ashamed," she said. "I wanted to tell you the truth, but he wouldn't let me."

"Who wouldn't—Prince Metternich?"

"Yes. I promised him. It was for Austria, you see."

"And I, too, wanted to tell you the truth," he smiled.

"And you are not an Emperor? Not anyone important?"

"Do you mind?"

"I am glad . . . so terribly, terribly glad."

"My little love!" He reached out his arms at that and she was close to him. For a moment her face was hidden and then she raised it to his.

"I love you," she whispered. "Is it wrong to tell you so?"

"Wrong? No! Right! Say it again, my darling!"

His lips were seeking hers, but even as he bent his head he saw someone coming towards them. There was no mistaking the tall figure, the majestic bearing of the man who always seemed to carry an invisible crown on his head.

As Richard stared, he felt Wanda stiffen in his arms and knew that she, too, had seen who was approaching. The Czar came closer. It was a moment of tension, a moment when Richard experienced again the murderous anger he had felt as he looked on those dented cushions.

Slowly he clenched his fists. As the Czar reached him the two men faced each other. There was a sudden silence and then the Czar burst out laughing.

"Richard! My dear Richard!" he laughed. "Have you seen your face? It is black, my poor fellow—black as coal!"

Chapter Twelve

RICHARD had felt Wanda stiffen in his arms with fear as the Czar advanced towards them. Now he knew, as the Imperial laughter echoed above the flames, that she was angry. But before either of them could speak, with one of those swift changes of mood which made the Czar so incomprehensible to his friends and enemies, the laughter ceased and with a very different expression on his face, he said:

"I owe you an apology, Comtesse. I had not the least idea, when I left you alone a little while ago in the Palace, that there was the slightest danger to you personally. I imagined the sounds I heard were intruding merry-makers and only when I returned to the Hofburg did I learn the terrible truth.

"If I had entertained the least idea that the Palace was on fire, I would have endeavoured to rescue you with the same gallantry as has, I know, been shown by my friend, Richard Melton."

There was no doubting the Czar's sincerity and as both Wanda and Richard knew, he was no coward when it came to physical action. But, while Wanda might be bewildered at the Czar's inability to hear what was being cried so loudly in the passages, Richard knew the reason only too well.

It was a closely kept secret of the Russian Court that the Czar was deaf in one ear. Shortly after he was born he had been taken away from his mother by the Empress Catherine the Great, who wanted to bring up her grandson to be a Spartan fully equipped to stand the physical strain which must fall upon the ruler of a militarized Empire.

In most ways the physical training to which Alexander was subjected proved beneficial; but in order to accustom him to the roar of guns, Catherine had him housed in a room at the Winter Palace where the windows faced the Admiralty. The child was forced to hear at close range the cannonade which took place at the Admiralty on every festive occasion, and festive occasions were very numerous.

Although Alexander became accustomed to artillery fire, the membranes of his ears proved too weak to sustain continual noise and the result was a deafness in one ear which was to remain with him for the rest of his life. His vanity made him ignore his disability and no one in his entourage was ever brave enough to refer to it.

"Will you forgive me for deserting you?" he asked now of Wanda.

The pleading in his words, the expression on his face and his almost magnetic charm made resistance impossible and almost despite herself Wanda found her antagonism melting away. It all seemed an ugly, unreal dream that this man should have attempted to rape her and that only a timely fire within the Palace itself should have saved her.

Before she could say anything, however, there was a sudden vibrating crash from the Palace behind them and the floor of a magnificent gallery, decorated with statues by Canova, gave way. A groan went up from the vast crowd watching the flames, and in the brilliant light of the conflagration their strained faces and wide astonished eyes gave them almost a macabre appearance.

The white snow-covered garden, the bare branches of the trees crested with frost, the marble fountains with their frozen water, made a strange, yet at the same time beautiful background for the burning Palace.

In the parts of the building where the fire had not yet penetrated, people were now flinging pictures and statues wildly into the gardens and court. If they escaped destruction by fire, they were often shattered to pieces on the flagstones or saturated with jets of water and slush which had already converted the ground into a quagmire.

Several battalions of infantry, which had arrived with the Emperor Francis of Austria at the head of them, were doing their best to preserve order and striving to prevent the progress of the flames. But the breeze was rising and it looked as if by the time morning came nothing would be left of one of the greatest treasure houses in Europe.

It was as if the spectacle was too much for Wanda, for with a little cry she turned towards Richard and buried her face in his shoulder.

"The Comtesse is tired, Sire," Richard said. "Have I your permission to take her home?"

As he spoke he lifted Wanda in his arms and with the light of the fire full on both their faces, the Czar and Richard faced each other. Their rank or lack of it was forgotten; they were just two men with a woman dividing them. The expression on the Czar's face was defiant. He resented that his overtures of friendship had gone unanswered.

He was, also, for one fleeting second, jealous of the penniless young Englishman he had befriended and to whom he had given his friendship. Then, it seemed as if he saw himself through Richard's eyes, saw the shallow, contrasting elements in his character of Christian humility and pompousness, sensuousness and spirituality, kindness and resentfulness. And because he was afraid of what he saw, he fell back on the one great asset he knew himself to possess—his extraordinary art of knowing the right way to approach other people, his remarkable ability to charm the hearts of all with whom he came in contact.

His lips curved in a gentle smile.

"But of course, my dear Richard," he said. "The Comtesse should be taken away at once from this scene of destruction. My own sleigh is at your disposal, take it with my blessing, and when the Comtesse is in a fit state to listen, convey to her my most sincere thankfulness that she is safe and unharmed."

Was it possible to withstand such magnanimity? Murmuring his thanks, Richard carried Wanda swiftly across the garden and through the crowd of spectators to where the sleighs, with their champing, frightened horses, were waiting for their masters.

Tenderly he lifted her into the comfortable cushioned seat, and then, settling himself beside her, allowed them to be covered by the heavy sable rugs which the Czar had brought with him from Russia.

It was but a short distance to the Baroness' house, but it took a long time owing to the fact that the roads leading out to the Razumovsky Palace were thick with

people. By this time the news had spread to all Vienna
that the Palace was on fire and everyone from the
highest nobleman to the lowest citizen was anxious to
see the spectacle, more magnificent in its wild beauty
than all the military parades, tournaments and masques
which had been performed to date.

For the whole of the journey Richard held Wanda
close in his arms and only when they were at length
within the city and the dawn was breaking, pale and
silver over the chimney pots, did she raise her face to
his and speak.

"Must you leave me?" she whispered.

He had thought perhaps she was asleep and had been
content to travel in silence. Now he put his hand under
her chin and turned her face up to his.

"My darling," he said softly, "I would stay with you
for ever if it were possible."

"And isn't it?"

The question was so low he hardly heard it and yet
he knew by the movement of her lips what she asked.

"I love you!" he said. "You know that, but what you
don't know is my position. I am penniless, Wanda, a
man without a country, an Englishman who cannot return
home."

"You are exiled?"

He nodded his head, it was impossible for him to
confirm the truth in words. If it had seemed bitter before to be barred from England for a crime he had not
committed, it was doubly hard now. He had a sudden
vision of Wanda in the house he loved, her laughter
echoing down the empty corridors, her little feet running
up the wide staircase.

For one moment he hesitated and then he said the
words he had never before said in his life.

"I want to ask you to marry me," he said. "God
knows I want it more than I have ever wanted anything
else in my life before, but it is not possible."

In the faint morning light he saw the sudden radiance
of her face; and then, because it hurt him too much to
see her happiness and know that there was no justification
for it, he looked away.

"I am homeless," he said. "I can ask no woman to
share that with me."

"But . . . but we love each other! . . ."

The words were somehow almost a cry. He turned to her almost roughly.

"Yes, I love you as I didn't believe it possible to love anyone. As I carried you through that fire, I thought to myself that if we died together it would not matter. It is going to be far harder to live apart."

"We cannot! There must be a way, there must!"

It was the cry of youth all over the world, the unquenchable belief that a solution could be found of every problem, however hard, the brightness of hope springing from a heart that had not yet known the bitterness of disillusionment.

Richard bent his head and his lips found hers. For a moment they clung together until, breathless, she drew away from him, her eyes shining.

"Everything will come right, I am sure of it," she cried exultantly.

He stared at her dumbly, not wishing to dispel her joy.

The sleigh drew up outside the Baroness' house. A sleepy footman opened the door and Richard helped Wanda up the freshly sanded stone steps. He would have said good-bye to her, but she clung to his arm.

"Please come in."

He could not resist the pleading in her eyes and so they entered the house together. The servants ran to light a fire in the small *salon* opening off the dining-room and the Majordomo promised that breakfast should be ready in a few minutes.

"I must go and tell the Baroness I am home," Wanda said. "You will not go until I return?"

Again the pleading in her voice was irresistible.

"I will wait," Richard promised.

She smiled at that and ran lightly up the stairs as if her feet were winged with happiness. Richard demanded hot water and when he looked at himself in the mirror was not surprised that the Czar had laughed at his appearance. His face was smeared and blackened, his hair untidy, his cravat a crumpled rag.

The Baroness' servants were apparently equal to any emergency, and when, twenty minutes later, he returned to the *salon*, he had shaved and washed, his borrowed neck-tie was spotless and immaculate, and his burnt legs had been bandaged.

Breakfast was ready, but there was no sign of Wanda; and then, as he hesitated, wondering whether to help himself to the hot dishes and to drink the steaming chocolate, Wanda came running into the room.

She had changed her evening dress for one of white muslin, and her hair, brushed until it shone like burnished gold, fell loosely over her shoulders. Her face was alight with happiness and her eyes seemed almost breath-takingly blue against the clear bloom of her unblemished skin.

She was so young, so fresh, so lovely that for a moment Richard forgot all the problems which had been troubling him and remembered only that he was a man and in love. He held out his arms and she ran into them.

"I was half-afraid you would have vanished," she said. "I thought I must have dreamed it all."

"Was ever a dream as delectable as this?" he asked, against her lips.

He felt her tremble as he kissed her, not with fear, but with a sudden ecstasy which seemed to sweep them both into a rapture beyond words. The very air they breathed was filled with an almost visible happiness as they drew apart and looked into each other's eyes.

"Tell me that you love me!" Richard commanded masterfully.

"I always knew that love would be like this," Wanda answered.

He took her hands in his and lifted them to his lips, kissing each one of her fingers until, laughing, she pulled him towards the breakfast table.

"You must be hungry," she said. "What a long night it has been!"

They sat down side by side and Richard ate with his left hand because he was holding hers with his right.

"The Baroness was awake," Wanda said as the servants came into the room to serve them. "I told her what had happened and when we have finished breakfast she wishes to see you."

Richard tried to force himself to remember his ignominious position, his poverty, and unenviable reputation; but he could think only of Wanda and the warmth of her little fingers clinging to his, the shining wonder of her eyes, her lips which seemed still to be quivering from his kisses. He had no idea of what he ate and drank, he only knew that it was the most delectable meal he had ever enjoyed in the whole of his life.

Yet later, as he climbed the stairs with Wanda towards

the Baroness' room, he wondered where he would find words to explain either to the Baroness or to Wanda that their love was doomed from the very start.

Wanda paused at the top of the stairs.

"Don't be afraid of her," she said softly. "I was, at first, but now I know she is gentle and lonely inside. She says sharp things with her tongue only because she is afraid of anyone feeling sorry for her. She has been very kind to me."

"Could anyone be anything else?" Richard asked.

She looked away from him and there was a shadow over her face.

"I have failed the Prince," she said.

"Prince Metternich?" Richard enquired. "He had no right to ask you to spy on his account."

"It was for Austria," she corrected him.

"I don't care if it was for Heaven," Richard answered. "It was outrageous of him to ask such a thing of you or for you to accept."

"The Prince was desperate," Wanda answered. "He told me so, and because I was new to Vienna—a face which had not been seen before—he thought I might succeed where he had failed. It was only a forlorn hope and, as you see, I have been no help at all."

"A good thing, too," Richard said sharply. "I shall tell Prince Metternich what I think of him and his schemes."

"No, no! I would not have you antagonize him," Wanda cried hastily.

Richard's lips tightened.

"We will go and see him together," he said. "I will not have you frightened by this man or any other."

"I am not frightened of him—really," Wanda answered, "but I like to hear you say that we will go to see the Prince, or anyone else . . . together."

When she spoke like that there was nothing Richard could do but put out his arms towards her, and as he kissed her he repeated the word silently but despairingly in his heart, "Together—together!"

But their plans were doomed to disappointment. Prince Metternich had decided to take advantage of a temporary lull in the negotiations of the Congress to enjoy a brief holiday. He kept his movements secret, knowing that to announce his departure would draw a storm of protest from everyone, including the Emperor Francis himself.

He had played a most exhausting rôle for so long that he felt that unless he got away for a few days he might be in danger of losing the few advantages he had gained by sheer tenacity, unremitting determination and against what at times seemed overwhelming odds.

It was not only the Congress that had exhausted him. He had lived strenuously since the beginning of the campaign against Napoleon. Day after day he had been in the saddle, advancing with the victorious armies. Without any rest or respite he had plunged into the negotiations in Paris, in London and now in Vienna.

The calls on his time socially, the irritations of the Czar's obstinacy, the machinations of Talleyrand, and the opposition of other statesmen had taken serious toll of his nervous energy. His left eye, in which he had caught a severe cold during the campaigns, had begun to trouble him again and had developed a slight droop. He knew that if he did not rest now he might collapse, and that as a sick man he would be unable to serve either his country or his own ambitions.

It was Julia who made the final decision. Count Szechenyi, who was Sophie Zichy's father, had properties near Wiener-Neustadt which she told Prince Metternich would be ideal for his retreat. The Count confirmed that he would be delighted to have the Prince and what was more, Julia was prepared to go with him.

For a moment when she announced this plan, Prince Metternich was silent, but she knew by the expression on his face and the sudden light in his eyes what he hoped of their journey and she knew that he asked her a question wordlessly.

"Yes, I will come with you," she answered, "but it will be as your nurse, as someone to minister to you, to look after you and you must promise to obey me."

"Have I ever done anything else?" he asked; and as he spoke his fingers tightened on hers and she knew that he had suffered because she had kept him at arm's length, waiting to be sure of his vow of fidelity, waiting, too, for what she considered the right and perfect moment for the consummation of their love.

Her grey eyes were very tender as they rested on his finely drawn face with the dark lines of exhaustion beneath his blue eyes.

"You have got to get well, my dear one," she said

and for the moment he had to be content with that for an answer.

Two days later they left the snow-covered capital in a *carrosse* and hurried southward. The countryside rolled past the windows, isolated hamlets, fertile farms, deep silent forests and wide silver rivers. He had forgotten that Austria could be so beautiful or so peaceful.

It was peace that he needed, he thought, and he felt as he had felt at their first meeting, that Julia brought him peace. Even after a few hours in her presence he could feel energy surging through his veins.

When they reached Wiener-Neustadt, they were transferred to an open sleigh and a Hungarian coachman swathed them thickly in warm fox furs. The sun was on their faces and the cold frosty air seemed as intoxicating as some rare wine.

The horses started to climb the white road into the mountains. The intrigues and gossips and irritations of Vienna seemed to have been left behind with civilization. Here there were only the rolling hills and the distant mountains, their glaciers dazzling against the blue of a winter sky. Here there was peace and the sudden feeling of being re-born into a pure and untouched world.

Finally they reached the property of Count Szechenyi near to Lake Neusiedel, that mysterious water which vanished sometimes for decades, only to reappear apparently replenished by the earth itself. In the last century the water had disappeared for so long that the peasants had planted their fields on the lake bed and even built their cottages there. Then the water had returned.

Now the lake was frozen over, but it seemed to have a fairylike quality about it, so that, as the horses and their sleigh galloped round it, their silver bells tinkling and the crack of the coachman's whip vibrating through the air, Prince Metternich wondered if he and Julia would also disappear as the water had done, leaving no trace behind them but the memory of their love.

At length the hunting lodge came in sight. It was a one-storied building, very substantial in appearance and built round a centre court. They were welcomed by the Count, who led them into the big, comfortable sitting-room where huge logs were burning in an open fireplace and where porcelain stoves in the directoire style also drove out the cold. The curtains were not yet drawn and Prince Metternich went to the window and looked out over the panorama of mountains and valleys, all white and silent and without a sign of habitation. It was just beginning to grow dark and the white fields beneath the hunting lodge were dotted with coveys of partridges appearing to be twice their natural size against the background of snow.

"Peace! Peace! It is all so peaceful here," he murmured to himself; and then with a sudden pang he remembered Vienna—what might be happening without his presence, what crisis might arise and he was not there to cope with it?

But even as the thought was there it was dispelled. Julia's hand touched his arm and he turned to see her smiling at him. The Count stayed for dinner, then announced that he had to leave for another part of his estate.

"You will not, I hope, be lonely without me," he said with a humorous twist of his lips.

When he had gone, Prince Metternich and Julia sat for a little time in front of the fire.

"You must go to bed," she said at length. "It has been a long day and more tiring than you realize. Tomorrow I have a great deal to show you. I love this place and I am always happy here."

"I think I had forgotten how to be happy until I met you," the Prince said.

"You work too hard, dearest."

"I like work," he answered. "Don't let us pretend about that, but to be with you is to be in Heaven itself."

He held out his arms for her and she let him hold her close against his breast, but when he would have kissed her lips she turned her head aside.

"Go to bed, my darling," she begged him. "We shall have so much to talk about tomorow."

He obeyed her because he knew that he was very near to collapse; but alone in his room he found his mind still troubled by the political manœuvres of the Congress. He found himself thinking of Talleyrand's sneering lips and crafty eyes, of Castlereagh's aloof impersonalness, which made him feel that he was dealing with a block of ice rather than a man. He could hear the Czar shouting at him as they quarrelled for the thousandth time over the question of Poland; he could feel himself irritated by the stupidity of King Frederick of Prussia and by the antics of the Spanish representative who was trying to make his country important by refusing to agree with anything or anybody.

Then, with a little jerk, Prince Metternich remembered where he was. He was here with Julia Zichy in a white world miles from anywhere, isolated together in the midst of a distant country; they were in fact alone as they had never been alone before.

He rose from his bed and, putting on a dressing gown of heavy silk brocade, walked quickly and impulsively down the corridor to her apartment. He tapped on the door but hardly expected an answer. He thought she must be asleep; then as he heard a gentle voice tell him to enter, he opened the door and saw that she was sitting up in bed supported by a great mass of lace pillows, reading by the light of three candles which stood on a little table beside her bed.

"I thought you would be asleep," he said.

She smiled at him and shook her head.

"I was tired and yet at the same time I was too excited by our drive and the thought of having you here alone, so I decided to read."

Prince Metternich sat down on the edge of her bed.

"I cannot sleep either," he said. "All the worries of the world seem to be crowding into my mind."

She reached out and took his hand in hers.

"Here you are not supposed to think," she told him. "If you stop worrying about the Congress your brain will be all the keener when you return. That is your only possible excuse for your absence from Vienna."

"That is not the only excuse for my absence," he said.

"There are others?"

"One other—that I wanted to be alone with you, alone with the loveliest woman I have ever known, the most perfect companion."

She smiled at that. When her eyes met his, he saw there was only tenderness and gentleness reflected in them. He was too great a lover and too experienced a one not to know that this was not the moment, when they were both tired after a long journey, for them to seek the springing fires of desire.

He sat there looking at her, at her dark hair lying in heavy waves on her white shoulders, at the sweet serenity of her heart-shaped face which seemed at times to remind him of the pictures of the Madonna hung in the Cathedral of St. Stephen in Vienna.

"What are you thinking?" he asked at length.

"I was thinking of you," she answered. "I think of very little else these days."

"Do you love me?"

"You know I do. So much that it seems to me there is nothing in the world but my love for you. I am yours—all of me."

Had he been different or less sensitive, he would have reached out towards her then; but there was a contact between them that had no need for physical expression. She was right, they belonged to each other, they were each of them a part of the other.

He sat for a long time, allowing the tender calm of Julia to flow through him, soothing away his worries and his irritations, his perplexities and his problems. Half an hour later, at peace in a manner that seemed somehow miraculous, he bent to kiss her good-night.

For a moment her lips, soft and warm, yielded to his.

"Good-night, my darling," she whispered.

Just for a moment he hesitated. At the touch of her a flame within himself flickered into life. Then he realized how tired he was, how in need of sleep.

"Good-night, my perfect one, my most beloved in all the world."

He lowered his head and kissed her breast where it curved beneath the soft lace of her nightgown; and then without looking back he went from the room and shut the door.

In his own room he felt sleep stealing over him like the waves of a tranquil sea. He abandoned his mind and his body to the soft rhythm of it and fell into a deep slumber which lasted until late the following morning.

"Yes, yes, I recollect both of them. Your father is dead?"

"He died five years ago," Richard replied. "It must be

Chapter Thirteen

"RICHARD MELTON! I seem to have heard the name."

"That perhaps is not surprising. I have waited on Your Excellency for six days hoping for an audience."

The Prince Talleyrand shrugged his shoulders.

"I am busy, young man, and . . . popular."

He smiled wryly at the last word and his thick lips parted to show his rotted and blackened teeth. He was a strange sight as he sat in the morning sunshine in the huge and elaborate bedroom. Two barbers were attending to his elaborate coiffure and his valet was pouring vinegar over his lame foot.

The Kaunitz Palace had housed many strange guests but never one stranger than Prince Talleyrand. The long path of diplomatic policy—and by no means a straight one—had brought him to Vienna as Minister of the newly created Louis XVIII. He had been preceded by a cook, two valets, two lackeys and his own musician, and from the moment he arrived his *salon* was the centre of opposition.

He gathered round him the discontented and he regaled them with his wit, his superlative food and an exhibition of his brilliant if treacherous art in diplomacy.

Looking at Richard with his small, deep-set grey eyes without any expression in them, the Prince subjected the tall, handsome Englishman standing before him to a scrutiny that was in itself an insolence.

"And what do you want of me?" he asked.

"A position in Paris, Your Excellency."

"And why should I give you that?"

"My father, whom you may recall as Lord John Melton, was at the Embassy in Paris for many years. You did,

I think, on one occasion, visit my late uncle, the third Marquess of Glencarron, in London."

"Yes, yes, I recollect both of them. Your father is dead?"

"He died five years ago," Richard replied. "It must be fifteen years since he was in Paris and yet I feel sure many of his friends will remember him."

"Few people have long memories," the Prince replied evasively. "Why should you wish to go to Paris?"

"I cannot return to England."

The Frenchman raised his eyebrows.

"Indeed! Are you exiled?"

"Yes, Your Excellency."

"Why?"

"For duelling, Your Excellency."

The Prince put the tips of his fingers together.

"Where are you staying in Vienna?"

"At the Hofburg. I am the guest of His Imperial Majesty, the Czar of Russia."

"So, you are housed in that camp, are you?"

"The Czar has been kind enough to befriend me," Richard said stiffly. "The Congress and its politics are no personal concern of mine."

"And yet, if the Czar is your protector here, it would seem that he might be persuaded to offer you a post in St. Petersburg?"

"I would prefer Paris, Your Excellency."

"So many people have said that," Prince Talleyrand replied, "but Paris is already overcrowded. I fear, young man, I can be of no use to you."

Richard bowed. He had expected nothing else from the first moment that he had set eyes on the Prince's cold inscrutable face. It had been absurd to imagine that this man, who had betrayed every master he had ever served, would be moved to do a kindly action from which he personally could gain no particular advantage.

Richard checked an impulse to say something bitter. His father had often told him how, when he was at the Embassy in Paris, he had helped Prince Talleyrand financially at a most crucial moment in his career. Well might the Frenchman affirm now that most people's memories were not long.

Richard went from the *salon* into the anteroom outside. There a crowd of visitors waited with bored faces and a deliberately assumed pose of indifference, as he himself had waited this past week. As he walked past, one man rose and together they descended the wide marble staircase with its gold banisters.

"Any luck?" the stranger enquired.

He was a middle-aged man with a weather-beaten face and Richard judged him to be a soldier who had fallen on hard times.

"None," he replied bitterly.

"I am not surprised," his companion remarked. "Talleyrand would rather cut his throat than speak a kind or helpful word. I was there when Napoleon Bonaparte in the presence of the whole Court called him 'a piece of dung in a silk stocking'. He was right and the Prince has not changed."

Richard laughed at the description, but he thought as he walked away from the Palace that hard words were no consolation. It had been a forlorn hope to imagine that Prince Talleyrand might in gratitude for his father's kindness in the past offer him a small position in Paris.

However small, however badly paid, it would have made it possible for him to ask Wanda to marry him. But without any prospects in the future, without the possibility of any settled income, how could he ask any woman to share his life?

Since the night of the fire at the Razumovsky Palace he had moved from the Hofburg to the Baroness Waluzen's house and they sat up every night, talking, planning and scheming; but they arrived always at precisely the same conclusion—that two people could not live on air.

Then Richard had thought of Prince Talleyrand, and having told the Baroness and Wanda of his intention to call upon the French Minister, he had gone to the Kaunitz Palace with high hopes and unquenchable optimism, only to find himself growing more despondent day by day as he was kept waiting for an audience and saw the crowds of other suppliants who were turned away.

Now, after waiting so long he was no further advanced in his search for security than he had been that first night when he had taken Wanda home after the fire and told both her and the Baroness the truth about himself.

"But we love each other," Wanda had said not once but a thousand times in the ensuing days when they had discussed the future.

"Love doesn't fill a hungry belly," the Baroness told

her; "love won't light a fire in the grate, or buy your husband a new coat when his is threadbare."

"Then what shall we do?" Wanda asked.

The despair on her little face, the trembling of her soft lips and the fear in her blue eyes forced Richard to appear more confident than he was.

"I will find something," he promised her. "Trust me— I swear I will not fail you."

It was so easy that way to bring the colour back into her cheeks and the happiness to her eyes, and yet when he was alone he admitted to himself that his head ached with thinking and he felt almost sick at the thought that he must fail her. What could he do? What was there for him to do?

It was hard to credit in the midst of so much lavish expenditure that poverty, dirt and hunger lurked just round the corner. Richard had heard talk of Comtesses and other noble ladies who had come to the Congress because it was their last chance of being social, who appeared at the banquets and entertainments blazing with magnificent diamonds which were entailed to their descendants and went away to sleep in a garret and starve until their next public appearance.

Now, as he thought of his own plight, he could credit that and a great many other things as well. He had not admitted either to Wanda or the Baroness why it was impossible for him to approach the Czar, who was the most likely person to prove benevolent and generous; but he thought they both guessed that Katharina barred the way to that solution.

He had seen the Princess at a Ball which he had attended in the company of the Baroness and Wanda and while she had smiled a him from a distance, there had been no excuse or opportunity for them to talk more intimately. Man-like, now the crisis was past, he began to forget about it. He thought, too, that Wanda had also erased from her memory those moments of terror in the Razumovsky Palace. She was too happy with him to allow anything to cloud their love and her joy, save the fear that they might be separated.

"I suppose you know you are spoiling her chances," the Baroness said tartly to Richard. "I had at least two eligible young men in mind for her and now she not only treats them as if they were invisible, but is curt to the point of rudeness when they ask her for a dance."

"I am glad about that. Do you blame me?" Richard enquired.

The Baroness looked at his handsome face and smiled. "I have told you before," she said, "that your love for each other is madness, but—I would give up my hope of Heaven to be young and mad."

Richard had grown to have a real affection for the old lady. Like Wanda, he realized that her caustic wit and sharp tongue were the only weapons left for her now that her beauty had faded and the men who had loved her had died or gone.

"Sometimes I remember that I, too, shall grow old," Wanda whispered to him once, "and when I think of those years ahead of me, I know that, unless I can have you or perhaps at the end only my memories of you, I would rather not live at all, I would prefer to die now at this moment when I am happy with your arms round me."

He kissed her then, wildly and passionately, feeling as if Fate was trying to separate them; that every moment, every second, was precious because tomorrow they might be parted.

"I love you, Richard. Oh, darling, do you think I would mind being poor with you?" Wanda asked, her mouth close to his. "I will cook for you, mend your socks and, if God is kind, bear your sons."

She blushed as she said that and hid her face against his neck. Richard, as he held her close, thought that in her sweet innocence she destroyed almost his last hope that somehow they might contrive to get married. How could he take upon himself to support not only a wife but a family? If they had been in England he might have risked it. He had friends who would never fail him and there would have been at least a roof over their heads and the nursery, where he had played himself, for his children.

But here, in Europe, they had nothing—just a few diminishing golden sovereigns and the loyalty and devotion of Harry. Despite his despair, Richard smiled to himself as he thought of Harry while he trudged through the slushy, snow-covered streets of Vienna.

Harry, who despite the fact that he disliked women and those he called 'the Guv's fancy morts', was already Wanda's devoted slave. She laughed delightedly at the way he talked, she flattered him by listening to his stories, and she found his sense of humour as irresistible as Richard did.

"He is so funny," she would say, wiping the tears of laughter from her eyes as she recounted to the Baroness or Richard some caustic remark Harry had made about their friends or acquaintances.

"He has no notion of how to behave," the Baroness would say stiffly, even while her eyes were twinkling. "He is not my idea of a servant."

"Nor mine," Richard agreed. "He is our friend."

Of one thing he was quite certain, if they were able to get married, Harry would fill the rôle of cook, house-maid and if necessary Nanny with the same humorous dexterity as he had enacted innumerable and varied rôles in the past. Yet what was the use of a servant without a house?

Richard sighed as he plodded on through the snow, envying for a moment those driving past him in the carriages and sleighs and quelling the thought that if he had still been at the Hofburg he could have commanded one of the many carriages which had been fashioned for the Emperor of Austria's guests.

It was nearly luncheon-time when Richard reached the Baroness Waluzen's house to find Wanda waiting for him. She knew by his face what was the result of his interview with Prince Talleyrand, and instead of asking stupid questions, as another woman might have done, she merely went to him and putting her arms round his neck, drew his face down to hers.

For one second he was too disappointed at the news he had to tell to respond even to her sweetness; then as he felt her lips seeking his, he held her to him fiercely, enfolding her in his arms as if he would never let her go.

"There will be something else. I know there will be something else," Wanda murmured.

"I was a fool to raise your hopes," Richard said roughly.

"We are neither of us going to give up hoping because of one small setback," Wanda answered.

There was something strong and resolute in her tone and as he looked down at her he thought that she had grown older and perhaps wiser these past days. Love had made her mature and for a moment he regretted the shy, lost child whom he had encountered that night at the Masked Ball. Then he knew that it was a woman he wanted, a woman who could help and comfort him, a woman who would be his companion through life, not just a plaything of the moment.

"I love you," he heard his own voice vibrate on the words and then, as she smiled her response, everything was forgotten.

"The Baroness and I drove to the Villa on the Rennweg," she said later. "Prince Metternich is returning sometime to-day so we can see him to-morrow."

"Is that good news or bad?" Richard asked.

"I don't know," Wanda answered. "Sometimes I think he will understand when I tell him that we love each other; at others I think he will be angry with me because I have failed him."

As she spoke, she reached up her hand quickly and pressed her fingers against Richard's lips.

"No, you are not to say what you think about that," she commanded. "I know you disapprove of the task Prince Metternich set me; but remember, if he had not asked my help, if I had not gone to the Masked Ball, we might never have met. It was Fate, darling, as I have told you before."

"It was Fate," Richard agreed, kissing her fingers, "and now Fate must go further and help me to find some way in which I can make money."

"I have prayed for that," Wanda answered, "and I cannot believe that my prayers will go unheard."

He held her once again in his arms and then luncheon was announced and they went in together with their faces so alight with happiness that the Baroness sighed again for her lost youth.

In the afternoon the Baroness took Wanda with her to a reception to which Richard had not been invited, and because he disliked being left behind, he went off in ill temper for a ride in the Prater. He hoped among his many acquaintances to find one who might be of use to him.

But although he talked with many people, kissed many white fingers and paid his respects to several visiting Sovereigns, the afternoon was a wasted one. He soon grew tired of making himself pleasant and galloped away from the crowds. He followed the Prater until it led him far from the city and out into the woods.

There he let his horse have its head and after an invigorating and exhilarating gallop along the snow-covered tracks beneath the leafless trees, he turned for home as dusk was falling. He felt happy as he rode back into the city. Wanda would be waiting for him and they had planned to spend the evening together at home.

He had worried so much lately that sometimes he felt his brain had lost the capacity to worry any more, but must let life take its leisurely course. To-morrow—there was always to-morrow to bring a change of circumstance, a lucky chance, perhaps a prize in one of the lotteries in which all Vienna indulged with their love for gambling.

Dark was falling and the roofs of the great houses were silhouetted against the sky in which the first evening stars were just appearing, Richard found himself whistling a little tune beneath his breath—then he recognized it. It was the waltz to which he and Wanda had danced that first night at the Masked Ball. 'An enchanted waltz' she had called it and certainly it had proved enchanted for both of them. It had bound them together with magical bonds which he knew would last for all eternity.

He turned in at the Baroness' drive gate and dismounted at the front door. He looked round in surprise because Harry was not waiting. Usually when he went riding the little man was hanging about, watching for his return and chivvying the grooms to attention. Because he himself had once been in the stable, he swore that he knew their lazy habits and slovenly ways whether they were in England or Vienna.

A footman opened the front door and a shaft of light came streaming out. When he saw who stood there, Richard heard him give peremptory orders to another lesser lackey and a few seconds later a groom came hurrying round the side of the house to take the horse.

Richard walked up the steps and into the hall. As he did so, Harry appeared from a door leading to the back premises.

"What's 'appened, Guv?" he asked. "Didn't you meet 'er Ladyship?"

"Meet whom?" Richard enquired.

"The Comtesse," Harry returned. "She got your message an' sets off in 'igh glee 'cos you were awaitin' for 'er."

"What the devil are you talking about?" Richard enquired. "I have not sent the Comtesse any message. I have been riding. You yourself saw me go off after the ladies had left me in their carriage."

"Yes, I know, Guv; but when they got back 'bout an

hour ago, a sleigh draws up, a slit-eyed bloke comes up to the door, says as 'ow you'd sent it for 'er Ladyship and she was to hop along at once and meet you at the 'Ofburg."

"At the Hofburg?"

"Yes, Guv."

"Are you sure he said that?"

"Gawd's truth! I thinks to meself that you must 'ave made it up with them Russian nobs after all. It queered me what your lay might be. Then I thinks to meself a meal's a meal, whoever pays for it."

"Cut your cackle, Harry, and get on with what happened," Richard said sharply.

"There ain't nothin' else to tell, Guv. 'Er Ladyship gets into the sleigh and rattles away."

Richard pressed his lips together. This was Katharina's doing, he was sure of that. What could she want with Wanda?

"Bring me my horse," he said sharply.

"Very good, Guv."

Harry disappeared to do his bidding and a minute or so later the horse was back at the door. Richard sprang into the saddle. The animal was still fresh, despite the afternoon's ride. It took him not more than ten minutes to reach the Hofburg, and nodding to the servants in the main hall, who knew him well by sight, he climbed the stairs to the Imperial apartments on the first floor.

He decided to ask the Czar first if he had sent for Wanda and what he required of her; but when he reached the Emperor's private *salon* he found it occupied only by an aide-de-camp.

"I wish to see His Imperial Majesty," Richard demanded formally.

"I am afraid that is impossible," the aide-de-camp replied.

"Why?"

"The Emperor is occupied."

Something in the man's manner and the slight giggle which accompanied the words made Richard stiffen with a sudden suspicion.

"Who's with him?" he asked sharply.

"I don't think I really ought to tell you," the aide-de-camp smirked.

"Tell me at once."

There was something in Richard's face which commanded the truth.

"It's a lady."

"I guessed that," Richard replied. "Who?"

The aide-de-camp looked over his shoulder before he replied and then, as Richard waited tensely, he answered:

"The Comtesse Sophie Zichy, and you wouldn't believe what has been going on here," he continued, only too eager to tell his tale now the first barrier was down. "The Comtesse was teasing the Emperor and saying that men were vainer than women and took longer to dress. He contradicted her, so she made a bet with His Imperial Majesty that she could change her clothes more quickly than he could. He accepted the challenge and sent an orderly to the Comtesse's house for the necessary garments. They are in there now," the aide-de-camp finished, pointing to the bedroom. "I suppose they will tell us when they come out who has won."

He giggled as he spoke and Richard turned from him in disgust. Without a word he went from the *salon* and down the corridor towards Katharina's bedroom. As he expected, she was resting in the big, cupid-decorated bed. Only a few candles were lit and she was lying back on her pillows with her eyes closed as if she were asleep. As Richard shut the door behind him and advanced across the room, she opened her eyes.

"Richard! What a surprise! I had given up hope that you would come to me."

"Where is Wanda?"

"Wanda? Who is Wanda? Oh, of course, that wench from the mountains in whom you are so interested. My dear, how should I know? I thought you were staying with her."

Richard came closer to the bed.

"What have you done with her?" he asked. "It is no use lying. I know it was you who enticed her away."

"I can't collect what you can be talking about," Katharina prevaricated.

She looked up at him, her fair hair falling against the lace pillows, the nakedness of her shoulders rising above the silken sheets. For a moment her eyes were wide as they watched his face, then they narrowed beneath the heavy lids and her lips parted.

"Have you really forsaken me, Richard?" she asked softly.

"I have asked you a question," he replied, "and I want an answer."

"This tiresome girl! Why should she come between us? She is pretty, I warrant you that, but so are a thousand other women. What can she give you that you have not already had from me? Is she passionate?—so am I! Does she desire you?—so do I! Does she love you? Oh, Richard, so do I!"

She held out her arms towards him as she spoke and now the sheets slipped back to reveal the beauty of her diaphanously covered breasts.

"Richard! Richard!"

Her voice was deep and hoarse with yearning, but his fingers closed fiercely, almost brutally, over her wrist.

"Answer me!" he said. "Where is Wanda?" Then as she did not reply he released her wrist and bent towards her. "Listen, Katharina. I am a desperate man. I have lost the woman I love and nobody shall stand in the way of my finding her. If you do not tell me where she is or where you have taken her, I shall kill you here and now."

His hands went out as he spoke and fastened themselves on her neck, the round, soft, white neck that he had kissed so passionately, that had throbbed beneath his lips, that held so proudly the exquisite beauty of her face.

"Answer me!"

His voice was raw then, as Katharina tried to scream, his hold tightened. She tore at him with her fingers, her nails leaving long, bleeding scratches on his hands, but she could not unfasten his grip and after a few seconds her struggles grew weaker. Her face was suffused with blood, her breath came pantingly between her lips.

"Answer me!"

Richard's voice seemed inexorable, the voice of someone devoid of all human feeling. Katharina tried to scream again, but it was impossible for her to force the sound from her imprisoned throat.

"Answer me!"

"I . . . I . . . will . . . tell . . . you." She was hardly able to breathe the words, but he heard them and relaxed his grip a little so that she could speak. "You've hurt me . . . dear God . . . how you've . . . hurt me!"

"Answer me!"

"Volkonski has . . . sent her . . . to Count . . . Araktcheef at Gruzino."

"Araktcheef!" Richard repeated the word in tones of horror. "I ought to kill you for that."

"My neck . . . my neck!" Katharina moaned.

Her lips were swollen and her face was still mottled purple and crimson, even now after he had released her. Her voice came only in a croak and she tried ineffectively to scream once again as he picked up the soft scarf she had worn round her shoulders and tied it over her mouth.

Having gagged her effectively he twisted her hands behind her back and tied them together with a handkerchief. As she lay writhing on the bed, half-naked and helpless, he straightened his shoulders and looked down at her.

"If I can't save Wanda," he said, "God help you, for I shall kill you, if it is the last thing I do on earth."

He walked from the room, shutting the door behind him. Outside he saw one of Katharina's maids whom he knew by sight. The woman smiled and curtsied at the sight of him.

"Her Highness is asleep," Richard said, "she does not wish to be disturbed for at least an hour and a half."

"I understand, Sir," the lady's maid smiled.

She was used to such orders and drew her own conclusions as to why they had been given.

Richard walked down the passage to Prince Volkonski's apartments. He entered without knocking. The Prince, who was seated at his desk, looked up in surprise; then at the sight of Richard's expression he rose to his feet.

"Good-evening, Melton. What do you . . .?" he began in his high, insidious voice.

Richard hit him without waiting for him to finish the sentence. Then, as Prince Volkonski staggered, for the moment too astonished to retaliate, Richard hit him again. They were about evenly matched in height and weight, but Richard had learnt boxing in Gentleman Jackson's Academy in Bond Street and the Prince was soft and flabby from over-luxurious living. He tried to defend himself, tried to ward off Richard's blows, but he was used to fighting with a sword and pistol and not with bare hands.

Again and again Richard hit him until with a terrific uppercut which seemed to lift him off his feet the Prince went down unconscious. After that it was but a matter of seconds before Richard had him gagged with his own cravat, his feet and arms tied with curtain cords.

Then Richard looked about him for a place of concealment. There was a big cupboard at one end of the room where the Prince kept his files and various books of reference. There was just room, by tumbling a number of them on to the floor, to shut the Prince inside. Richard slammed the door, locked it, and threw the key out the window.

His knuckles were bleeding when he came out of the Prince's room and went back down the corridor towards the Czar's apartment. His blood was up by now, he felt that nothing, not even a regiment of soldiers, could stop him. He walked past the sentries. There was nobody in the salon and he guessed that the aide-de-camp had gone downstairs to escort the Comtesse Sophie to her carriage.

He walked across the room and opened the door of the Czar's bedroom; then the impetuous words he was about to speak died on his lips, for Alexander was asleep. He was lying on his bed, wearing his brocade dressing-gown, his legs covered by a gold and sable-lined spread. There was the contented smile of a satiated man upon his lips. He looked younger and more vulnerable than when he was awake.

For a moment Richard stared at the sleeping Emperor; then, as he stepped towards him, something on the table by the fireside glittered in the light of the flames. It distracted his attention and in that second his plans were changed.

He knew what the ring was. It was one of those used by the Imperial couriers when they travelled between St. Petersburg and Vienna on the Emperor's business. It was understood that a man who carried such a symbol should be given every attention because, while the ring was in his possession, his commands and orders were given in the Emperor's name.

The Czar turned over and murmured in his sleep. Richard stood very still; then he reached out his hand, picked up the ring from the table, and went from the room, closing the door behind him.

Chapter Fourteen

HURRYING down the staircase of the Hofburg Palace, Richard met the aide-de-camp returning, as he had suspected, from seeing the Comtesse Sophie Zichy into her carriage. He nodded to him coolly, but the young man was anxious to stop and gossip.

"They were in His Imperial Majesty's bedroom for an hour and three-quarters!" he recounted with glee.

"Indeed!" Richard answered indifferently, and hurried down the stairs with what he hoped was an absent-minded air that would not arouse suspicion.

When he reached the main hall, he turned down the passage which led towards that side of the Palace where the stables were located. The Czar's private grooms, sleighs and horses occupied a large part of the Imperial stables. The rest of the Sovereigns had been content to use the three hundred carriages thoughtfully provided for them by the Emperor Francis and were more than delighted with the fourteen hundred thoroughbred German horses which had been brought to Vienna specially for the Congress.

But the Czar, in his usual grandiose manner, had brought a large number of his own horses, carriages and sleighs with him. The fact that his most generous host found it hard to house so vast an entourage did not trouble him in the slightest.

It was fortunate that Richard knew the Head Stableman personally and that they had a mutual respect for each other as being able judges of horseflesh. He sent for him now and extended to him his left hand, on the third finger of which glistened the gold ring he had taken from the Czar's room.

"Secret and urgent orders of His Imperial Majesty," he said in a low voice.

The Head Stableman looked over his shoulder as if he was afraid of being overheard.

"I am at your service, Mein Herr."

"A sleigh left here this afternoon by orders of Prince Volkonski. It was to pick up a passenger at Baroness Waluzen's house and carry the lady to Count Araktcheef at Gruzino."

"That's right, Mein Herr; the sleigh left about an hour and a half ago."

"His Imperial Majesty has changed his mind. He wishes me to intercept the sleigh and bring back the passenger."

"I understand, Mein Herr."

"How many horses were drawing the sleigh?" Richard asked.

"Two, Mein Herr. Two of our best Arabs."

"Give me four!" Richard commanded.

The man hesitated and his eyes went towards the crowd of servants standing around the stables with little or nothing to do. Richard knew that he was wondering which among them were competent to drive a four-in-hand fast and at night.

"I will drive myself," he said.

The Russian's lips broke into a reluctant smile.

"You'll find them a handful, Mein Herr."

"Time is pressing," Richard said curtly.

He glanced up, as he spoke, towards the Palace as if he half-suspected the Czar might be watching from one of the many brightly illuminated windows. His words seemed to galvanize the Head Stableman into action. A torrent of words poured from his lips as order followed order and men sprang to obey them.

It was only a question of minutes before a narrow, finely constructed sleigh was brought into the courtyard and four black horses with their arched Arab necks and long black flowing manes and tails were harnessed together.

"I shall want a coat," Richard said.

A driving-coat lined with sable was produced as if by magic. A Russian cap, trimmed with the same fur, was offered to him and he thrust it on his head.

"I have chosen two grooms to go with you, Mein Herr," the Head Stableman said when the horses were practically ready, "two of my best men. They are both of them

capable of driving if you prefer it. They both speak a
little Austrian."

"Let them sit in the sleigh," Richard answered.

He knew that however good the Russian coachmen
might be, they would be afraid of travelling at the speed
at which he intended to go. There were dire penalties for
a groom who upset a sleigh or carriage or who overdrove
one of the Czar's horses. Wild though Russian drivers were
as a general rule, in the Emperor's service they were
forced for fear of punishment to a caution which was in
fact foreign to their natures.

The sleigh was ready. Every moment that he had waited
had seemed to Richard to pass like an eternity, in case
Volkonski or one of Katharina's servants came into the
yard and prevented him from leaving. Both of them would
be well aware as to where he was going. From both of
them in the future he could expect a revenge which would
mean death.

No-one, as Richard knew, could insult Volkonski and
live. His power was tremendous, for he had the ear of the
Czar and everyone in the Russian Court was afraid of him.

But there was a man who was stronger still and much
more to be feared, and his name was Araktcheef! But as
Richard, with the reins in one hand and a long driving-
whip in the other, guided the excited horses through the
narrow gates of the Hofburg Palace and out into the snow-
covered street, he did not dare to let his mind rest on
Wanda and where she was being taken.

The horses occupied his mind for some miles to the
exclusion of all else. Fortunately they were used to being
teamed together and he was an outstandingly brilliant
whip. Even his worst enemy could not deny that he was a
Corinthian when it came to handling the ribbons, and
though it had not been often in his life that he could
afford a four-in-hand of his own, his reputation made his
friends eager to secure his services when they had a wager
to win or when they were in a hurry to get to Newmarket
for the Races.

After a few wild prancings and rearings which made
the grooms grip the sides of the sleigh and mutter beneath
their breath, the horses settled into a steady gallop and
Richard could begin to plan his journey. He knew it was
a question of time, first to save Wanda from falling into
the hands of Count Araktcheef, and secondly to get her

back to Vienna before Prince Volkonski sent another sleigh to intercept them.

So long as they were on Austrian territory and in the open, Richard felt that he could deal with the Prince, but he was well aware that Volkonski would eventually resort to the stab in the back or the blow in the dark if he could not obtain his revenge in any other way.

What was terrifying beyond expression was the idea of Wanda coming into the clutches of Count Araktcheef. A soldier whom a great number of people already looked upon as the Czar's evil genius, Araktcheef was a man of malice and spitefulness with no friends because no-one except the vilest toadies could tolerate him. Even the easy-going, self-seeking members of the Russian Court could not pronounce his name without contempt and the more respectable and dignified among them made no secret, in private, of their hatred for the Czar's favourite Minister.

But the Czar looked on the Count as his friend and trusted him implicitly. Araktcheef had showed everyone a letter written from Paris earlier in the year, which the Czar ended:

I can truly say that there is no one in whom I have equal confidence and from whom it has pained me so much to be separated. Always, for all my life, your devoted friend,

Alexander.

For the last seven years Count Araktcheef had held the post of Minister for War. His influence was growing all the time. Clever as a serpent when it came to intrigue, he had made himself the Czar's mentor, counsellor and watch-dog, and no one had the courage to warn the Emperor that there was a very different side to the Count's nature.

The Czar had stayed frequently at Gruzino, Count Araktcheef's own estate; but Richard knew, as did the rest of the Court, that the Count's mistress was bundled out of the way when the Czar was expected, and that the Bible-reading Alexander was never taken to see the Art Gallery at the end of the garden, which Araktcheef had filled with a unique collection of indecent pictures. The Czar, too, knew nothing of the frequent floggings of the serfs or the harsh punishments inflicted upon married women who were unable or unwilling to bear children.

Terrible stories were whispered of what went on at

Gruzino. Only last month Richard had heard how a girl of sixteen had been flogged to death to please the sadism of Araktcheef while her companions were compelled to stand round her and chant the prayers for the dying.

The Czar knew nothing of this any more than he knew of the tragic misery which was inflicted upon his people by the experiment Araktcheef was making with what were called 'the colonists'. Thousands of peasants had been incorporated in the Army, housed in barracks and made to till the soil in uniform and be subjected to Military discipline.

The Czar believed that men who were properly housed with their families and who were given the right tools and the right seed would turn out to be expert farmers. What he did not know was that Count Araktcheef worked his colonists so hard that a large proportion of them died from sheer overwork, others were herded together in barracks in such horrible promiscuity that husbands and wives could find no corner for connubial seclusion.

Overseers arranged their marriages for them, compelling them, when they saw any symptoms of jealousy, to draw lots for their wives. The result of these cruelties was that family after family deserted the settlements, hid themselves in the swamps and forests, and died there.

Richard had seen Count Araktcheef on several occasions, but he had always avoided the man for fear that his instincts should get the better of him and he would strike the wide, sneering smile from the Russian's crafty face. It was not his business what went on in foreign countries, and though he had drawn his own conclusions from the whispered tales of horror and brutality which were passed continuously round the Imperial circle, it had not been his place to interfere or express any comment while he was an honoured guest of the Czar.

But now all that he had listened to, all that had been left unsaid, came rushing into his mind, so that he was filled with a terror such as he had never known before at the thought of Wanda in the hands of such a brute.

It seemed to him inconceivable even now that Katharina's jealousy should have led her to such lengths; and yet he could realize now the truth of the trite saying he had learned at Eton: 'Hell has no fury like a woman scorned'.

As they reached the open road, the fear within his heart made him whip up the already galloping horses until their hoofs seemed almost to fly over the powdery snow. He knew that the two grooms were tense and fearful in the sleigh as it swung precariously round corners and when it seemed that only a miracle could save it from being overturned.

But Richard's superb horsemanship saved them from disaster. The miles were being eaten up and the moon, shining clearly through the frosty night, made the road ahead as clear as if they travelled by daylight.

On, on they went, and as each mile passed Richard found himself praying that he would soon overtake Wanda and her escort. He was well aware that the first sleigh had a long start, but owing to his reckless yet superb driving the distance between them must be growing appreciably less. He felt as if the anxiety of his own heart might bridge the miles and comfort Wanda in her terror and fear at being kidnapped.

Of one thing he was thankful. She would not know what was ahead of her when she arrived in Russia. He thought of her little face, her wide, trusting blue eyes raised to his, and he vowed in that moment he would save and protect her for the rest of his life.

She was his; he loved her and she loved him. How, he asked himself now, had he been such a fool as to wait so long without marrying her? What did money matter? Better to starve together than to risk the misery and the danger of being separated.

He remembered now on that first night when they had supped together at the 'Golden Vine' she had said:

"The people one loves grow dearer and more precious."

How right she had been! She had grown dearer and more precious to him until the thought of life without her was too hideous to contemplate.

'Wanda, Wanda, I love you! I am coming to you'—his heart called to her, feeling that his desire for her bridged the distance between them.

On, on. The horses were lathered now with sweat, but he would not spare them. On, on! Over a land strangely ghost-like in the rays of the moon, past forests silhouetted darkly against the horizon, the fields white beneath the snow made it seem as if all life lay shrouded by a heavy pall.

On, on! And now at last he saw ahead the lights of the first posting inn.

Intricate arrangements had been made so that the Czar

could keep in touch with his Government at St. Petersburg. Posting houses with horses and men were situated all along the route so that the Imperial couriers travelled with almost unheard-of speed from capital to capital. It was, however, not only affairs of State which brought the messengers speeding along the road. The Czar sent messengers backwards and forwards on the merest pretext.

"The Emperor thinks of nothing except his uniforms," a disgruntled aide-de-camp confided to Richard one day at the Hofburg. "For the love of God, man, keep this to yourself, but to-day I found him trying on eight or nine pairs of Hussar's trousers—in despair at seeing they were all too tight or too short! A courier has been despatched to St. Petersburg to bring back another uniform. He will arrive too late! This was pointed out to the Emperor, but he would not give up and sent him notwithstanding!"

As Richard turned into the yard of the posting house, he prayed that one of those frivolous errands would not have deprived the post of all its fresh horses. Wanda's sleigh had already come and gone. Two would have depleted the number available and he required four of the very best to carry him on.

As the sleigh drew up in the light of several flaring torches, grooms and ostlers came running. There was no delay, no question asked. As the men unharnessed the sweating, exhausted team and led them into the stables, others were brought to replace them. When Richard walked into the inn he found hot food and wine ready for him. He had to admit reluctantly that the Czar's arrangements were perfect down to the last detail.

"A sleigh has passed through here," he said to the innkeeper. "There was a lady in it. How long has it been gone?"

"A sleigh stopped about half an hour ago, Mein Herr," the man replied, "but I don't know who the passenger might be."

"Why not?" Richard enquired.

"The lady, if it was a lady, Mein Herr, did not leave the sleigh."

Richard pressed his lips together. This meant that Wanda was being kept a close prisoner. It would be on Volkonski's orders and he wished now that he had hit him harder. He was well aware how tired and cramped one became after sitting for a long time in either a carriage or a sleigh. But Wanda had not been permitted to enter the inn.

"Was the lady given anything to eat or drink?" he asked.

"I think not, Mein Herr, but I'll make enquiries."

Richard did not wait for any more. He had eaten a few mouthfuls of food in the time that it took the ostlers to change the horses. Now he gulped down a glass of wine and went back to the sleigh. He saw by the faces of the grooms that they would like to have protested against being hurried so quickly from the warmth and comfort of the inn, but they had been too well disciplined to complain. They said nothing; but as they climbed back into the sleigh their faces were eloquent of their dissatisfaction.

On again now. The road was more difficult than before, climbing up the sides of mountains, dropping down into deep valleys; but the horses were fresh and of a fine quality, having come from the Imperial stables in St. Petersburg.

On, on! Now they were passing through a desolate countryside without a sign of human habitation. There were great forests ahead, dark and menacing, in which they were obliged to slacken their pace, because even the moonlight could not penetrate the close density of the trees.

Then, as they moved slowly in the darkness, the horses shying uneasily at a broken bough or at the hoot of an owl, Richard heard the baying of a wolf.

Wanda had heard it some time earlier when her sleigh had entered the forest and the horses had suddenly reared up on their haunches and only with repeated beatings had been persuaded to go forward again. At first she had not known what the sound was, but when she did understand the meaning of that strange, eerie howl and the terror of the horses, it seemed to her no worse than the agony of fear she had been experiencing ever since the sleigh which had fetched her from the Baroness Waluzen's house had carried her past the Hofburg and out of Vienna.

At first she thought there must be some mistake. She turned to speak to the man driving behind her.

"You said Mr. Melton was expecting me at the Hofburg Palace," she said.

He did not answer her, but stared straight ahead, his eyes on the horses he drove.

"The Hofburg," she called to him. "Didn't you say Mr. Melton was expecting me at the Hofburg?"

Again he did not answer and she felt as if an icy hand clutched her heart. Almost instinctively she half-rose. As she did so a man's hand came down on her shoulder. For a moment she could hardly believe that he was touching her, forcing her back into her seat. The impertinence of being handled by a servant was almost more than she could credit.

Then, with a sudden clarity, she understood. This was a trap. Richard had not sent for her. How could she have been so stupid, so foolish, as to believe for one moment that he would ask her to go to him at the Hofburg? It was the Czar who had done this, the Czar who was punishing her for resisting him the other night.

Then, even as she accused him, she saw Katharina's face as vividly as if the Princess stood before her, and she knew who was responsible for everything. She remembered now that she had seen Katharina watching her two nights before when she had gone with Richard to see the ballet *Flore and Zéphire* at the Opera House.

They had been sitting with the Baroness in her box when the Czar, accompanied by several members of his suite, had come into one opposite them. Katharina was among them and Wanda had watched the older woman without saying anything to Richard. As he was sitting in the back of the box, she did not know whether he had noticed the Royal party, but her new-found jealousy would not permit her to mention Katharina to him.

Again and again she found her eyes being drawn across the Opera House to where Katharina sat. She was looking exquisitely beautiful that evening, Wanda thought, with a little stabbing pain in her heart. She wore a neckace of huge emeralds above a *decolletage* so low and so daring that she appeared to be almost naked above the waist. There were emeralds glittering in her ears and a tiara of emeralds and diamonds on her head.

She was smiling at the Czar and she had evidently said something to amuse him, for he laughed and turned to whisper something in her ear. It was at that moment Wanda realized that Katharina had recognized her and Richard who sat behind her in the shadows. She saw Katharina's face change, she saw the smile fade from her lips, her eyes narrow and an expression so venomous change her that for a moment her beauty seemed to vanish as if a cloud passed across the sun.

'She hates me,' Wanda thought and added defiantly, 'and I hate her, too.'

It was hard to make herself watch the ballet with Senorita Bitollini in the principal part. Afterwards she could not recall what she had seen or what she had heard. She was only conscious of Katharina's hatred vibrating towards her from the Royal Box.

She felt as if those dark eyes stabbed at her. She found herself remembering tales she had heard of witches who could injure their victims at a distance, of magic which, by mysterious rites and incantations, practised by natives in the jungle, left the victim incapacitated without visible wounds and without mortal weapons.

She could feel Katharina's hatred and malice without looking at her, feel it as if a cold finger touched her back, feel it, as her old Nanny would have said, 'in her bones'.

When they had left the Opera House and she was sitting beside Richard in the carriage driving home, she chid herself. He was holding her hand beneath the fur rug, his fingers were strong and reassuring. He had said nothing, he had done nothing to make her think he had even seen Katharina. Whatever there had been between him and the Princess in the past, it was over now. It was ridiculous for her to worry.

Surreptitiously so that the Baroness should not see she rested her cheek against his shoulder. It had been a movement to reassure herself. But he noticed it and his fingers had tightened on hers.

"You are not tired?"

The question, tender with concern, made her smile.

"Shall we go to the ball at the Apollo Hall?"

The Baroness laughed.

"Have you not had enough parties lately that you must join the *hoi polloi*, the sweepings of the streets, at a place of public amusement?"

"The rarefied atmosphere of the great makes me yawn," Richard answered. "There are to be Tyrolean singers at the Apollo to-night. Shall we go and hear them?"

There was a boyishness about his enthusiasm which the Baroness could not resist.

"Youth is contagious," she grumbled, "so I suppose I must agree."

But she had enjoyed it as much as they had. A public Ball was a change from the exclusive pomposity of the entertainments which were planned to dazzle the visiting Sovereigns. Here the Viennese were enjoying themselves lightheartedly with an enthusiasm which came from a sheer love of music and a natural gaiety. Polonaises and mazurkas were danced with joyful abandonment which had something childish and spontaneous about it.

There were no wonderful jewels, few gorgeous uniforms and no formality. And yet it was an evening of fun as Wanda had not found at the Balls given at the Hofburg or the Razumovsky Palaces or any of the other great mansions which had been commandeered for the entertainment of the nobility.

The Apollo Hall was in itself a fantastic entertainment.

"We must look at the Turkish kiosk!" Wanda exclaimed. "I've heard people talking about it."

"There is also a Lapland hut and a Chinese pagoda for you to see," Richard answered, having been there before.

"I don't want to miss anything," Wanda cried excitedly.

Every style of architecture had its place in the galleries surrounding the great hall, while in the centre of the huge supper room there was a rock with a waterfall springing from among the flowers and ferns and flowering into stone pools filled with various kinds of fish.

The Baroness had spoken scathingly of those who frequented the Apollo Hall, but she was surprised to find a large number of the Emperor's distinguished guests enjoying themselves by rubbing shoulders with the middle class, flirting with little shop-girls and imagining that their incognito was impenetrable.

Wanda danced with Richard and he held her close to him in a manner which would have caused comment at the more formal Balls.

"I am happy, so happy that I want to go on dancing for ever," she whispered.

"Another enchanted waltz?" he teased her.

She shook her head.

"It is different from that first night. Then you were a stranger and I was afraid of you, even while you attracted me. Now I love you. Oh, Richard! I am too happy to put it into words."

"If you look at me like that," he answered, "I shall kiss you."

"I don't suppose anyone here would be shocked . . . except me!" she answered provocatively.

"Are you flirting with me?" he enquired.

"I hope so," she replied, "if this is what flirting means."

"It is," he replied, "and if you ever do it with anyone else, I warn you that I shall beat you or suffocate you to death with kisses."

They laughed at that. It had been so easy to laugh. Everything had seemed to be touched with some special magic of excitement, happiness and joy. It was only later when she was alone in her bedroom that Wanda remembered Katharina and the hatred in her eyes.

She knew now that it was Katharina who had had her kidnapped by a trick. Already the sleigh had carried her out of Vienna and they were travelling too fast for her to contemplate screaming for help to some passer-by. Perhaps, Wanda thought, she could throw herself from the sleigh into the snow. But she decided that it was too risky. Not only might she injure herself, but there was also every likelihood of her being stunned by the fall and being picked up again before she could run to safety.

The fur rugs enveloped her and would, she decided, prove an almost insuperable obstacle to escape. There were two men on the sleigh, the driver and a groom, and now, since one of them had touched her, she was afraid of their violence.

She had always been afraid of Russians—they were not like other men—and as she remembered some of the things that Harry had said about them, she began to feel more frightened than ever. It would be fruitless to question them as to where they were taking her; but as they galloped over the open countryside, she knew with a premonition that could not be denied that her destination was to be Katharina's country.

She wanted to scream then, not only in fear, but in defiance. This was a violation of all civilized behaviour. It was incredible, unbelievable that it should be happening to her, Wanda Schonbörn, in the nineteenth century.

'We might be living in medieval times that I can be spirited away without anything being done to prevent it!' she told herself angrily.

Then she remembered something Richard had said when he and the Baroness were talking one evening about the Russians.

"We can't judge them by European standards," he remarked. "They are orientals and their civilization is medieval. In another five hundred years they may have reached the standard that we have reached now. In the meantime, it is no use expecting them to be anything but—savages."

Wanda shut her eyes for a moment. What was she personally to expect from savage, uncivilized people? She felt herself tremble. The hatred in Katharina's eyes had been unmistakable, and although the Princess was left behind in Vienna, when she reached Russia she knew she would be unable to escape from the violence of that hatred. It was to Russia that the sleigh was taking her, she was sure of that now, and she began to pray as she had never prayed before that she might be saved.

She wondered how soon it would be before Richard found out that she had gone. Harry had seen her go, that was her only hope.

'Let him find me, dear God! Let him find me!'

Having her eyes closed in prayer, Wanda did not see the Inn until the sleigh slowed down and came to a standstill in the lighted yard. Then she opened her eyes in astonishment at the lights and the grooms running to attend to the horses. With a sudden wild hope in her heart she sat up. Here was a chance to escape, to cry for help. But even as she moved, a heavy hand came down on her shoulder.

"If you make a sound," a coarse, guttural voice said fiercely in her ear, "I shall cover your mouth with my hand."

That was all, but she knew that the man meant what he said and she could not bear to contemplate the horror of it. With his high cheekbones and slit, Mongolian eyes his face was like that of some heathen idol, she thought, and felt herself tremble with fear beyond anything she had ever known in her short, sheltered life.

Fresh horses were harnessed to the sleigh. The men took it in turns to go into the Inn, one always remaining on the sleigh behind her. She knew by the way in which they returned wiping their mouths with the backs of their hands that they had eaten and drunk. Nothing was offered to her and she could not have taken it even if it had been. Her throat was closed with fear; she was conscious only of that heavy hand on her shoulder and the voice in her ear.

Then they went off again, driving into the darkness, the cold wind whistling in her face. After some miles a piece of harness broke and there was a long delay while the sleigh was brought to a standstill and the Russians mended a broken trace. Wanda thought that if Richard was following, this would enable him to catch up with her. She kept looking over her shoulder at the road down which they had come.

'Please, God, let him find me . . . please, God, please, please!'

But her prayers were apparently unheard. The broken trace was repaired, the road behind was empty and they set off again. Now their route lay up the steep hills and down again into deep valleys. Their pace was slower, the horses in some places picking their way with difficulty.

Finally they came to a great forest and as they entered the dark impenetrability of it Wanda heard the Russians talk to each other for the first time since they left Vienna. She could not understand what they were saying, for they spoke in their native tongue; but she knew by the tone of their voices that something was amiss.

Then she heard the baying of the wolves and the horses pranced and reared as they heard them too. Only the whip, used cruelly and persistently, drove them forward and made them obedient to the man who wielded it.

The baying came again and yet again Wanda looked back over her shoulder and saw that the Russian behind her had drawn his pistols and was holding them ready in his hands. The wolves were drawing nearer. Now she could see that they were running through the trees on either side of the sleigh, keeping level with the horses. Their bodies were little more than black shadows flitting between the tree trunks, yet the night was suddenly hideous with the sound of their tongues.

The horses were bolting now, there was no need to whip them, no need to urge them on; they were terrified, speeding through the darkness, striving to escape.

Wanda held her breath. The pack was closing in, coming nearer and nearer. Then the leader of the wolves sprang across the roadway. The horses stopped suddenly, rearing in the air.

There was a crash as the sleigh slithered to a standstill, quivering, shaking and nearly overturning itself. There was the sudden report of a shot, another and yet another.

Then Wanda found herself standing, clinging to the front of the sleigh, while the Russians fired and the horses plunged, twisted and reared before the snarling attacks of the hungry wolves.

Chapter Fifteen

RICHARD heard the shots and drove his team forward at such a speed that it was only by a miracle that they kept on the road. Without receiving any instructions the Russians in the sleigh began to prime their pistols and Richard wished that he himself had not come away unarmed.

Then, as they swung precariously round a corner, Richard was just able to pull his horses to a standstill, averting by a hair's breadth a collision with Wanda's sleigh which stood in the middle of the road, encircled by the snarling wolves.

The trees in this part of the forest were not so thick and the moonlight managed to percolate through the interlocked boughs to show all too clearly what was happening. The whinnying horses, wild with fright, were rearing amongst the debris of broken harness and woodwork, the sleigh-driver and his attendant groom were firing indiscriminately and without taking aim into the shadows, while Wanda, white-faced and frozen by sheer terror into immobility, stood clinging to the front of the sleigh, her cloak of white ermine making her conspicuous against the darkness.

The sudden appearance of another team of horses made the wolves, timid enough when the odds were against them, withdraw to a safe position amongst the trees. They did not go far and it was easy, if one looked carefully, to see the glitter of their eyes and the slobber from their jaws. They were waiting, ready to attack if the time should seem propitious; but they were prepared, for the moment, to allow the travellers a respite.

"Get to the horses' heads," Richard shouted to his grooms, and they sprang to obey him, hanging on with difficulty as the horses began to shy and whinny, sensing the lurking danger on the other side of them.

When his team was more or less under control, Richard threw down the reins and stepped into the snow. As he passed one of his grooms, he took from him a loaded and cocked pistol, and holding it in his right hand, walked to where Wanda's escort stood staring at him.

He heard Wanda breathe his name in a choked voice, but he did not look at her, speaking only to the Russian driver standing at the back of the sleigh with the broken reins and a smoking pistol in his hands.

"His Imperial Majesty, the Czar, commands that this lady be taken back to Vienna," Richard said in a tone of authority.

"I have my orders from His Highness Prince Volkonski," the man replied in slow, broken Austrian.

"His Majesty is not concerned with the Prince's instructions," Richard retorted sternly.

He held out his left hand as he spoke so that the moonlight could glitter on his ring. He saw by the expression on the man's face that he recognized it, but he repeated:

"I am the Prince's servant, Mein Herr, and the lady must go to Gruzino."

"You will take your instructions from me, for I give them in the name of the Czar," Richard replied.

As he spoke he raised the pistol he held in his hand, and, although the Russian's secretive, Mongolian expression did not alter, Richard knew that he surrendered to the inevitable. The pistols of both Prince Volkonski's men were empty and besides, the Czar's name was too awe-inspiring, too omnipotent, to warrant opposition. Knowing without the need for words that he was victorious, Richard turned towards Wanda.

"May I escort you to my sleigh, Madame?" he asked formally, offering her his arm.

He saw her check the impulsive words which had risen to her lips and restrain the overwhelming relief which made her want to throw her arms round his neck. With a dignity which made him proud of her, she answered in a soft voice:

"I am ready to obey His Imperial Majesty's commands."

Then her trembling fingers were on his arm and he was leading her through the snow to his own sleigh. He handed her in and covered her with a rug before he turned to the senior of his two grooms.

"Tell those fellows they are to take their horses slowly to the next posting inn and to wait there for further instructions," he said. "Our other groom had best go with them. That will allow one to drive and two to keep the wolves at bay until they are out of the forest."

"Very good, Mein Herr."

The man, still hanging to the horses' heads, gave the orders in fluent and forceful Russian. Then, as the grooms let go of Richard's team, he managed to turn them with the dexterity which had made him a Nonpareil with the ribbons. As Prince Volkonski's grooms watched them in surly silence, Richard's man sprang on to the back of the sleigh and they galloped away back on the road down which they had come.

Only as they came out of the forest and into the open country did Richard check the speed of his horses.

"His Imperial Majesty suggested that we return to Vienna by a different route from that by which we left," he said. "He does not wish anyone to know that this lady has returned. How can we reach the south gates of the city?"

"There is a turn to the left a little further on, Mein Herr."

"Do you know the road?" Richard enquired.

"Yes, Mein Herr, I have travelled it once or twice."

"Good." Richard drew the horses to a standstill. "You can drive," he said.

The Russian took the reins while Richard climbed into the sleigh. As he settled himself in beside her under the heavy rug, he heard her draw in her breath excitedly. She turned her face towards him, framed by a little bonnet of velvet trimmed with ermine, and he could see in the light of the moon that her eyes were shining like stars.

"You came!" she whispered. "I was praying that you would come and save me."

"Did you doubt it?" he asked, forgetting in that moment his own fears that he might be too late, that he might fail to deliver her from the horrors of Gruzino.

"No, I was sure you would do so," she answered. "Yet at the same time I was afraid—terribly afraid."

"My darling, it is my fault. I should have married you a week ago," he said, "the night after I rescued you from the fire at the Razumovsky Palace."

She was silent for a moment at that and then her hands sought and found his.

"Richard! You mean . . . can you mean that you will marry me now?"

"The very moment we arrive in Vienna," he answered. "I have got to be sure of you, to be in a position where I can protect you."

"Oh, Richard!"

There was no need for her to say any more. The happiness on her face seemed to transfigure her.

"I love you, my darling," he said, "Will that always be enough for you?"

"Always," she answered. "What does anything else matter except that we love each other?"

"If you really believe that, then nothing else will matter. Dear God, I wish I had more to offer you!"

"You have everything I want and need," she replied. "When you came towards me just now, I thought that there had never been a man like you—so brave, so strong and clever enough to find me after I had been spirited away from the Baroness' house in that terrible manner. How did you know where I had gone?"

"Harry told me that a sleigh had come for you," Richard replied.

"The driver said that you were waiting for me at the Hofburg."

"Harry told me that, too. I went to the Hofburg and found there had been a mistake."

"It was so stupid of me not to suspect it might be a trick," Wanda murmured.

She wondered if she should put her suspicions into words that it was Katharina who had sent the sleigh for her. Then she decided to say nothing. It was best not to mention names. They were talking in whispers and it seemed impossible that the man standing behind them with the wind in his face could hear anything, yet one never knew.

Wanda gave a little sigh of utter contentment. Richard was here, he had saved her, that was all that mattered. And now she was to marry him, to be his wife. She would be safe! While to bear his name and to belong to him would be a wonderful happiness beyond words.

She dropped her head against his shoulder. She was thinking only of her utter and complete contentment. But Richard was concerned with other and more frightening things.

"As soon as we are married," he said slowly as if he were thinking aloud, "we must leave Vienna. We had best go to Brussels, I think. I have a slight acquaintance with the English Ambassador and I might persuade him to help us."

"Why must we leave Vienna so quickly?" Wanda asked wonderingly. "The Baroness would be pleased to have us stay with her; I am sure that she is fond of us both."

"No, we must leave."

Richard did not wish to frighten Wanda by explaining in what jeopardy he had placed his own life. He did not wish her to know that there was every likelihood of her becoming a widow almost as soon as she was a bride. Prince Volkonski would never forgive the indignity of being pummelled into unconsciousness and locked in a cupboard.

Katharina, too, would want her revenge for being trussed up and gagged.

"No, we must get away," Richard said again.

There was something so decisive in his voice that Wanda said no more. She was not really concerned with their destination. Once they were married she was content to let him decide and plan their lives, asking only that she should be with him, wherever he might wish to wander.

"If only we could go home!" Richard cried suddenly.

It seemed to him intolerable that the peace and security of his own country were forbidden him.

Well might the English laugh at foreigners, he thought, with their high emotions, their vendettas and vengeances, their intrigues and conspiracies. In the clubs of St. James's they would laugh at the idea that he must go in fear of his life because a Russian Princess loved him and a Russian Prince disliked him.

They would not believe the stories he could tell of plot and counter-plot, of kidnappings and last-minute rescues, or of the desperate measures they must now take to escape retaliation. No-one in England would credit such things, and yet they were happening to Richard Melton, an ordinary Englishman, and to the woman he loved—an unimportant girl by the name of Wanda Schonbörn.

"If only we could go home to England!"

Richard repeated the words, following the train of his own thoughts, which brought him back always to the same point, to a yearning desire for home and for his own people.

"Is there no hope of that?" Wanda asked.

"None!"

He had told her already what had occurred that night when he had gone in search of his cousin and had been made the scapegoat of a crime he had not committed.

"Suppose you went to the Prince Regent yourself and told him what had happened?" she suggested.

"That is what Harry is always asking me to do," Richard said, "but Prinny would not believe me."

His voice was so bitter for the moment, remembering how easy it had been for the Prince Regent to be gracious in the past when he had been in favour and his reputation unblemished.

"Curse all Princes, Kings and Emperors," he said. "Why need we concern ourselves with them? All we ask is to be left alone, to live out our lives in obscurity and happiness."

"We are happy," Wanda said soothingly. "So perhaps it would not be fair if we had everything else as well."

He smiled at that and his dark thoughts went from him and he turned to look into her eyes.

"You are right," he said; "it would not be fair that I should have you and anything else as well."

"Something will happen to help us, I am sure of it," Wanda said. "We have been through so much already and yet we have found each other and we are together."

"And we will be together for ever," Richard answered. "Will you promise not to tire of me?"

"I shall never do that," she replied. "I shall only be afraid that you will find me dull and inexperienced, without the wiles or graces of the other women you have known."

"You are not to compare yourself with them," he cried masterfully. "You are different—utterly different from anyone else. I love you and I ask only of the future that we can be together with our love—in safety."

"Of course we shall be safe once we are married," Wanda said confidently. "Why should you doubt it?"

He would not worry her with his fears, so he evaded the question.

"We will be married as soon as we reach Vienna," he said, "and we will leave for Brussels tonight. Do you trust me?"

"You know I do."

"Then do not ask for too many explanations for the moment. As soon as we arrive, we will go and see Lord Stewart, the English Ambassador. We can be married at the Embassy."

There was silence for a moment and then Wanda said in a very low voice:

"Would you be angry with me if I asked a favour?"

"Angry?" Richard questioned. "My darling, you must not be afraid of me. Of course I should not be angry, whatever you asked of me."

She stirred in his arms at that and looked up at him confidingly.

"Then—could we go first to see Prince Metternich?"

She felt him stiffen.

"Please," she cried hastily. "You promised that you would not be angry! But because of the Prince's kindness to me, and because, too, of my mother's fondness for him, I would like to ask, if not his permission, his blessing on our marriage. Please, Richard, please!"

The soft pleading in her voice swept away his antagonism.

"It shall be as you wish," he answered.

She would have thanked him, but he added quickly:

"No, you are not to thank me for something which I have no right to refuse. You must not spoil me into becoming selfish and autocratic. I will spend my life, my little love, in trying to make you happy; but I have a reason for wishing to be married with all possible haste, so you must forgive me if I seem impatient."

"We will go to the Prince first," Wanda said, "and then straight to the Embassy."

He drew her closer into his arms.

"All I want is to be sure of you," he said. "Nothing must separate us now—nothing!"

Close in each other's arms, as trusting as two children might have been in the Fate which had brought them together again, they slept for the last part of the journey. Daylight was breaking as they entered the city by the south gate.

"Drive to Prince Metternich's villa," Richard commanded, as the Russian driver would have swung the horses towards the Hofburg.

The team was tired out, but the driver managed to make them travel in style down the beautiful avenue which led to Prince Metternich's private house and to draw up with a flourish at the door. Richard stepped out of the sleigh as the Majordomo hurried down to see who could be arriving at such an early hour.

"See that the Russian driver of this sleigh has breakfast and that the horses are rested in the stable. I do not wish them to return to the Hofburg for some hours."

The Majordomo's face did not change at this strange request.

"Very good, Sir. You have an appointment with His Highness?"

"No," Richard replied, "but he will wish to see the Comtesse Wanda Schonbörn. Please inform His Highness that she is here and craves an audience. It is of the utmost import."

He turned to assist Wanda from the sleigh. She was stiff and cramped and would have fallen if his arms had not gone round her. But her lips were smiling and her eyes were bright with laughter.

"My legs have forgotten how to obey me," she said, "but I am not complaining. I have enjoyed our journey together."

Richard suppressed the thought in his own mind that the journey might have had a very different ending. It was no use thinking of the past. There was the future to be considered and time was of vital importance.

Gently he helped Wanda up the steps. As they entered the big, beautifully proportioned hall, she looked down at her crumpled gown and her hands went to her bonnet.

"Could I tidy myself before I see the Prince?" she asked of the Majordomo.

A housekeeper in rustling black silk was produced in a few minutes. She led Wanda away while Richard also retired to wash and make himself presentable.

"There is no hurry, Sir," the Majordomo informed him. "His Highness usually breakfasts about 8.30 and it is not yet a quarter to eight."

"Then find me a barber," Richard commanded, "and a fresh necktie."

"Your clothes can be pressed, Sir, while you are being shaved," the Majordomo informed him.

Richard smiled as he undressed. It seemed to him that he was always borrowing neckties or being shaved in other people's houses. He remembered the night after the fire, when he had been obliged to clean his blackened face in the Baroness Waluzen's house and then had sent for Harry to come and join him.

Harry would be worrying now, he thought. But the little man would be pleased at the news that they were to leave

Vienna. He had never liked what was popularly supposed to be the gayest city in Europe.

When Richard was washed, shaved and arrayed in his freshly pressed clothes, he was led to a small room overlooking the garden.

"His Highness has been informed that the Comtesse is here, Sir. He will be down in a few minutes," the Majordomo informed him.

Alone, Richard walked across to the window and looked out on the snow-covered lawns. He was beginning to worry now as to what the Prince would say when he learned of the events of the past week and was told that the girl in whom he was interested because he had loved her mother was going to marry a penniless, exiled Englishman.

There was no time, however, for his thoughts to be heavy upon him before the door opened and Wanda came in. She had discarded her bonnet and cloak and was wearing a dress of pale blue mousseline cut low in the neck to reveal her favourite pendant of turquoise and diamonds. Her hair had been skilfully dressed, her complexion was exquisitely clear and she might, Richard thought, have stepped from a Parisian bandbox rather than have spent a night of terror and danger in an open sleigh.

She ran towards him and, as the lackey shut the door behind her, Richard put his arms round her.

"I love you," he said fiercely. "Are you certain nothing else matters?"

"Quite, quite certain," she smiled. "Oh, my darling, I love you, too. I have not had time yet to thank you for saving me."

"I didn't do it entirely for your sake," he answered.

Her eyes widened at that.

"Why then?" she enquired.

"For my own," he said. "I wanted you. I need you, I adore you. Do you imagine I could bear to lose you?"

He held her closer still as he spoke. His lips sought hers and they clung together, forgetting everything but the rapture of their love, the ecstasy of a rising passion.

He felt the fire of desire ignite an answering flame in her, so that her breath came quickly and excitedly and her lips opened softly beneath his kisses. Her body was trembling against him, not with fear but with a new and strange emotion which made her pulses throb and her eyelids feel warm and heavy.

"To-night you will be my wife," Richard whispered

hoarsely against her mouth, and then his kisses seemed to demand the surrender of her very soul.

They did not hear the door open and someone come in. It was instinct more than anything else which told them they were not alone.

With a start they jumped apart to find that Prince Metternich was standing beside them. He was wearing a dressing-gown of sapphire blue velvet, his hair was beautifully arranged, and there was an alert vivacity about him which made it almost impossible to believe that he ever relaxed in sleep.

"I heard that the Comtesse Wanda Schonbörn wanted to see me urgently," he said in an amused voice. "Is this the reason—for such urgency?"

Flushing, Wanda sank in a deep curtsy.

"Please forgive us for not hearing you come in," she said.

"Love is perhaps deaf as well as blind," the Prince murmured, and his eyes went towards Richard.

"Richard Melton, at your service, Your Excellency," the latter introduced himself.

The Prince held out his hand.

"I knew your father some years ago when he was in Paris." Then he turned to Wanda again. "What have you to tell me?" he asked, "or can I guess?"

"We came because we are going to be married to-day," Wanda told him; "but I wanted you to know first, and I wanted you to meet Richard."

"To be married!"

There was a frown on the Prince's forehead.

"Yes," Wanda said quickly. "I love Richard and he loves me, but he feels that it is of the utmost importance that we should be married to-day . . . at once. We have to leave Vienna, you see."

"Indeed! This is news to me," the Prince said. "Perhaps, young man, you will explain yourself."

"I think, Your Excellency, I can do that more easily if I see you alone . . ." Richard began, only to be interrupted by Wanda.

"No, no, I refuse!" she cried. "I know that you think to spare my feelings when you recount what happened at the Razumovsky Palace, but I have nothing of which to be ashamed. I want the Prince to know what has happened and I am not afraid to hear you tell it."

Wanda moved as she spoke and slipped her hand into

Richard's. His fingers closed over hers and he smiled down at her.

"Very well, then. We will tell him everything together," he agreed. Then he looked at the Prince with a touch of defiance on his face.

The Prince looked from one to the other and raised his eyebrows.

"If it is to be a long story," he said at length, "it would be best for us to sit down."

"Thank you, Sir," Richard replied.

They crossed to the fireplace and while the Prince seated himself in a high-backed wing chair, Wanda and Richard sat facing him on a brocade and gilt sofa. The Prince listened attentively as Richard recounted all that had happened since he and Wanda had met that first night at the Hofburg.

He told how he had impersonated the Czar, how he had fallen in love with Wanda and how Katharina had discovered that she was a spy. He told what had happened at the Razumovsky Palace and how the fire had broken out in time to save Wanda from the Czar, of their stay with the Baroness Waluzen and what had happened yesterday evening when the sleigh, purporting to come from him, had carried her away from Vienna *en route* for Gruzino.

As he spoke, relating his story simply and without elaboration, Prince Metternich's eyes never left his face, until finally he finished:

"That is all, Your Excellency. I have decided that the only thing for us to do is to get married immediately and to leave Vienna. When Wanda is my wife, I shall be in a position to protect her. But I am not so foolhardy as not to realize that I have made two very bitter enemies. I intend that we start for Brussels to-night where I shall throw myself on the mercy of the British Ambassador there. He may be able to help me to obtain employment of some sort."

"You are exiled from England?"

"Yes—exiled!" Richard answered. "For a duel I did not fight, for the death of a man with whom I had no quarrel."

"What happened?" the Prince asked.

Richard explained briefly.

"I know your cousin," the Prince said. "Duelling has a hold on him as another man might become a slave to drink."

"There was nothing for me to do at the time but to accept the conditions he proposed."

"No, I can see that," the Prince replied. "There was no alternative under the circumstances. But that forces me to ask you a pertinent question. How do you propose to keep a wife?"

"I can answer that frankly," Richard answered. "I don't know. I can only hope and pray that fortune will favour me."

"And if it doesn't?" the Prince enquired.

As Richard did not answer, Wanda sprang to her feet.

"We will manage somehow," she said. She crossed the hearth and knelt beside the Prince's chair. "I love Richard. I want, above everything in the world, to be his wife. Please give us your blessing."

"And if I refuse?"

"You could not be so unkind or so cruel," Wanda protested. "Now that Richard has told you everything, you must understand what we mean to each other. Indeed, if he did not wish to marry me I should want only to die."

"That is all very well," the Prince said in a hard voice. "But you have still got to be housed. You still have to eat, to clothe yourselves."

"Richard will find some kind of employment when we get to Brussels."

"Richard knows, as well as I do, that employment for a man who has been brought up only to be a gentleman is a rare phenomenon," the Prince retorted.

"Nevertheless, whether I have employment or not," Richard answered, "I intend to marry Wanda to-day."

The eyes of the two men met.

"I forbid it!"

"Have you the right to do that?" Richard asked.

"I think I have," the Prince replied slowly.

"No, no, you could not be so cruel." Wanda put out both hands as she spoke and laid them on the Prince's arm. "Can you not understand what this means to us?" she pleaded. "I was made for Richard and he for me. We love each other. Have you never been in love that you can deny us something which means more than life itself?"

Her voice broke for a moment, but still the Prince did not move, did not look down at her. And then urgently she continued:

"You loved my mother. I know that, and she loved you. I did not understand how much or what it meant until I came to Vienna. Then I heard people talking . . . I saw the Baroness looking at me, I heard her murmuring strange things . . . and then . . . I understood!"

The Prince turned and looked down at her.

"What did you understand?" he enquired.

"I understood . . . or thought I did . . ." Wanda faltered, "that I was born of love! Your love for my mother . . . hers for you. Am I right?"

She seemed to tremble at her own temerity. The Prince bent towards her and put his hand under her chin to lift her face to his. Blue eyes looked into blue eyes and then he said:

"You are right—my daughter."

Wanda gave a little cry.

"I am glad . . . glad! I thought it must be so, and yet it seemed presumptuous even to dream of such a thing. But now you have told me, I am proud . . . terribly proud to call you . . . Father."

The Prince bent down and kissed her forehead. Then he raised his head to look at Richard.

"Does that answer your question as to my authority?"

"An unofficial authority!" he answered a little stiffly.

"Naturally," the Prince agreed. He rose to his feet as he spoke and drawing Wanda to hers, put his arm round her. "Listen, little Wanda," he said, "this situation requires thought. Will you give me an hour—perhaps less—to think things over and to see if I can find a better solution than the one this young man of yours has suggested?"

"There can be no better solution than that we should be married," Wanda said hastily.

"There might be a better one than that you should wander penniless over the map of Europe. All I ask is time to think." As he spoke the Prince glanced at the clock over the mantelpiece. "I have guests for breakfast," he went on, "they will have arrived. I will give orders that a meal shall be served here for you two alone. When I return, a solution may have occurred to me. Will you trust me?"

Wanda glanced at Richard, then she turned impulsively towards the Prince.

"We will wait," she said; "but on one thing we are both determined—we must be married at once."

Her eyes were anxious as she spoke, fearing the Prince would be angry with her for defying him. Instead he smiled.

"Give me an hour," he said.

"On one condition," she replied.

His eyebrows went up at that.

"A condition?" he enquired.

"Yes," she replied. "The condition being that when the hour is over, whatever solution you may have come to about our future, you will be present at our wedding . . . to-day."

The Prince threw back his head and laughed.

"I warn you, Richard," he said, "you will have to be a very masterful man to rule your household, for your wife will, if you are not careful, twist you round her little finger as she twists me."

"Then you agree!" Wanda gave a little cry of sheer joy. "Oh, thank you, thank you! I knew you would understand."

She would have kissed his hand, but the Prince took her in his arms and kissed her cheek.

"You are a shameless schemer," he scolded. "I cannot think from where you get such talent!"

Wanda laughed up at him in delight.

"My eyes are not the only thing I inherited, *mon père*."

"Minx!"

The Prince kissed her again and went from the room. He did not, however, go at once to the breakfast room where his guests were waiting for him. Instead, he went to the desk in his private sitting-room and took a letter from a locked drawer. It was a bulky letter of many pages, and he had sat until the early hours of the morning writing it.

He stood staring at the envelope, which was addressed to the Comtesse Julia Zichy. It had been too late last night when he had finished writing it to send it to her house, and now he hesitated. He had written it under the mad impulse of the moment, baring his heart and soul to her, revealing his innermost, secret self as he had never revealed himself to any woman before. Last night he had felt that he could go on no longer loving her with an unrequited passion which seemed to tear his very self asunder.

He had thought of Julia despairingly and he had known with some strange clairvoyant conviction that their time together was short, the sands were running out. He was certain, against all logic, all common sense, but with an undeniable presentiment that the day would come when he would lose her, not to any other man, but to death.

He had been afraid then, as he had never been afraid

before. Afraid of his own loneliness, afraid of receiving the ashes which had been his letters, of having nothing left but the memory of their love.

Driven by his fear, he had rushed to his writing-desk and put down on paper all that he felt, all that he longed for, all that he desired. He had told Julia that he could not live without her, that he vowed himself to her service and offered her the fidelity she demanded—not only of his body, but of his very mind and soul. He wanted her as he had never wanted a woman before. He offered her in return his whole life.

In the morning light, the terror which had inspired him last night seemed less poignant; and yet, as the Prince stared at the letter, he knew it must go. He had written it in the heat of the moment, but the reasons for the letter were still there this morning, as strong and undeniable as they had been the night before.

He rang the bell. A lackey came hurrying to his summons. He gave the letter into his hand and commanded that a groom should ride swiftly to the Comtesse's house and wait for an answer. As the man went from the room, the Prince closed his eyes. It was a last desperate throw of a man who gambles everything. If she refused him now, he knew that he could go on no longer—he could not live without her.

Then with an effort he returned to the mundane affairs of every-day diplomacy; his guests were waiting and he walked slowly towards the breakfast room.

In the room where the Prince had left them, Wanda and Richard faced each other across the breakfast table. Although both of them were grateful for cups of steaming hot coffee, with great clots of cream swimming in it in true Viennese fashion, neither of them was hungry.

They talked at first animatedly; then, as the time passed and the Prince did not return, Wanda kept glancing at the clock. Half an hour, three-quarters! What, she wondered desperately, could be keeping him?

"Don't worry, darling," Richard said consolingly as he saw the anxiety in her eyes.

"But I do worry," Wanda answered. "I am so afraid that the Prince will find some reason to prevent our marriage."

"Nothing can prevent it," Richard answered. "Haven't I told you that a thousand times? You are mine, mine, and no one shall take you from me."

She held out her hands to him and he carried them to his lips, then leaned across the table so that he could kiss her mouth.

"I have had enough of foreign intrigue and foreign prevarication," he said. "By to-night you will be my wife and an English-woman."

She laughed at that, but tenderly.

"Are you quite certain that you are not making a mistake in marrying a foreigner?"

"There is only one mistake I am making and that is in being such an unconscionable time about it."

"I love you," she said.

"I love you," he answered.

The words, spoken as they looked into each other's eyes, had a magic which turned everything to gold. Then, as they stared at each other, the door opened and the Prince came in, followed by someone else.

"The hour is not yet up," he said, "but I have found a solution!"

Wanda and Richard rose to their feet.

"A solution?" Wanda questioned.

"To your future," the Prince answered. He put his arm around her and turned towards Richard. "Richard Melton, there is a gentleman here who informed me quite by chance that he has been looking for you for the last three days."

"Looking for me?" Richard enquired.

He turned to look at the man who stood in the doorway and recognized the English Ambassador, Lord Stewart. There was no mistaking his eccentric appearance or the languid manner of his address, which was so fashionable amongst the dandies who surrounded the Prince Regent.

"You're a demmed elusive chap, Melton," he drawled as he moved across the room towards Richard.

"I am sorry I have put you to any inconvenience, my Lord," Richard replied. "You wished to see me?"

"I was informed that you were in Vienna," Lord Stewart replied, "but I had no idea where to find you."

"And now you have done so?" Richard enquired.

"I have news that might be of interest," Lord Stewart replied. "Your cousin, the Marquess of Glencarron, is dead."

"Dead!" Richard ejaculated. "But—how?"

"A duel in which he received a mortal wound," Lord Stewart replied. "But before he died he gave certain information to the authorities which has cleared your name."

"Oh, Richard!"

Richard hardly heard Wanda breathe the words. He was staring at Lord Stewart as if he had been turned to stone.

"The way is clear for you to return to England," his Lordship continued. "What is more, His Royal Highness, the Prince Regent, commands your presence at Carlton House. I have been desired, in his name, to convey this information to you—my Lord."

There was a sudden silence. Then Richard spoke with admirable composure.

"I thank your Lordship."

Wanda gave a little cry.

"Then you can go back to England! It is just what you wanted."

"Just what I wanted," Richard repeated. He smiled down at her and turned again to Lord Stewart. "May I request your Lordship to arrange for my marriage to the Comtesse Wanda Schonbörn before we start our journey home?"

"One moment," the Prince interposed. "You have not asked my permission and my blessing."

"You will not refuse it, Sir?" Richard enquired.

"On the contrary," the Prince answered. "I am delighted to give permission for my ward, Wanda Schonbörn, to marry Richard Melton, Marquess of Glencarron. Didn't I tell you I would find a solution?"

Wanda's eyes were round as she looked up at Richard.

"I do not understand," she said. "Is it true that you are indeed a Marquess?"

"Quite true," Richard answered. "Does it make any difference?"

"A great deal," she pouted. "I did so want to cook for you and darn your socks, and now you will be rich and there will be no necessity."

Regardless of the presence of Lord Stewart and the Prince, Richard put his arms round her.

"Women are never satisfied," he said, "but you can't escape me now. It is too late. We are to be married to-day."

Wanda gave a little sigh of utter happiness and laid her head against his shoulder. Richard looked up to say something to the Prince, but found that his attention was no longer on them. A footman had entered the room carrying a letter on a gold salver.

He handed it to the Prince, who tore it open with fingers which seemed to tremble with impatience. The letter contained only one word, written with an exquisite precision in the centre of the page:

"To-night!"

ON SALE WHEREVER PAPERBACKS ARE SOLD
— or use this coupon to order directly from the publisher.

BARBARA CARTLAND

V3587	The Kiss of the Devil $1.25 £	
V2751	Kiss Of Paris $1.25 £ (#38)	
V3474	A Kiss Of Silk $1.25 £ (#30)	
V3450	The Leaping Flame $1.25 £ (#70)	
V3174	Light To The Heart $1.25 £ (#56)	
V2965	Lights of Love $1.25 £ (#46)	
V2966	The Little Pretender $1.25 £ (#19)	
V3122	Lost Enchantment $1.25 £ (#52)	
V3196	Love Forbidden £ $1.25 (#51)	
V3519	Love Holds The Cards $1.25 £ (#12)	
V2750	Love In Hiding $1.25 £ (#4)	
V3047	Love Is An Eagle $1.25 £ (#49)	
V3429	Love Is Contraband $1.25 £ (#13)	
V2611	Love Is Dangerous $1.25 £ (#31)	
V2824	Love Is The Enemy $1.25 £ (#9)	
V2865	Love Is Mine $1.25 £ (#43)	
V3451	Love Me Forever $1.25 £ (#14)	
V3079	Love On The Run (#50) £ $1.25	
V2864	Love To The Rescue $1.25 £ (#11)	
V2768	Love Under Fire $1.25 £ (#39)	
V2997	Messenger Of Love $1.25 £ (#22)	
V3372	Metternich: The Passionate Diplomat $1.25 £	

Send to: PYRAMID PUBLICATIONS,
Dept. M.O., 9 Garden Street, Moonachie, N.J. 07074

NAME _____

ADDRESS _____

CITY _____

STATE _____ ZIP _____

I enclose $_____, which includes the total price of all books ordered plus 50¢ per book postage and handling for the first book and 25¢ for each additional. If my total order is $10.00 or more, I understand that Pyramid will pay all postage and handling.
No COD's or stamps. Please allow three to four weeks for delivery.
Prices subject to change.   P-16